ELIZABETH BUTLER

The Colonel's Widow

Reviewers Said -

From opening paragraph to happy ending, *The Colonel's Widow* crackles with action and steams with romance.

— Lynn Crandall, Author *Silver Wings*, Precious Gems

ELIZABETH BUTLER brings Arizona and the old west to life with her great story and touches of warmth and humor.

-      Patricia Barnes, Owner, The Paperback Store

A gripping story of two people who's lives were torn apart by the Civil War and how they found each other, re-discovered themselves, and forged a new and stronger life together in the process.

- Sandy Fitzgerald, Reviewer for *Romancing the Prairie*, Newsletter of Prairie Hearts Chapter of Romance Writers of America

ISBN: 0-9675767-0-9

ACKNOWLEDGEMENTS

I'd like to thank my husband, daughter, son-in-law and members of my writing group for encouragement. They were there to pick me up when I was down and never let me forget that I am an author.

DEDICATION

To my Mother-in-law

Mable J. Deavers

1914-1998

She loved to read and was a constant encouragement
To me and she loved Arizona as much as I do.

The Colonel's Widow

Elizabeth Butler

Prologue

March 3, 1866 – Outside Springfield, Illinois

Amanda Green shifted uncomfortably on the needlepoint - seated oak chair in the huge farmhouse dining room. It had been theirs – hers and Simon's. *What am I going to do now?* A whiff of fresh coffee wafted to her and she rose to pour a cup. She didn't miss the servants they'd once had - she wasn't used to them anymore. Like the seven petticoats she wore, they were part of her life that seemed almost a dream that had happened long ago.

She started toward the kitchen Simon had insisted on being built in the house even if it did heat up in the summer. They'd spend that time in town anyway, he'd said. One day a kitchen next to the dining room would be in every home, he'd predicted. A knock sounded at the front door from the brass knocker he'd insisted on having installed. She paused. *Who could that be? Who knew she'd returned?* Jed, her brother and his wife had wanted her to spend the night, but just as determined to start her new life, she'd refused and ridden to the farm.

Changing directions, she walked down the short hall to the front door passing furniture still covered with cloths to protect it from dust. Floorboards creaked beneath her boot-clad feet. Although she'd decided to don one of her former house dresses which fit her loosely, she hadn't been able to force herself to lace the high-topped kid-leather narrow boots she'd once worn. Stepping to the window the length of the door, she peered out. Three people who looked faintly familiar waited outside. She opened the door. "Yes?"

"Mrs. Green?" The man, a crutch under each arm, a pinned up trouser leg telling the story, stepped in front of the two women.

Amanda glanced past the group to the wagon sitting in the drive, one normally used to move furnishings, feed, and necessities, not the best conveyance to move people. "Yes, I'm Amanda Green."

"Well," the man balanced himself on the crutches as he removed the battered black felt hat, "I guess you don't remember us? I'm Arnold Baxter and this is Mrs. Satterly." He pointed to a white-haired woman bent over a crooked cane. "This is Opal

Worthington." He motioned to the third person, a woman about Amanda's age who she vaguely remembered seeing around Springfield.

The younger woman smiled showing dark holes where teeth had once been.

"Yes, I remember you. Won't you come in? I just arrived last evening and don't have things unpacked, but I've a fresh pot of coffee on the stove."

"Thank you ma'am, but this isn't a social call."

His words made a shiver run down Amanda's back. Yes, she knew these people – all depositors in Simon's bank.

"Move out of the way, Arnold." The older woman pushed her way around his crutches. "I knew you'd pussy-foot around with this." She stepped up to Amanda, her blue eyes sparkling with something Amanda could only call determination. "We want to know what the chances of getting our money back are now that your man is dead? We're sorry about that, but a lot of us are missing loved ones too and doing it without money. Look at Opal there, got seven youngin's and no man to support her. All her savings and ours were in that bank when your husband closed it promisin' to get our money back as soon as the war was over. It's over and he's dead, but we still need our money."

For a moment, Amanda couldn't think of a thing to say. She'd expected this, but not quite this soon. Sometimes she'd even thought this might be part of the reason she'd agreed to stay to the end helping clean up the hospital tents, see the last patients gone. Her thoughts drifted back to the night she'd learned Simon was going to loan a large portion of the assets in their Springfield bank to Maurice Oldham, a businessman who had just appeared one day saying he planned to open a bank in Arizona Territory and seeking investors. She'd been against the idea from the beginning and she and Simon had had one of their rare arguments over it.

"I haven't had a chance to talk to my brother, Jed, about it."

"Well, we have," Mrs. Satterly again. "He said there was nothing he could do. He just took his orders from Mr. Green and he gave our money away to that man out west."

The others nodded, their eyes accused. A memory from long ago returned. She'd been sitting in her father's store. Even now she could almost see the barrels of flour, meal and dill pickles, smell the aroma of cinnamon, ginger and peppermint tea, hear his voice boom above the clatter of horse-drawn carts three-feet outside the front door on the cobblestone street. "We aren't always guilty of what comes to us, Mandy, but sometimes we're responsible just the same." He'd shown his responsibility by providing a home for his in-laws when they'd lived beyond their means and lost all their money. They often didn't appear to appreciate his labors and sometimes even made fun of him because he put work ahead of the social functions in which they delighted.

What kind of responsibility did she have to Simon's depositors? She'd enjoyed the fruits of his status in town, worn fashionable gowns, had been part of the more affluent residents in Springfield. If she'd been a depositor, what would she expect the bankers' widow to do? "I don't know what I can do," she heard herself saying, "but I'll try."

"We can't ask anymore than that ma'am." Mr. Baxter tipped his hat, grasped his crutches then turned to leave.

The two women followed. Mrs. Satterly leaned heavily on her cane. Opal Worthington's shoulders didn't seem to be drooped quite as low.

Amanda watched them leave. She'd never really thought of going to Arizona Territory, but....

One

Arizona Desert - July 1, 1866

Sheriff Wade Denton tied his horse and mule to a mesquite tree hidden by the boulders, then looked toward the rocks through which the rider, who had followed for half-a-day would have to pass. He'd learned during the War a man couldn't stay alive not knowing everything about who was around. He climbed to the tallest boulder and crouched. He hated hand to hand combat, but he didn't intend to be shot in the back.

The rider approached slowly.

Wade felt his muscles coil, ready to spring. Self-preservation, the code they'd lived by for years, filled him. Beneath him a hat moved. A horse's hoof, muffled in the sand, clicked against a rock.

He sprang.

In mid-air, he knew he'd made a mistake. He recognized the horse. Amanda Green's frightened blue-eyed gaze caught his as he tried to slow his descent. Her weather-beaten leather hat tipped back on her blonde head. He saw her blue shirt and black trousers, then he was on her, dragging her from her gray speckled horse, Pepper.

The sand cushioned their fall somewhat, but Amanda didn't give up easily. With tiny fists she beat at his chest. She pulled his hair and when he tried to push her to the ground, she bit near his right hand.

"Stop, stop," he yelled. "It's me."

But, she didn't stop. She pushed and kicked with her legs, then opened her mouth to bite at his left arm.

"Amanda, it's me, Sheriff Denton."

Suddenly, all fight left her. Lying motionless on the ground, she glared up at him with vengeance.

"What're you doing, trying to kill me?"

"No, I just wanted to know who was following me."

"Do you accost everyone who follows you?"

"No."

"Well, get off me."

Amanda's gaze burned into his. Red lips, flushed from the tussle, invited him. For more than a week she'd been hounding him, seemingly unaware of the affect she had on him. It was more than he could take.

Instead of moving off her, he lowered his body over hers. His lips covered hers with, a deep, sensuous kiss that made his head whirl, and his heart race. Her lips were soft and warm. She tasted sweet, just like he'd known she would, but he could feel her pushing against his chest. *Damn! What's gotten into me?* He jerked his head away.

Smack! Her open hand plowed into his cheek.

His jaw burned. His ears rang. She carried quite a punch. He stared down at her.

Shock registered on her face. "I'll thank you to get off me, Sheriff Denton." Wrath replaced shock.

Humbly, he stood, offered a hand that she pushed aside. Still tasting her, he brushed his pants off, then retrieved his crumpled Stetson. As he worked the creases out he wondered what had gotten into him. Slowly, he turned toward her and slipped the hat on. "I'm sorry, but...what the hell are you doing here?"

"Looking for Maurice Oldham," she said quietly. Her hat had fallen off and silky strands of hair billowed wildly around her head, mingling with the sand and dust. Amanda looked too young and vulnerable to be in this godforsaken territory - alone.

"What makes you think I'm searching for Oldham?" He thought he'd made it out of Mineral Wells by himself. What he didn't need was this woman who had barely reached adulthood and disguised herself as a man on his tail.

"Well." She sat up and reached for her battered hat. "I guess you might call it 'woman's intuition', Sheriff." She slapped the hat on her head, then looked at him. The anger had disappeared and a slight grin lifted her swollen rosy lips.

"Well, your *intuition* is going to get you into *big* trouble." He spat the words at her.

"Is that right, Sheriff?" She stood, plopped her hands on her slim hips and eyed him.

"Yes, that's right. I was hired for this kind of work and I don't need any help." He didn't like the expression. It was just like the one she'd worn the day she'd arrived in town demanding to know where Oldham, the former banker was.

"Are you looking for Oldham?"

He couldn't avoid her blue gaze. "Yes, but if I'd wanted you to come along, I'd have invited you." He walked toward the tree where he'd tied his horse and pack mule. He was wasting time he didn't have.

"Don't you think I know that?"

He heard quick steps behind him. *Damn, didn't she ever give up?* "But...."

He stopped and pivoted slowly, trying to ignore the plea in her youthful eyes the memory of her warm lips under his and the fact she probably couldn't survive here alone long. "There are no *buts* about this." He looked around her, out over the valley. He didn't see signs of the Indians he'd noticed earlier, but that made him nervous. "Apaches and Mexican bandits haunt this area, and I don't want to take care of a woman." He turned his back to her again, but had only taken a couple of steps when she ran in front of him blocking his path.

"You don't have to take care of me. I'm self-sufficient. I've read about the dangers in the newspapers." Lifting her chin slightly, he saw defiance darken her eyes. "I have as much right to search for Maurice as you."

He'd seen this same expression when he'd first met her five days before outside his office. "Then hunt. It's a big desert. You don't have to do it with me."

"I wasn't doing it with you."

He halted. "But, you were following me."

"Yes," her voice softened slightly. "I thought you'd lead me to him."

"Lead you to him?" Now he'd heard everything. He couldn't believe what her words implied. What's more, he didn't like them. Did she really think he was in cahoots with Oldham, a bank robber? What kind of man did she think he was?

She stepped toward him. "Yeah, the way I understand it, you've been Sheriff of Mineral Wells for awhile. Why did you decide, all of a sudden, to look for the town's most wanted man?" Her eyes condemned. "I was told that's what you were hired to do, but you hadn't done a thing until I came to town."

"I don't have to answer to you." He strolled around her and walked toward his horse.

"Maybe you don't, Sheriff, but you have to answer to the residents. They've been patient."

Although he wanted to ignore her statement, he couldn't. Obviously, she'd been talking to someone who knew what happened in Mineral Wells. Sometimes, he sensed folks suspected him of being involved with Oldham, but none had confronted him openly. He had arrived in town to a very cold trail. Not many people wanted to talk about the disappearing banker and their money. For months, he'd been an observer, given few clues. After awhile, he had decided more people were involved in trying to bankrupt the town than just Oldham. He didn't intend to tell Amanda. It would only make matters worse.

Stopping again, he turned around. "What do you want?"

"To find Oldham. Get some of my husband, Simon's money back. God rest his soul." Humbleness passed over her face that hadn't been there a few moments before, her voice sounded more like a plea than a demand.

He'd always had a soft spot for a desperate woman, couldn't resist trying to help no matter how much trouble they might cause.

"I need the money," she said, quietly, "and the others need it too."

"What others?" *Why did he ask? Why didn't he just ride off?*

"Mrs. Satterly, Opal Worthington, Old Mister Baxter, are a few. They're people who had savings in Simon's bank. Mrs. Satterly, she's a widow all broken down with the rheumatism. Opal Worthington's a widow now too, got seven children to feed. Mister Baxter lost his right leg in the War, can't work anymore. I can name others. It was their money Simon loaned to Oldham."

"I'm sure they need it, but money can be replaced." *Damn! I can't be drawn into this story enough to let her come along. It'd be suicide for both of us. A man alone can hide, two people riding together would be a moving target.*

"It'd take years for them to make enough money to replenish what Simon gave away. In the meantime, what do they do?"

The question fell like a boulder between them. Her logic was sound. With low wages, a woman with children, a widow, and an old man would find it hard to survive. But he couldn't let this five-foot-four inch willowy frame standing before him risk her life for money. He admired her desire to help and couldn't ignore her determination, but it was dangerous enough for him on this desert without having her along.

A light dusting of freckles danced on her nose.   She looked young and wholesome. Since that first day he'd wanted to protect her even though the glint in her eyes told him she'd rather care for herself. He remembered her soft lips under his. What had he done? He shouldn't rest until she rode away permanently. Having her with him was deadly. If she didn't cause trouble, like she already had, she'd sure as hell interrupt his tranquility.

But he couldn't send her away. They were at least sixty miles from Mineral Wells. Since she'd made it this far with no trouble, he wanted to send her back, but clearly, she was determined to go on, with or without him and if she did find Oldham, could she survive? *Probably not alone.*

Wade gazed out over the desert again, but saw only cactus, a dust devil and desert bushes - no Apaches. As far as he knew, Oldham hadn't killed anyone, but letting Amanda chase him or anyone alone was the same as offering her as sacrifice.

Amanda watched him stare at her. Was he going to allow her to ride with him? *Men! Woman had to be careful around them. One minute they'd ask for help, the next, smother you with their need to protect you.*

"Just how much money did Simon entrust to Maurice, Amanda?"

"A lot." *He didn't need to think she'd give him a figure. If he knew how much, he'd probably knock her over the head and take it himself.*

"How much is a lot?"

"I don't think I want to tell you." She clamped her mouth shut.

"Why not?" He walked toward the mesquite tree where he'd tied his horse and pack mule.

She'd have to be careful or she'd lose this battle, but she couldn't hold back. "Maybe you helped Maurice."

He slowly pivoted toward her a dark expression in his brown eyes told her he didn't appreciate the accusation.

"You could be riding to meet him. You didn't tell anyone where you were going." Her desperate words rushed out. Her heart pounded and she felt flushed. *He has to let me ride along he just has to.*

"You're about the most exasperating person I ever met." He turned away and stomped toward the horses again.

"I could help, Sheriff." She hated pleading, but didn't see any other way. "I'll bet you don't even know what Maurice looks like."

He took the canteen and two canvas bags from his gear. "I have a picture."

"Hand drawn posters aren't good likenesses, and you know it. I can identify him." She felt like she was gaining momentum.

Wade started to take a drink, but looked at her instead.

At least, he was listening. "I shoot well too and make a great campfire stew."

He hung a water bag on the red roan's head and one of oats on the mule, then tipped the canteen to his lips.

She walked to her horse that had been standing several yards away since their scuffle.

Wiping the moisture from his lips, he put the cap back and gave her a sharp look. "I can't tell you what to do, but stay out of my way. I stopped to rest my horse. Don't cause any trouble, and don't get too close."

"I won't." Excitement filled her and she couldn't suppress her smile. She led Pepper past him, to a nearby tree and moved the canvas bags from the horses' back to her head so she could drink.

Digging into the saddlebags she retrieved the last of the biscuits and meat Gladys Richardson had packed. For a moment she reflected on what had happened since she'd arrived at Mineral Wells a little over a week before. Gladys owned the hotel and seemed to be the only person in town welcoming another woman. The men, including the sheriff, had out right told her to keep moving. That drew her suspicions and all had been tight-lipped when she asked about Oldham. It was if they'd signed a secret pact. She didn't like it.

Amanda drank long and deep from her canteen, savoring the water that revived and cooled her. A cool breeze ruffled her hat and filtered through the over-large shirt. A bee buzzed a tiny desert flower a few feet away. The hum of insects told how alive the desert actually was. She began to relax, but hoped they came upon a stream soon. A shake of her canteen told her finding water had to be a priority. Pepper would need water too. She hadn't counted on this dry desert.

With the last of her meat and biscuits, she walked to the tree and sat leaning against the trunk. Her confidence rose. At least the sheriff hadn't run her off. She bit into a hard biscuit and let her thoughts drift.

Mineral Wells had proved to be just another one of Oldham's scams. He'd made it sound like a growing metropolis. Instead, it was a dusty spot in the road, hardly big enough to be called a town. But he'd proved to be exactly what she'd feared, a liar and a cheat. He wasn't where he said he'd be, and he hadn't left the money. He'd learn she didn't give up easily.

Glancing at the sheriff, sitting under a tree several yards away, she noted that he'd covered his eyes with his hat. He would learn too. She turned to the desert wondering what he had been watching earlier. Heat ripples glided along the sandy surface. Sagebrush dotted the soil, but otherwise, she saw nothing. Biting into a piece of tough meat she looked at her companion again.

Wade Denton was long and lanky, dressed in light brown trousers and a matching shirt. A glittery star denoted his occupation. The straw Stetson, battered from their tussle, covered his head hiding his sandy hair and proud brown eyes. She detected the hint of a Southern drawl in his voice.

Interesting. Of course, this part of Arizona territory had been Confederate, but she hadn't expected to run into one of them as sheriff, not that it mattered. She'd learned during the war even enemies could help sometimes.

Dark stubble covered Wade's hard jaw. It had been rough against her soft chin when he'd kissed her. *Cold.* The sheriff looked authoritative and cold, but there had been nothing cold about that kiss he'd given her. She touched her lips and let her thoughts drift back to the incident.

She'd never been kissed like that before, certainly not by Simon. Her pulse-rate quickened just thinking of Wade Denton's body on top of hers. *If she hadn't been so angry....* Yes, if she hadn't been so angry, she might have reacted differently. Probably a good thing he'd caught her off-guard that way. She couldn't afford to let some wayward emotion get in the way of her mission - the reason she'd come to this part of the country.

Letting her gaze travel to the sheriff, she noticed the six-shooter strapped to his right hip. He probably wouldn't hesitate to use it.

She found him attractive in a rough way, but that didn't matter either, she had no time to think of anything except why she'd come to Arizona Territory - get Simon's money back and return it to his depositors. The sheriff would learn that Amanda Green didn't quit until she got what she wanted.

Leaning against the tree, she sighed and closed her eyes. She wiggled around as she tried to find a more comfortable spot. An eye popped open. She'd better stay awake. He might break away if she dozed. She glanced at him. He must be napping. He hadn't moved since she'd first looked at him. Bone tired from the long ride a nap seemed like the best thing to do right now.

"Eeeee." The scream brought Wade out of a rather pleasant nap. Through the cholla, prickley pear and palo verde branches he saw Amanda Green, dancing around a mesquite tree. She slapped at her clothes, pulled at her trousers and shirt.

Sleep disappeared and the unhappy realization that he was no longer riding alone returned as he jumped to his feet and darted across the desert to her. "What is it?"

"Something's biting." She slapped at her back, brushed at her legs.

"Stop, Amanda, stop." He started to unbutton her shirt.

"Don't." She stepped back wincing.

"Don't be silly. You've got to get out of those clothes. You're covered with ants." *Fool woman, didn't she know what they could do to her? This wasn't the time for modesty!*

Still wincing, she gave in.

He stripped the shirt from her then unbuttoned her trousers. Without a word he slid the chemise over her head. She didn't resist and he was glad.

"You sat in a nest of sand ants. They're all over you." Turning her around, he brushed at her back. "Out of them." He pointed to her pants.

She hesitated, giving him an imploring look over her shoulder.

He whirled her around and stared her in the eye. "Don't be a fool."

Turning away from him, she slipped out of the trousers, then the drawers. Red welts covered her beautiful silky skin from head to toe. She had to be in misery.

"Stand still." Compassion filled him. As gently as he could, he wiped the intruding ants from her body, all the while mindful of the softness of her skin.

Amanda started to scratch.

"You've got to quit that, honey. Scratching them will make the itch worse."

"What am I to do?" Tears rushed to her eyes. Her cheeks grew flushed.

"I guess you didn't know anything about Arizona ants?"

She shook her head. Silky strands draped loosely over her thin shoulders.

Wade swallowed hard. "I'll make a poultice with the baking soda I have in my saddlebags. That should help soothe the pain and itch." He strolled to Pepper and untied Amanda's bedroll. "This will have to replace your clothes until the itching eases." He draped the blanket around her shoulders, trying to ignore the lithe body beneath. She was beautiful, no doubt about it and she was starting out to be just as much trouble as he'd expected, but he couldn't manage to feel anything but sorry for her. At the moment, she didn't feel anything except pain.

In a cup he mixed baking soda and water. "If this doesn't work, mud probably will." When he'd blended it sufficiently, he looked at her. She stood a few feet away, cheeks still red, but the tears had disappeared and again he saw staunch perseverance in her expression. "Turn around."

She pivoted.

He dabbed it on the bites, trying to be as impersonal as he could. Amanda grimaced, but didn't whimper. He had to admire her ability to deal with adversity, not to mention her other obvious attributes.

When the bites had been doctored, he pulled the blanket close around her and tucked it securely under her chin. "I'll see to your clothes now." He needed to put some distance between them, but he couldn't help remembering that they were the only two people for miles and miles - probably not a good idea to stay here long. "I wouldn't move on today, but we need to be closer to water." He wiped what was left of the mixture out of his cup. "I'm concerned about those riders I saw earlier, too. Are you able to ride?"

"Yes," she replied firmly. "I'm feeling better already."

"Good." He rubbed sand in the cup to finish cleaning it, then picked up her infested clothes. They still felt warm from her heat and they smelled earthy and clean just like she had when he'd tackled her. Why had he kissed her? Why hadn't he sent her away? If she'd made it this far, she could make it back to Mineral Wells. Beating the clothes against a rock, he pushed the questions away. If she was with him, he'd know she was safe.

Two

Four hours later, Amanda started to ride past Sheriff Denton to chose a campsite about a hundred yards or so away.

"Where are you going?"

"You said not to get close. I don't intend to." The incident with the ants seemed to have cracked his hard veneer some, but she had no intentions of becoming a nuisance nor did she plan for him to leave without her. She was somewhat embarrassed by the situation, but nowhere had she read about ants that would bite so.

"We shouldn't make two fires." His voice sounded gruff, almost angry again. "More than one will attract too much attention. I'll build the fire. You can use it."

He'd chosen a place near the edge of the rocks. Behind them, the mountains protected them from attack. In front they overlooked a breathtaking view of saguaros, cholla and prickly pear cacti all now casting long shadows across the sandy soil. The sun had slid behind the peaks, but still reflected amber on distant mountains. Weariness filled Amanda as she slid from Pepper's back. It had been a long hot afternoon's ride. Even the shadows didn't cool the air much.

She tied Pepper to a tiny bush then started to gather twigs. She dropped the twigs near where he'd placed several stones in a round circle. "I don't want to be any trouble."

His dark gaze met hers. "Too late for that." He stood tall and strong above her, silhouetted against the reds and oranges of the setting sun.

Again, Amanda's heart pounded like the snare drums she'd heard during the War. Why did this unfeeling man affect her this way? Whatever compassion he'd had earlier had disappeared.

"I don't want to get in the way, Sheriff."

"Then you should've stayed in Mineral Wells, or wherever it was you came from." He added some branches to the fire.

"Springfield, Illinois." She walked back to Pepper and began to remove her saddle. "I got out here by myself, without any trouble, too." She felt bound to tell him.

He glanced at her and shook his head. "Your record hasn't held. You had a big enough problem this afternoon to last awhile."

Amanda glanced up at him.

He was looking at her, his eyes filled with humor.

Her heart leapt. "I did at that." She smiled self-consciously as the memory of him brushing ants from her body returned.

Maybe this wasn't such a good idea after all. Except for Simon and wounded soldiers, she didn't have much experience with men. Would Sheriff Denton think she was like the women who lived at the edge of army camps? Even though he was a sheriff, he was also a man. She'd been told more times than she could remember that they wanted only one thing from a woman. That is, all of them except Simon.

Slipping the saddle from Pepper's back, she hoped she didn't have to worry about that. She had enough to be concerned about, just trying to find Oldham.

She took a few steps toward the campfire and dropped the saddle on the ground. From the saddlebags she pulled a tin of coffee and a pot, then dumped grounds inside and added water. Replacing the lid, she walked to the blaze that leapt cheerfully up from the twigs. *Maybe I can redeem myself with a pot of great coffee.*

He looked up at her. Their gazes collided in the waning light. An almost predatory expression crossed his face. A tinge of restlessness moved deep within her.

The sun had drifted below the mountains. Shadows cooled the air and an occasional whiff of breeze made the blaze flicker in the darkening night. A thin curl of smoke billowed toward Amanda who sat across the fire from Wade. The aroma of burning mesquite tickled his nostrils.

He tried to relax on the blanket he'd spread several feet away from the campfire, but it wasn't easy. He had trouble keeping his mind on Oldham, the reason he was here. Glancing at Amanda again, he couldn't believe he'd actually insisted she camp with him.

Funny how the best plans can fall apart in the space of a day. Alone, this morning, he'd planned how he'd travel to Mexico in a couple of days, find Oldham, then return to Mineral Wells. Unfortunately, he'd noticed the rider following him. If he hadn't acted so hastily.... If he hadn't kissed her.... If she hadn't sat in those ants....

"Tomorrow, we'll search for water," he said. "What we've got is almost gone. The horses will need to drink and graze." Leaning against a rock, he forced his mind to what needed to be done, rather than the sultry curves of his companion.

"My canteen's almost empty too." She glanced at him across the fire while she continued to work with her hair.

She'd loosened the braids and let the blonde strands fall freely to her shoulders. Her hair glistened, almost coppery in the campfire light. She combed through the tresses and let them billow around her head in the light breeze. Did they feel soft and silky, like they looked? Combing, parting, working the long strands into a rope she draped it down her back.

Did she know he was watching? *Damn, just what I need, a distraction when I'm chasing a criminal.* He stood and walked to his saddlebags. Digging the gun cleaning gear out he stepped back toward the fire and reached for his six-shooter. He ran the ramrod through the firearm and forced himself to think of the night sounds.

Crickets chirped in the nearby bushes. An owl hooted in the distance. The flames of the fire dipped. He heard the rustle of an animal in the darkness behind Amanda. Tensing, ready to pounce, he squinted trying to see what made the noise, but nothing stepped into the light. He heard it move away.

Focusing on the gun, Wade fought his conflicting thoughts. Why would a woman like her travel out here by herself, even if she did need money? Why did she feel such an obligation to her friends? Had her husband made her promise to clear his name? No real man would make his wife do something like that.

"How do you feel?" He quit cleaning his pistol and looked across the fire at her. "Has the itching stopped?"

"For the most part." She smiled.

A dimple in her left cheek creased inward reminding him of her youthfulness, but he'd always had a weakness for dimples. Sarah Jean Studyvent, his former fiancee had them. That was one of her most attractive attributes. *Damn. He didn't want to think of her. He'd left her and their plans in New Orleans. He didn't want to think about that now, or ever.* Pulling the cleaning rod out of the gun barrel, he said, "I'd suggest, you pick your seats more carefully in the future." He didn't really want to spar with her again, but it made him nervous to realize he had no idea how much she knew about surviving in the desert.

"I think I've learned my lesson on that one." She flashed him a grin. "I learn quickly."

He moved uncomfortably. It had been a long time since a woman had bantered with him. "Didn't you realize how much water you'd be needing?" He reloaded the gun.

"No, I didn't. Sure gets dry out here though." She leaned against the saddle. With her hair freshly braided, she looked neat and orderly. Her eyes sparkled with humor and she sighed lightly, like she belonged in this place.

Wade became nervous. He wasn't used to noticing this much about a woman. "Do you know where to look for water?"

"Of course." Her blue eyes caught his. "I search for trees or mountains."

"Trees or mountains?" *Now he'd heard everything.*

"Yes, and if water is scarce, it can be found in the desert at night. Place a piece of canvas over a hole in the sand. Put a rock in the middle and a pan under it. By morning, there will be water." Enthusiasm filled her voice and a soft smile curved on her full lips.

A memory of how they'd tasted under his returned. Ignoring the thought, he slipped the gun into the holster, then put his cleaning gear away. "Where'd you hear that?"

"I read up on it a bit, before I left Springfield. My father was a sportsman too." She wound the long braid on the top of her head and secured it with hairpins. Her profile seemed molded against the darkening night and for the first time in years, he remembered what he was missing. As a child, he'd seen his parents laugh together, his dad's husky and almost secretive whispers his mother's light, nervous laugh. He'd noticed a special look between them and once he'd wanted that kind of relationship too, but no more.

He looked away from her and stood. Walking to the pile of twigs and logs he concentrated on rebuilding the fire. He watched the brush ignite, but couldn't keep from asking, "Do you believe everything you read?"

"What are you getting at?"

That defiant tone had returned to her voice.

"It might not be true." He moved his saddle to his blanket. If he lay down, maybe he could think of something other than her. "Sometimes that works, but when it's as dry as it is now, there's very little moisture in the sand, even at night." He propped himself against the saddle, pulled a cigarette paper from his pocket and rolled a smoke. His hand shook and he got too much moisture on the paper, but he put it between his lips and lit it anyway. Wouldn't do to let her notice how distracted she made him.

"We did it during the War." Her voice floated to him through the darkness.

"What war?"

"The War Between the States."

Staring across the blaze at her, he sat up.

She'd slid down onto the blanket and appeared to be getting comfortable for the night.

"What do you mean, you did it during the War?"

"I mean, I did it." She opened her eyes and rose to her elbow. "I went to war with Simon. He was a Colonel in the Union Army. Died three days before Shiloh of hospital gangrene. It got into a cut on his leg. After that, I nursed."

"Nursed?"

"Yes, nursed. A lot of northern wives did. With Simon dead, I didn't have any reason to go home. He'd closed the bank. There wasn't that much money left after he made the loan to Maurice. He promised the depositors he'd come to Arizona and get their money as soon as the war ended. My brother Jed had worked for him, but he'd gone to work for another bank. Simon had sold the house in town and I didn't know a thing about farming. So I continued on with the nursing after he died."

Wade lay back against the saddle. *Wouldn't you know it? A Yankee! Just my luck to get trapped out on the desert with a beautiful woman who's a Yankee with a hero for a husband.* The minute he'd seen her, he'd known she'd be trouble. She hadn't wasted a moment proving him wrong. "Too bad, he died so young." He wished the war hadn't been mentioned. There wasn't a thing about it worth remembering as far as he was concerned.

"Oh, Simon wasn't young."

He opened his eyes and rolled his head toward her.

Her gaze was taking in the starry sky above.

"He wasn't?" *She'd been married to some old codger. An old Yankee. No wonder he died.*

"He was a friend of my fathers."

The thought of her in bed with some dried up old prune made Wade's stomach churn. He gritted his teeth, inhaled the cigarette smoke, and tried to relax and let the knot in his stomach unwind.

"It was too bad he died." She yawned. "Simon was a good man. He felt very responsible to his depositors. That's part of why I want to get their money back. I knew he shouldn't give Maurice any money, but Simon wouldn't listen to me."

"Maybe, he thought being a banker, he knew better." Wade blew a smoke ring into the night sky and a smile slipped out, imagining the old Yankee having his hands full with this one.

"Oh, I didn't argue with Simon about everything, just Maurice." She sat up for a moment and looked at him like she was trying to convince him she didn't fight Simon. Remembering the punch she'd given him earlier, he doubted it. She lay back down. "They talked and planned for days. Then, the afternoon before Maurice left, Simon took a loan from our bank. Told me, he knew Maurice could be trusted. Within a year we'd have two or three times our money back because Maurice was going to find gold in Arizona Territory just like had been done in California a few years before. He'd be rich. We'd all be rich. We got one short letter from him." She turned on her side, toward Wade and closed her eyes.

Snuffing the cigarette out on a rock, he slid down on the blanket, letting the fatigue filling his body rule.

"Goodnight, Wade." Her voice was soft, almost seductive.

"Goodnight." He closed his eyes. A long lost memory engulfed him as he pulled his hat over his eyes, blocking the vision of her. It'd been a long time since anyone had told him goodnight. His mother when he'd been young, fellow soldiers on the battlefield.

What would it be like to say goodnight to someone every night? Again the memory of Sarah Jean Sturdyvent, his former fiancée returned. Except for the dimples, he couldn't visualize her anymore. Dark hair, auburn he thought, but when he'd last seen her, it had seemed darker. Like everything else about her, even her hair had been different.

The hurt and anger he'd felt leaving the Sturdyvent home seemed to have lessened, but it'd been hell and he'd vowed not to forget. He wouldn't put himself in that kind of position again. No, Sarah Jean Sturdyvent, Amanda Green, or another woman, it didn't matter. They were all women. Any one of them could open him up for anguish. Agony that was worse than any he'd suffered in the war, worse than loss of the family plantation, worse than losing the Confederacy.

He heard a rustle across the fire and moving his hat back slightly peaked. Amanda's back faced him and he could see the rising and falling of her breathing. Again covering his eyes with the hat, he willed himself to go to sleep. Maybe he could figure out a way to lose her somewhere along the way. It'd sure be worth the try. Thinking about her or any other woman was a waste of time. He'd come to Arizona to get away from females. Until now, he'd done a pretty good job. But his mind continued to race. Thoughts of her lips under his, her body, her flashing blue eyes fought with his need to sleep.

Three

"We'll go to Ft. Bowie," Sheriff Denton said, glancing at Amanda.

Around them, cactus wrens flew from one plant to another an ant carried a tiny piece of hardtack away and the early morning sun began to warm the desert.

"Ft. Bowie? I didn't know there were any forts around here." She rolled her bedding into a tight bundle although she sensed his gaze following her every move. She tried to ignore his perusal and the quiver in the pit of her stomach. She hadn't slept well and he was the reason. Tying the bundle behind her saddlebag she concentrated on readying Pepper or their days journey.

Stepping around the horse as she adjusted the stirrups, she glanced at the sheriff. Their gazes met and locked. Unconsciously, her attention moved to his lips. For a moment, she remembered how they'd tasted the day before, salty, with a hint of tobacco. Her heart pounded in tune to the woodpecker working on a palo verde tree a few feet away. She willed her heart to slow and walked to the opposite side of the fire.

"Seems to me, there's a lot about this Arizona desert you don't know." His voice had taken on that stern authoritative tone again.

"Yes, but I'm willing to learn." She didn't want to start the morning arguing.

He looked at her like he would an unruly child. "One thing you'd better learn is everything in Arizona either bites, sticks or stings. Smart people watch where they sit, check their bedroll at night and give the cactus plenty of room."

Amanda didn't like the tone, but he did know more about living here than she did. Her sitting in an anthill proved that. "I'll remember that."

"Do you really think Simon would want you out here?"

So he's taking a different tactic this morning. Maybe its time I give him an idea what Simon was really like. "Simon didn't want me to do anything unless he approved and I've had enough of that. One person shouldn't be telling another every move to make. This is a free country. Even the slaves are free anymore."

"They are at that." He eyed her with a question in his dark eyes.

She ignored it and continued to ready herself to leave. He might as well know right now that she didn't intend to let a man, any man, push her around again. With everything packed, she pulled her bag of mush and a small pan from the saddlebags and walked to the fire where she made her breakfast. After it was cooked, she sat on a rock and dipped into it as he ate a slimy mixture he'd told her was gravy. "Where is Fort Bowie?"

"'Bout a days' ride east."

"Why go there?"

"We need food, and maybe Oldham's been through there."

"Good. I'd begun to wonder if you were taking me in circles." She finished the mush and started toward Pepper.

"And just why would you think I'd do a thing like that?" His brown eyes had grown stormy and she sensed he didn't like her thought. He'd finished eating too and was rubbing sand in his tin plate.

"I've heard that the best way to get rid of someone out here is to lead them in circles. You can't say you wanted me along." She stashed her bowl then readjusted the saddlebags.

"You're damn right about that." He crossed to his saddle. Picking it up, he groaned slightly. "But I ain't the kind of man who would leave a helpless woman out in the desert, by herself, with a bunch of Apaches around."

"Apaches?"

He stopped near his horse, and looked at her over his shoulder. "Yes, Apaches, the most ruthless of the red men in this area. I wouldn't want to meet up with them. What they do to white men shouldn't be done to anyone. And white women...?" He placed the saddle on the horse's back and cinched it down.

Amanda swallowed hard. She'd been so determined to make things right, she'd never completely considered the dangers she might be putting herself in coming on a trip like this. By Wade's seriousness, she knew he wasn't telling her this just to frighten her. Maybe she should listen to him.

"If you're planning to use that pan again, I'd suggest you wipe it out with sand, while it's still wet." He walked back to the fire. "We might not come upon water for awhile." For several minutes he worked covering the fire with sand and stones.

"I couldn't possibly eat out of a pan that's been cleaned with sand." Amanda patted Pepper's neck and wondered when they were going to leave. If this was dangerous country, maybe they should get out of it.

"Suit yourself." He shook his head, and his voice had taken on a complacent one. Without another word he swung into the saddle, clicked and moved away from their camp.

Amanda hastily mounted Pepper and followed. What was it about him that made her want to defy him? She could've brushed some sand in the pan, but taking his suggestion seemed akin to an order to return to Mineral Wells. She just couldn't do it.

The shadows had begun to lengthen again when they passed a mountain range, with one tall peak. They'd been riding in a southeasterly direction all day and had hit a dry riverbed that went through the San Simeon Valley. The lush, delicate grasses gave the horses something to munch on and occasionally, they came upon small pools of water.

As they rode, Amanda watched their surroundings carefully, trying to be sure they actually headed for the fort, but it was no use. All the mountains and grasses looked the same. She still thought Wade might be taking her in a circle.

He'd stopped riding several times to let the horses eat and drink. At noon, they let the animals graze for over an hour. They followed the wash for several miles through a narrow pass. From it, they came out onto rolling hills. Keeping his distance, Wade stayed ahead of her.

Amanda had been content to let him stay there, but as the afternoon wore on, she grew impatient. She'd thought they should have been at the fort already. "How much longer before we get there?"

He pulled up short on the horse's reins and waited for her. Pushing the hat back on his head, he leveled his gaze on her. "Probably four or five miles." The Southern drawl softened his voice.

"You're traveling very slowly?"

"I'm trying to keep myself alert to be sure we're alone." He spoke as one would to an inquisitive child asking too many questions.

"What do you mean?" Amanda hadn't seen a thing or sensed a need to be cautious.

Agitation crossed his face. He took a deep breath and leaned forward in the saddle. "We're in Apache country. Just because Fort Bowie's here doesn't mean all the Indians are gone. A band of renegades could be on us before we know they're around."

"Oh." She glanced around. The desert looked empty. Studying Wade, she realized he still hadn't relaxed. Was he really worried about her safety? She forced herself to look away. This rough, businesslike sheriff wasn't interested in anything except doing his job and at the moment she was part of that. "I didn't realize we were in any danger."

"How did you make it across this country alive?" He stared at her, the question in his dark eyes.

"I took the train to Independence. Then joined a wagon train to Santa Fe." She raised her chin slightly. He had to know she wasn't inept. "Then, I struck out on my own. I'm not as naive as you think, Sheriff. I just don't know anything about this part of Arizona Territory. I didn't study beyond Mineral Wells."

"Well, I think it's time you learned." His no nonsense attitude told her he thought this was serious business.

"I'll watch for Indians." Her voice sounded meek. She looked around, but except for them, all she could see was creasote bushes, green grass and cacti.

"You should. This is savage country. You need to remember that." He paused for a moment, his gaze still on her, sighed then shook his head. "Actually, I doubt they'd do anything worse to us than we did to ourselves." He turned away and spurred his horse.

Amanda urged Pepper to catch up with him. "During the War Between the States?"

He stopped. "Yes." The word rang with bitterness. He spurred his horse and rode away.

Amanda cantered up behind him.

He slowed and their horses matched their gates.

"Were you a soldier?"

"Yes."

"On which side?" She had to hear him say it, although she suspected she knew.

"The losing one." He clicked to his horse. They trotted toward a rise a few hundred yards away.

Amanda and Pepper followed, but didn't try to catch him. Obviously he felt bitter about the war, but she'd never felt either side won. A memory of the wounded and dying returned. No, the South may have surrendered, but nobody won. She rode up to the top of the rise where he'd stopped. A large building made of adobe loomed on the horizon - Fort Bowie. Humanity looked good to her.

"The store has been here awhile." Wade loosened his reins to give his horse his head as they rode slowly toward the building. "We'll pick up supplies and replenish our water at the spring. If they haven't seen Oldham, we're heading back to Mineral Wells tomorrow."

Amanda cringed. That wasn't what she wanted to hear, but this probably wasn't the time to argue. She let her gaze follow the direction he pointed. At the bottom of the hill a tiny green valley surrounded by more than a dozen palm trees spoke of continual water.

He stopped in front of the adobe building with a roof made of saguaro skeletal wood covered with palm leaves and dismounted. Bunches of dried red peppers, garlic and onions tied to the logs decorated the porch spanning the store length. Rough-hewn log benches offered weary travelers shade and rest. Through the glass paned windows, Amanda saw barrels, jars, buckets, guns, and other supplies inside. The sign above the door declared 'Tully, Ochoa, & Co.'

"It's almost as big as a town."

"No, it's only a trading post near the fort. Our business may not welcome here." Wade tied his horse to the hitch rail. "One of the owners is Indian, Chihuahua. I'm not sure how they'll take to a woman, particularly one in pants so, stay with me." His firm voice sounded irritated again.

She bristled. She'd sensed he, like most people she met didn't approve of her wearing trousers. Now his attitude proved it, but they were comfortable and easier to ride in than a dress. Anymore, she didn't care what other people thought, particularly Wade Denton. She'd come to search for Oldham. Slipping off Pepper she tied the horse to a hitch rail and tried to suppress the surfacing excitement. They just might be very close to Maurice Oldham. Without another word, she followed the sheriff inside.

Gooseflesh popped up on her arms. After having been in the heat so long the building felt very cool. The scent of fresh coffee, cinnamon and spices filled her nostrils bringing back memories of home. She breathed deep. In her carefree and happy days her father's store in Boston had smelled like this.

Wade strolled to the counter near the back. "Which building houses the commander?"

"The one with the flag out front." A rotund baldheaded man stood. His wiry mustache drooped on the left side and his dark eyes roved over them cautiously, measuring. "The captain should be there."

"We'll see in a few minutes." Wade leaned against the counter. "Do you have any sodie water? It's been a long dry ride."

"Got some, and it's cold." The man reached beneath the counter. "Two."

"You and the missus can make yourselves comfortable in there, if you want." He pointed toward an open door a few feet away.

His words burned in Amanda's ears. She expected Wade to set the storekeeper straight, but he didn't.

Instead, he slapped two coins on the table, took the bottles, and motioned her into the next room.

She tried to meet his gaze to let him know she didn't appreciate him not telling the storekeeper the truth, but he didn't look at her as she passed him and stepped ahead into a room unlike any she'd ever seen. Decorated in red and gold and trimmed in black, the room could have been in one of the best hotels in Boston. A large billiard table filled the center. Around it, small tables, surrounded by chairs silently awaited card games.

The storekeeper stepped inside looking a bit embarrassed. "I hope you don't mind, resting in the same room with a billiard table, Missus." His cheeks had grown pink and he had beads of sweat on his head. "This is the best we have to offer. It's the only pool table in the eastern part of the territory. I had it shipped from St. Louis." Pride filled his voice.

Amanda admired his humbleness as well as his desire to please her. She didn't want to offend him although she considered straightening him out on the missus part, but remembered Wade's warning. "I'm not in favor of gambling, but we won't be here long." She sat on a leather horsehair padded chair and sipped the drink.

"Should I go for the captain?"

"No, we'll visit him as soon as we finish our sodies." Wade leaned against the pool table, a casual air about him that hadn't been there before.

"Then I'll leave you to yourselves." He walked away.

The storekeeper had barely disappeared when Amanda hissed, "Why did you let him think we were married?"

"Because it's safer."

"Safer?"

"Yes, safer." He took a long drink seemingly unmoved by this inference.

She flushed. What had she gotten herself into?

"Not many men around here would understand a woman traveling alone. I'm not sure I do. If the soldiers think you're my wife, they'll leave you alone." He emptied his bottle. A glint of humor flashed in his dark eyes.

She sensed he enjoyed having her in a situation she couldn't control. "But, I didn't have any trouble before."

He sat the bottle on the table between them and leveled his eyes on her. "You weren't on a desert outpost with a hundred or more female starved men before."

"So, I wasn't." She sipped her sodie water, and turned away from him. She began to warm again, not from the heat, but from what he insinuated. Or was this a ploy, a way to get rid of her? If the sheriff had any ideas about losing her, he'd better change his mind. "What do we do now?"

"I'm going to ask the captain if they've heard or seen anything of Oldham. We'll restock our supplies and water and leave in the morning. If the captain doesn't know anything, I'm starting back to Mineral Wells."

"That's what you said earlier, but we can't go back until we've found Oldham."

"Mrs. Green." He scowled. "I'd like to remind you I'm the sheriff here. If I say we're going back we are. If no one has seen Oldham, it's unlikely he came this way. He's been gone six months. I don't want to stay away from town too long. If he decides to return, I want to be there. I have my doubts he took all the money with him."

Amanda gave him her complete attention, but her mind whirled. Rarely had they discussed Mineral Wells, but he'd never speculated anything about Oldham and the money before. "What do you mean? Where would the money be?"

"If I knew that, I'd have the case solved." He stood and walked to the billiard table, picked up a cue and set the balls. Bending, he shot, then turned and looked off somewhere above her. "According to Gladys, Oldham left town late one night on horseback, no saddlebags, clothes or food. That doesn't sound like a hardened criminal to me." He took some chalk and rubbed it on the cue tip. "I don't think he's in this alone. The money might even still be in town." Turning back to the table, he bent and hit the balls again.

"Who do you think is involved with him?" Amanda jumped up.

"If I knew, I wouldn't be out here, Mrs. Green." He straightened, turned and scrutinized her from head to toe. "For all I know, it could be you."

"But...but, I wasn't there when the money disappeared." Anger rose in her. How could he think such a thing?

Nonchalantly, he turned away and hit the cue ball again. Balls fell into several pockets. Laying the cue on the table, he swiveled. His gaze caught hers and held her in place. "How do I know you didn't plot with him before he ever came here? You didn't have to be there to be involved. Maybe you're just mad because he spent the money or hid it where you can't find it."

She couldn't believe her ears. He didn't really think this, did he? But before she could ask, he strolled away.

"It's time I went to see the captain."

Amanda seethed as she ran after him. Wade Denton didn't need to think he could get rid of her that easy.

The post commander's tiny office was small but tidy. Against the wall, in the corner near the front, sat a small cot with a linsey woolsey blanket. A round table surrounded by four straight chairs with caned seats was placed near the cot indicating the captain had occasional visitors. In the right corner a wash bowl and pitcher sat on a smaller table and the left corner, a United States flag. *Better accommodations than an enlisted man.*

Wade stood in front of the captain, trying to suppress his frustration. "But, I need to leave her here, Sir." He didn't want his voice to sound like a plea, but he felt desperate.

"Can't do it, Sheriff." The captain who had been sitting behind a rolled topped desk, stood and walked around it. Meeting Wade's eyes, he asked, "Why did you bring her along? Most men would make their woman stay at home."

A rush of anger gripped Wade, threatening his patience. He should have expected this from a northern officer, but the war was over. Since they were now on the same side, he'd hoped the man would understand.

"She's not my woman." His face warmed.

The captain's eyes twinkled. "Then why did you tell the storekeeper you were married?"

"I didn't." Wade paced around the room. "He assumed. I didn't correct him. I figure, a man and woman travelin' together should be married."

"Yes, normally." The captain watched him, but didn't relent.

Wade wished he'd kept up the charade, but when he'd tried, the captain had flatly refused to consider keeping Amanda.

"You a service man?"

"Yes, I served the Confederacy." Wade raised his head a little higher. His service record matched or bettered that of any man he knew. He'd had enough failures, he didn't intend for this Yankee to look down on him for being on the wrong side.

"Then, I'm sure you know an Army post is no place for a lady." The captain strolled back to his desk. "This post is pretty far from civilization. Some of these men haven't seen a single white woman in a year or more. To leave her here is asking for trouble. I don't plan on any."

"It wouldn't be more than a month or so."

The captain's right eyebrow lifted. "How long does it take women hungry men to fight over a female?"

Wade sighed. "Can we spend the night?"

"Down by the spring." The captain sank into his chair and flipped through the pages of a document he'd been reading when Wade entered.

"Have you seen Oldham?" Wade didn't want this visit to be a total loss.

"Can't say for sure. Had an incident several months' back. What does he look like?"

Wade pulled the crude drawing from his pocket.

The captain scowled, then looked at him. "Could be."

"What did he do?"

"Shot a man." The captain folded the paper and handed it back to him.

"Which way did he go?"

"Toward Mexico. We followed him to the border, then came back. Don't have any jurisdiction over there. One of the men was in Tucson a couple of weeks ago though and he thought he saw him there. I've wired the sheriff to keep a lookout for him."

Four

Sitting on a crude wooden bench in front of the post headquarters, Amanda gazed out over the camp. It was made up of a dozen or less adobe buildings with flat roofs. She glanced at the too heavy wooden door behind her wishing she could hear through it. Wade had insisted she wait here and she didn't like it. *Trust him? Not her!* And his insistences that he speak to the commanding officer alone made her think he hoped to leave her. *No way!* Over and over, she ran through her mind what she'd tell the captain if Wade ordered her to stay. He didn't think she had a reason to be here. She knew she did.

She looked away from the closed door, and noticed a building about half way down the street. A hint of smoke wafted up from the metal stovepipe. A whiff of something fried floated to her. Her stomach growled. Restlessness gripped her. Standing, she let her gaze travel over the buildings to a small cabin at the furthest end of the street. A horse tied outside marked it a livery stable. Their animals needed water and Wade couldn't leave without them.

She stepped off the tiny wooden porch, untied the reins and started down the nearly deserted street leading the animals behind her. She passed one soldier otherwise she was alone.

As she neared a cabin, the screened door burst open and a rooster darted out.

The bird wobbled into the street. It flopped, stood, then staggered.

A private wearing an apron and carrying a hatchet burst through the door. He ran after the bird yelling. "Stop! Stop!"

The frightened bird darted toward Wade's mule.

Panic filled Amanda.

For a moment, the mule stared at the chicken, then the bird darted between his legs. The mule bellowed, kicked, and bucked.

Dust billowed beneath the angry animal's feet.

Scurrying across the street, the rooster slipped beneath a building.

To keep from being kicked Amanda jumped away from the mule. The reins slipped from her hands.

The angry mule brayed, then bucked again.

Pepper and Wade's horse that had been standing docilely to the side joined in the fray.

Wade's gelding reared then ran down the street.

Pepper followed.

Amanda watched helplessly as their mounts disappeared.

The soldier stepped off the porch and joined Amanda in the middle of the street.

Realizing she needed to do something, she grabbed the mule's reins and tried to calm him. "Whoa!" She pulled the reins, but the angry animal continued to buck. Her hat slid off. Immediately, the mule stomped it into the sand.

"Give him room." The soldier shouted.

Amanda heard laughter behind her.

"Never saw a mule dance like that before," a male voice chuckled.

Speaking to the mule as calmly as she could, Amanda ignored the jeers.

Finally he stopped bucking.

Catching her breath, she brushed her hair away from her face as she continued to hold the reins.

"Yeah! Good goin'." The heckling soldiers had formed a circle around her, but she ignored them. She continued to speak soothingly to the mule.

As quickly as the jeering had started, the crowd quieted.

Amanda realized the mule wasn't the object of their attention anymore. She was.

"Did ya ever?" one soldier asked.

"A woman in pants," a husky voice added.

An eerie stillness crept over her. Amanda wanted to run, but she had no place to go.

The crunch of boots on the rocks interrupted the silence.

Turning toward the sound, her gaze collided with Sheriff Denton's stormy one.

"What are you doing?"

"I tried to water the animals." Her voice sounded weak, even to her ears. She lifted her chin a little higher meeting the angry sheriff's gaze without flinching.

"You could've waited for me." He took the reins from her.

"I could have, but they were thirsty, and I was restless." Her reasoning didn't seem as sound as it had when she was sitting on the captain's front porch, but she couldn't back down in front of all these men.

The anger in his eyes had turned them to ebony stones.

"I was doing fine until that chicken...." Glancing around she saw no chicken. Frustration filled her. "It was here."

The expression on his face told her reasons didn't matter. The silence suffocated her. She realized the fascinated soldiers were listening to every word. Lifting her head proudly she met Wade's glare without wavering. The anger she'd seen there a few seconds before seemed to have diminished. For a moment she thought she saw compassion, understanding, but no, it couldn't be, could it? The sheriff rather liked to see her in trouble, didn't he?

She dusted her trousers off and scanned the crowd. The men were waiting almost like they expected her to burst into tears or something. Well, she'd been through worse things than this. Picking her hat up, she plopped it on her head and stepped closer to Wade.

"Where are the horses?"

She pointed in the direction they'd disappeared.

He sighed.

"You can use one of our mounts to retrieve the animals, Sheriff," the Captain said.

Amanda started toward the livery. "I'll go. I'm the one who lost them."

"No, you won't." Wade caught her arm. His expression had changed, grown determined.

"It was my fault."

"I said no, Amanda." He stepped to the hitching post, securely tied the mule then walked toward the livery.

"You'd better come with me, Mrs. Denton, while your husband finds your mounts." The captain took her by the elbow and turned her toward his quarters.

"But...." She glanced at the mule standing docilely near the water trough. He looked like he'd never been excited.

"The troops aren't used to having a pretty women around. I try to keep an orderly camp. Back to work, men." In a whisper, meant only for her, he added, "It's not everyday my men get to see a woman in pants, Mrs. Denton."

"I'm not...." She glanced at him.

The warning in his eyes kept her from completing the sentence.

"I'm sorry about the animals." Amanda spoke from the blanket she'd spread beside the tiny spring. A soft breeze caressed her skin. The evening star twinkled like a crown jewel in the west. She looked at Wade. He'd been gone more than an hour retrieving the horses.

He grunted, but didn't speak as he worked building the fire.

They had eaten with the captain, pinto beans, fried potatoes and Indian fried bread. Since making camp, Wade hadn't spoken to her.

Amanda couldn't stand anymore silence. "Has the captain seen Oldham?"

"He's not sure." Wade sat on a rock and pulled his gun out.

"Not sure?" Excitement filled her as she watched him begin to clean the firearm again. "You sure clean that pistol a lot."

"Never know when I'll need it." He still hadn't glanced at her.

"Had the captain heard of Oldham?" She sensed pushing would only cause him to clam up, but she wanted to know more.

"Maybe."

"Oh?" Excitement filled her and she had to know more. "Where is he? Did he have any suggestions how we might find him?"

"No."

"What did he say?" She stood and walked around the fire toward him. Her agitation grew. She had a right to know whether he'd learned anything about Oldham, and she intended to find out – now!

He glanced at her, but didn't move. "The captain said this is no place for a woman." Wade's dark uncompromising gaze clashed with hers.

"Did you tell him I have a lot of money invested in this?" She continued to stare at him. The least he could do was tell the captain how important it was that they found Oldham.

"I did." He ran a ramrod down the gun barrel. "He agrees with me." His voice sounded flat, uncompromising. "This desert is no place for a woman."

Amanda knelt in the sand, a few feet from him. Somehow, they had to settle this, before he insisted she return to Mineral Wells. She had no intention of pleading, but they had to come to some kind of agreement. "He must've heard something?"

Wade stopped for a moment and looked at her. Anger disappeared and his eyes lost their fire. "He said a man was shot a few months back. They followed the suspect to the border, but he went into Mexico and they couldn't. One of his men saw a man they thought was the same one in Tucson a couple of weeks ago."

"Good, then that's where we're going next?" She smiled, not trying to hide her excitement.

"No, I'm taking you to Mineral Wells." His stare grew cold.

By the expression on his face, Amanda knew he didn't intend to change his mind. "Why?"

"Do you really have to ask?" He stood and slipped the gun into its holster then moved toward the fire. Kneeling with his back to her, he fumbled in the right pocket of his shirt, and pulled out cigarette papers. Opening the pack, he slipped one thin paper off, then closed it and put it back in his pocket.

"Yes, I have to ask."

He took a tobacco pouch from his pants pocket and sprinkled some on the paper.

Amanda's irritation increased. What was the matter with him? How would she convince him she desperately needed to find Maurice?

He rolled the paper into a tube shape around the tobacco then licked one side of it. Placing the cigarette loosely between his lips, he picked up a twig and held it in the fire until it glowed red, then he touched it to the tip.

"Obviously, you've never survived on nothing." Amanda didn't try to hide the frustration in her voice.

Drawing the smoke into his lungs, he blew it out through his mouth, then turned to her. "You don't know anything about me, Amanda." The smoke curled away from his lips and disappeared into the darkening night.

"No, I don't, but I'm desperate. Without Oldham, I don't have a chance of getting the money back." She let her words soak in as she watched him. If he insisted they return to Mineral Wells, she'd just have to go to Tucson by herself.

Silence wrapped around them. He slowly smoked the cigarette and finally tossed the butt onto the ground. Standing, he took a step and ground the remaining fire into the sand. "Is that right? Don't you know an unmarried woman shouldn't be out in the desert alone with a man?" He moved toward with the grace of a cat about to pounce. "You're driving me crazy, Amanda." Stepping closer, he bent over. His angry lips covered hers, as he slipped his arms around her pulling her to meet him.

Breathlessly, she clung to him as the force of the kiss took her wind. Naturally, she slipped her arms around his neck and felt her body responding to his. Any caution she'd ever had disappeared, as she tasted the warmth of his hungry mouth. Blood rushed to her head. Her heart pounded in her ears and she felt the thump of his beneath her breast. The anger had vanished as she returned the kiss fully. His hands roamed freely down her back, singeing through the shirt into her skin. She tingled with the warmth. Her head whirled, then as quickly as he'd pulled her to him he pushed away.

"You can't stay, Amanda. We're starting back to Mineral Wells tomorrow." Anger had returned to his eyes.

"Just because you keep wanting to kiss me?"

"Partly."

"Simon rarely kissed me on the cheek. Touching of any kind was wicked he'd told me."

"Well, I guess that was Simon's problem." He stepped a little further away.

"It might be sinful, but it sure does feel good." Warmth rushed to her cheeks. She probably shouldn't have said that, but she really wouldn't mind if he kissed her again.

"Yeah, I've noticed." He stared at her, his mouth a tight line.

"But, he wouldn't turn around if he thought it was Oldham." She didn't waver under his glare. "You'll be more than a two weeks starting to track him again."

"So I will." He walked to his saddle and sat.

"Well, I'm not going." She stepped around the fire to her blanket. "You can't make me, Wade Denton. I didn't come all this way to turn around now."

Wade leaned against the saddle and looked at her.

"I'm going on, with or without you." She sat on her blanket waiting for him to respond.

He didn't.

She lay down, took a deep breath, cleared her throat and then closed her eyes. What did he mean about her making him crazy? Why did she feel all weak-kneed and woozy when he kissed her?

Pushing thoughts of Wade and the sensations he'd produced out of her mind, she tried to forget the feelings he'd awaken. She'd never known anyone who excited her like he did. But, she had to find Oldham, get the money back.

Glancing across the fire, she saw that he had stretched out. He leaned his head against the saddle like he had the night before. Their kiss didn't seem to have affected him. If they continued to ride together, when she argued with him, she'd keep her distance, she couldn't afford to be in a titter all the time around him.

Three days later, Wade pulled his horse up beside Amanda's and stopped. "I think we'll start riding early in the morning and right before sunset." His gaze traveled her length. "The heat's hard on the horses. If Oldham is around, he's probably traveling then too."

Did he have any idea how miserable she felt? "It is quite hot." She wiped her brow with a bandana, but showed no other discomfort.

He watched her every move. A slight smile creased his lips then he raised an eyebrow. "You won't admit it's too hot will you?"

"It isn't." Sitting up straighter, she met his gaze without wavering. She hoped her resistance didn't encourage him to travel on, but she didn't want him to see her weakness. "I don't especially like it, but if you want to ride on, I can." She'd caused him enough trouble without complaining.

"Well, some of us know when we've had enough. I have and so have the horses." His voice sounded curt. He turned his horse toward the mountains, lifted his right hand and pointed. "According to the map I have, there should be a creek in these hills."

"I could use a little freshening."

Wade stopped and smiled the first genuine one she'd seen on his face since the first night she'd ridden with him. Pushing his hat back, he leaned on the saddlehorn and shook his head. "Amanda, you're as stubborn as any man I ever knew."

She didn't know whether to thank him or be angry, but decided the statement was a compliment. "Thanks, Sheriff."

"It wasn't meant to flatter you." He spurred his horse and pointed him toward the taller hills. "What will it take for you to give up?"

If she hadn't been so hot, she'd have told him she never quit. Instead, she clicked to Pepper and followed him.

They rode for a couple of miles over flat sandy soil that was occasionally spotted by a creasote or jojoba bush, but little else. Not even birds or lizards disturbed the open spaces. In the distance, the boulders seemed to get bigger, more irregularly shaped and towering. The trail disappeared near the edge of the rocks.

Amanda admired how Wade found the narrow canyon he guided his horse through. She didn't see it and wouldn't have guessed it lay ahead in these craggly rocks. Shear cliffs rose several hundred feet above them on either side of the passage. Shadows fell across the entrance. The air felt cooler. Jojoba and creasote bushes clumped together interrupted prickly pear and cholla cactus dotting the landscape. Ahead a saguaro stood sentinel. The land didn't look so barren and lonely.

Suddenly, a shot pierced the silence. Startled, Amanda screamed and watched, horrified as Wade slumped forward in the saddle. Instantly, his horse bolted and Wade's limp body slipped to the ground.

Amanda jumped from Pepper holding the reins tightly. Behind the frightened horse she huddled and waited for the next shot.

Silence.

Wade lay deathly still in the sand.

Using Pepper for cover, she worked her way to him. She touched his neck. His face was ashen. At first, she didn't feel movement. Fear engulfed her. A faint pulse moved under her sensitive fingers. She rolled him over. Blood stain marked his right shoulder and the sand beneath it.

She heard a noise. Glancing toward the sound, she saw a cloud of dust.

Riders circled then escaped through the canyon entrance.

She looked back at Wade. He needed attention. Blood oozed from the wound. She'd seen too many other men wounded. He needed the bullet out - now.

Amanda tied Pepper to a nearby bush then ran back to Wade. Lifting him slightly, she leaned him against a rock.

He roused. "What happened?"

"Someone shot you."

"Oh." He fell back.

Slipping her neckerchief off, Amanda tied it around his shoulder. Her heart sank. She didn't see signs of water nearby, but in the distance, a small grove of sycamores offered hope.

Wade's horse and mule had disappeared. Their tracks led toward the trees. Wiping sweat that formed on her forehead away, she ran to Pepper and untied her. She pulled on the reins and led the horse to the wounded sheriff. Bending over him, she asked, "Can you hear me?"

He nodded slightly.

"I've got to move you closer to water."

He didn't respond.

Leaning over him, she said, "You've got to help me. You're too heavy." Sliding his good arm around her shoulders, she started to lift. "Stand!"

He didn't move.

"Please, Wade, you've got to help me help you."

Slowly he began to rise.

She leaned him against Pepper. His knees started to buckle, but she righted him. She knelt behind him, grasping the back of his knees and tried to raise him.

He didn't budge.

Relaxing for a moment, she took a deep breath then lifted again.

Gripping the saddle horn with his uninjured arm, he pulled.

She pushed.

Once she'd draped him over Pepper she stepped back and caught a breath. The bandana on his shoulder was no longer blue, but black with blood. Hastily, she led Pepper toward the sycamore trees and hopefully water.

Amanda pulled the cork off the whiskey bottle and lifted it to her lips. Alcohol burned as it slid down her throat, but she began to calm. A misshapen piece of lead, still wet with Wade's blood, lay beside the blanket. The air smelled of singed skin from the cauterized wound. Her hand shook. She stuffed the cork back into the bottle.

Would her best be good enough? Memories came flooding back, of all those men she couldn't help, no matter how she tried. The smell of his blood reminded her of war horror, the sight of arms and legs lying in piles. The doctors had removed, hoping to save the men. Many times, she'd stepped away from the hospital tents just far enough not to disturb delirious men and lost what little food she'd consumed that day.

Wade had called her stubborn a little while before. Without her determination he'd be dead now.

He slept.

Is he healing, or has he passed out again?

Night sounds filled the air as she picked up some twigs to make a fire. An owl hooted. A stream gurgled, but Amanda had only found a tiny lake and Wade's mule nearby. Pepper snorted. The mule swished its tail. Stars twinkled overhead. Although she'd kept Wade's Colt Peacemaker close all day, no one had come near them in this desert oasis.

Putting some side meat into the pan on the fire, she plopped down beside him. Fatigue overcame her. Lying down, she fell asleep.

Five

Amanda pondered her predicament as she stirred the broth. She was a long way from the fort and even further from a town. What if Wade didn't survive? Although she knew the general direction they'd ridden from Ft. Bowie, she wasn't sure she could make it back alone and there was the matter of Apaches. She shuddered. She couldn't think of it. Wade had to survive. If he didn't she'd decide then whether to continue toward Tucson or return to the fort or Mineral Wells.

A sliver of moon hung on the horizon, but morning crept over the eastern edge of the mountains. The chilled breeze brushed lightly against her arms, heightening her senses.

Wade moaned on the blanket behind her.

She turned.

His eyes were still closed. He'd been feverishly moaning for hours.

She could do nothing but wait and hope his body fought the infection.

"No!"

She watched him.

"No!"

Dropping the spoon she ran to him. "What is it?" She leaned over and touched his forehead. It was hot. She took a cloth she'd been using and ran to the lake where she dipped it in the cold water than placed it on his hot brow.

"Don't do that to him!"

She sat down, bent closer. This wasn't the first time she'd seen a wounded soldier cry out in his sleep.

"I said don't do that to him!" He sat up, opened his eyes and swung his unhurt arm at an unknown assailant.

Amanda tried to grab his flailing arm, but even injured, he was strong. Walking behind him she slipped her arm around his chest and laid him against the blanket.

His arm dropped to his side and he drifted off to sleep again.

Wade blinked, but let his eyes close. He ached from head to toe. Obviously, he'd been dreaming, but where was he? Opening his eyes again, the surroundings came into focus. Bits and pieces started returning. This was some kind of canyon. Overhead he saw a tree. His gaze followed the branches, until azure sky came into view, then a buzzard flew overhead.

Not yet, he grimaced. He wasn't dead. Blinking, he rolled over slightly. His backside felt like he'd been lying in one place for a week and the rest didn't feel much better. How long had he been here? Amanda? Where was she? Had she been hit too? His stomach churned as the thought hit him. No. He wasn't exactly sure why, but an inner peace filled him. She was alive. Glancing at his shoulder, he saw the rag, proof she'd taken care of him. What had she covered under there? Vaguely, he remembered a whiskey bottle being pushed down his throat. She'd been digging around in his wound, and hadn't been too gentle, either.

He didn't see her, but a crumpled blanket indicated she wasn't far away. Then he saw the campfire and a small lake beyond. His gaze returned to the whiskey bottle. He reached for it, but pain shot through him. "Damn!" He fell back. Why hadn't she left it a little closer?

He tried to relax and let the pain subside, but didn't feel much better. Overhead, the vulture had disappeared. *That's good, I'm not ready to be buzzard food yet.* His stomach growled. He saw a small flame under a tin pan above the fire. Amanda had something cooking. With his good arm, he tried to sit, but pain gripped him again. He decided to wait. Lying quietly, for a few moments, he wondered who had shot him. Water splashed. Turning toward the lake, he looked past the fire.

The pool of water glistened cool and clear in the late morning sunlight as he focused on the source of the sound.

Amanda glided gracefully on her back across the pool. The water made her fair skin look milky and unflawed as she reached the opposite shore where she dove beneath then resurfaced several yards closer to where he lay. Diving deeply, she resurfaced several seconds later, then swam vigorously toward camp.

About half way across, she stopped and stepped to shore. Picking up something, she turned and glided back into the water. Plunging in again, she stayed beneath the surface long enough he began to wonder if something had happened to her, but gracefully she pulled herself up on a flat rock and began to rub her hair lavishly. Foam appeared around her head and floated down her shoulders onto her breasts.

Her flawless skin shimmered in the light. Firm taut breasts pointed toward the sun and the suds caressed them. Sliding back into the water, she disappeared, resurfacing quicker this time. The suds cascaded over her shoulders. Delicate blond strands of hair fell nearly to her waist. Tresses of gold glowed like ripe wheat after a gentle summer rain.

Wade felt movement in his lower body. He had ignored these feelings for a long time and he had survived. Why did she have to reawaken them now? He let the scene fade as pain ripped through him. Continuing to watch could only cause one thing, more pain, intense and different than the one in his shoulder. Glancing down again, the true meaning of his injury came to him.

He'd been concerned about trying to take care of her, while she'd obviously saved his life. *Typical for him.* The water reminded him of his brother. That day, it'd been warm and sunny just like today. He'd done everything he could to save him, but his best wasn't enough. After traveling a long way to forget he couldn't let one woman make him vulnerable to that kind of pain again. But, his eyes involuntarily popped open and he focused on her.

The memory of how her lips tasted invaded his thoughts. They'd been soft and sweet, when he'd kissed her, like the rest of her body looked now. Turning away, he wondered how long it had been since those kisses. *Yesterday, the day before?* He wasn't sure. How long had he been out?

He focused on the lake again. She'd stopped swimming and appeared to be watching him. Then she dove in reminding him of dolphin he'd once seen off the coast of Florida. Letting his head fall against the blanket, he tried to blot the vision from his mind. She was magnificent, the most beautiful woman he'd ever seen. When he'd met her that first day, in Mineral Wells, he'd thought she was a boy. There was nothing boyish about her!

After a few moments, his gaze sought her again. She wasn't in the pool, but near the boulder where he'd seen her disappear. Dressed in white underclothes, she combed her hair. The tresses fell forward as she bent toward the water, reminding him of fine spun silk he'd once seen in San Francisco. The fabric had been soft and smooth in his rough hands, just as he knew those golden strands would be. Sunlight filtered through her hair, making it shimmer. Again, his body reacted to the sight of her.

She was alluring like no other woman. Or, was it the injury? *A dream?* He hoped so. Drifting off to sleep, his mind waged a war. He was a failure. Everyone who'd relied on him had suffered; his brother, Fred Bessler, his mother and now Amanda. Sarah Jean had been right to reject him. Even here in this beautiful oasis he'd let Amanda down. But just before he fell asleep the sensations she'd awaken returned, stronger and more intense.

Amanda ambled back to camp, leaving her clean clothes on the rocks to dry. The sun beat down on her, but the rocks and water offered protection she hadn't felt in the open desert. The air wasn't nearly as hot as the day before. She felt fairly safe although she carried Wade's six-shooter strapped to his belt around her waist.

A tiny lizard scurried in front of her, but the buzzard she'd noticed earlier had disappeared. Azure sky, clear and bright, made her eyes ache when she looked into it. Never before had she been in such a beautiful place that could be so dangerous.

Walking toward the campfire, she glanced at Wade. He seemed to be sleeping peaceably. What had he been dreaming? Did it have something to do with the war? At the fire she removed the pan of broth she'd been cooking.

Earlier she'd caught Wade's horse and retrieved the saddlebags. Trying not to disturb him she stepped to the bags and removed a frying pan. He thrashed restlessly on the pallet, but she hoped he was getting some healing rest. Placing a small piece of the dwindling bacon in the skillet, she listened to it sizzle. The scent filled the camp.

"Smells good." His voice sounded weak, but steady.

Turning toward him, her heart leapt with joy. "You're awake!"

"I'm starved." His gaze met hers and he smiled slightly.

The spark in his dark eyes gave her hope he would survive, but it was still early. One couldn't always tell. Too many times she'd seen men appear to be improving then take that terrible turn for the worse. Wade couldn't do that - he just couldn't.

"How's your fever?" She crossed to him and placed her hand on his forehead. He felt cooler, but the physical contact made her skin singe. "I've got broth." Pulling her hand away she walked to the fire and retrieved the simmering pot. She tried to ignore the fact her heart beat faster than it had a few minutes before, but she couldn't disregard the reality that while he was asleep, she'd thought nothing of touching him, now she felt self-conscious when she did.

"What did you do to me anyway?"

She looked at him.

He pointed toward the shoulder.

"The bullet was deep." She picked up the pan and walked back to him. Sinking down beside him, she pushed the uncomfortable thoughts away. She was a nurse. She did whatever she had to see her patients got well. She offered him a spoonful of broth.

"It feels like you cut my shoulder off." He sipped hungrily.

"I never removed a bullet before."

"Well, you didn't have to experiment on me." His voice was harsh, his eyes angry.

"If I hadn't, you wouldn't be talking to me now." She dipped into the pan.

"I wouldn't?" He sounded surprised.

"No, you wouldn't. You'd have bled to death."

The anger disappeared. "I guess, I owe you my life then, Amanda Green." His voice sounded husky.

"Don't get melodramatic on me, Sheriff Denton." She pushed the spoon between his lips. "I didn't do more than anyone else would have."

"Did you see who shot me?"

"No, I was too busy trying to keep from being hit myself."

"Maybe it was Oldham."

"There were two of them. I saw through the dust when they rode away." She fought to keep her voice sounding impersonal. It wouldn't do for him to know how frightened she'd been.

"You haven't seen anyone since they left?"

"No, we've had the place all to ourselves." She dipped the last of the food for him.

"Thanks, Amanda." He slid back down.

"You'd better rest now." She used the efficient tone she'd developed during the war. "You need a lot of rest to help rebuild the blood you've lost."

He let his head drop back to the pallet and closed his eyes.

She wasn't sure he'd heard her.

* * *

He was lying on the cot, a filthy blanket wrapped around him. The moans had awakened him again. Glancing at the cot beside him, Wade tried to blot the vision from his mind. His best friend, Fred Bessler, lay there. His leg had been amputated above the knee, but Wade could see the blood seeping onto the rag tied over the stump.

"Guard!"

Quiet.

"Guard!" He had to get help. "Where the hell is the doctor?" He woke up.

Glancing around, Wade saw he wasn't in the prison. A lather of sweat wet his shirt. He fell back against the blanket and took a deep breath. Then, someone moved near him. His eyes popped open.

She stood over him, the blue eyes piercing into his looking like an angel, an avenging angel. Then he remembered. He was under a tree in Arizona Territory. This was desert, not Libby Prison. The sky was even brighter than her eyes.

He looked at her again. She was a Yankee angel that's what she was. Amanda Green had saved him, but she wasn't an angel at all. One day, she'd kicked, hit, and tried to bite him. He'd discovered she'd been following him that day. How long ago was that?

"Are you all right?" She placed her cool hand on his hot brow.

"Yeah. Just a dream." He closed his eyes and wished it hadn't happened. This wasn't the time for a reoccurring nightmare, but he didn't have control over them and he didn't want her or anyone else to know.

"I think your fever is breaking again. Lie back so I can put a cool cloth on your forehead." She took the cloth from his head, then walked away.

He let his head drop back against the blanket, closed his eyes and finally slept.

The next time he woke, Wade felt better. It was about dark, but he felt stronger. The fire crackled and flickered in the waning light. A cricket chirped in a nearby bush and in the distance a coyote wailed. He smelled the wood smoke and soil on which he lay. Yes, he was going to live. Pushing himself up on his good arm he watched her.

She sat with her back to him, her figure silhouetted against the flames. What had she made of his outburst? Had he frightened her? Her shoulders were hunched foreword and she seemed to be far, far away. Why had a beautiful young woman like her traveled to this barren land alone? Of course, he knew the reason she gave him, but why was she so desperate? It didn't make sense.

His head started to clear, but his shoulder still throbbed. He owed her a lot - she'd saved his life. "What's the matter?"

She jumped restlessly, and turned toward him.

"I didn't mean to scare you."

"I'm surprised you're awake. You were sleeping restlessly." She eyed him, a haunting expression in her blue eyes.

"I know that. What's the matter with you?" She was hiding something, he was sure. Of course, she had a right to be jumpy, but she hadn't been until now.

"Oh, nothing." She strolled toward him, but her eyes didn't agree with her words. They said something had happened and she didn't want to tell him what. "Why do you ask?"

"When I spoke to you, you appeared to be deep in thought. You jumped like I'd shot you."

She knelt on the blanket near him, usually she didn't do that unless she was feeding him. She smelled musty, like she'd been riding. Her hands were fisted together in front of her like she was holding some secret.

"What's the matter, Amanda?"

"I thought I'd see if I could find any clues about who shot you. I found more than I bargained."

"What do you mean?"

"A body. Probably prospector, but...his face has been blown away. Up in those rocks." She pointed to the boulders behind and above them. "I haven't been able to figure out why they left us, and I guess, I'm scared."

"It's a little late to get frightened now." He touched her hands. They felt cool and clammy and he wanted to warm them. "You can handle things, you've already proved that."

She took a deep breath and appeared a little calmer, but glanced toward the rocks again.

A prospector dead? Other than the Apaches he'd seen the day she'd caught up with him, their trip had been lonely. "Have you seen anyone else?"

"No, but the men who shot you may know we're still here if they're outside waiting for us to leave."

"I'm feeling better. I can't chase anyone yet, but I can shoot, if I have to." Somehow he had to let her know he'd take care of her.

"Normally, I don't get squeamish, Sheriff, but that man, maybe it's because this is such a pretty place. It's hard to imagine horrors here." Her voice seemed to echo through the coming night.

"I know." He looked above them. Stars twinkled overhead. The pool of water made a gentle gurgling sound. He glanced at her.

She watched him.

He wanted to take her into his arms and reassure her everything would be all right, but his strength ebbed. He lay back against the blanket. "I don't intend to let my guard down again."

"That makes two of us." She smiled.

Suddenly, he wanted to know more about her. That Simon--had he made her promise to clear his name? How could a man who loved a woman expect anything like that? Could there be something between her and the former banker she hadn't told him? Had she been using the money as a way to search for her lover? "Where'd you learn it?"

"What?"

"How to take a bullet out?"

"It's the first one I ever took out on my own." She looked uncomfortable and rose to her feet.

"But...?" He wanted to hear her story, but realized he was going at it the wrong way. "You said you nursed. Nurses don't usually remove bullets on their own. Where'd you learn it?"

"I'd rather not talk about it, Wade."

"Why not?"

"It's not a pleasant memory."

"But, if you're digging around in me for bullets, I have a right to know where you learned." Frustration rose in him. He wasn't sure why he pressed the issue. Didn't he have a right to know?

"I told you I was a nurse during the war. Now does that satisfy you?" She walked toward the fire.

"All right." He leaned against the saddle and watched her silently move around the camp. She added some jerky and water to the pan before stirring the fire.

Why wouldn't she talk about the War? She'd helped on the winning side. It couldn't have been as bad for her as it was for him, could it? Of course, she'd lost her husband and she obviously felt some guilt for that. "I thank you for saving my life," he called, although he'd already told her twice.

If she hadn't been along, he'd have died. He remembered Fort Bowie and how he'd tried to convince the captain to keep her there.

He'd only been thinking of his resolve to stay away from women. The one thing he'd never wanted was to be grateful to one of them. They needed and expected things he couldn't give. The memory of his grief-stricken mother's face after his brother's death returned. Such anguish he couldn't describe. Although she'd pulled Wade to her and told him she knew he'd done everything he could, he hadn't been able to convince himself he couldn't have saved his brother's life.

Amanda turned toward him, but he couldn't see her eyes. "It was no more than I would have done for anyone else."

Damn, don't you think I know that? He concentrated on the millions of stars overhead. Somewhere deep down, he wished she'd wanted to save him for himself, not because she saw him as any other soldier she'd helped. Loneliness overcame him like he hadn't felt since he'd left the cold damp confines of the prison. He willed himself to sleep. He had to think about getting well, not about Amanda Green.

The next three days passed slowly for Amanda. To her relief, no one came into the canyon. She buried the prospector and searched the place where she thought the shot that hit Wade might have come from. The hoof-prints in the sand near the prospector proved there had indeed been two riders.

Wade continued to improve, although he still spent most of the time sleeping. He hadn't moved away from the blanket.

With broth from a rabbit she'd shot, Amanda prepared a tantalizing stew made of wild greens spiced with leeks. She hoped the sheriff would be well enough to travel within another week.

Occasionally, her thoughts drifted to her mother and Simon. If she'd listened to them, she wouldn't know how to do any of these things, but in Boston, where her mother wanted her to be she wouldn't need to. Was it wrong to be like she was? She'd tried not to think about it much, but having time on her hands always brought the questions back. She forced her thoughts away from her troubling memories to Oldham, but she had no desire to search for him alone.

Leaning against a sycamore tree, her head bobbed sleepily in the late afternoon heat. A bee buzzed around a hedgehog cactus, its bright pink blossom offering a tasty source of nectar. A hush fell over the little oasis. Amanda forced her eyes open, willing herself to stay awake. Now she understood why people living here took siestas. As she started to stand, she heard water splash. Following the sound with her eyes she saw Wade.

A few feet away, he leaned into the water, washing his face and hair. Relief flowed through her. After the second day, she'd thought he'd be all right, but when he continued to sleep, she started to doubt her diagnosis. Obviously, she'd been correct. She stood and walked toward him, but hesitated a few feet from where he bent into the lake. Her stomach quivered as she watched him wash himself.

He'd taken his torn shirt off and used it to dampen his head. His taut back muscles rippled in the afternoon sunshine. Amanda couldn't pull her eyes away. He was strong and virile, but she had seen plenty of barebacked vibrant men before, why did he affect her this way?

Simon would say these feelings were wrong and without a doubt her mother would agree. Only her father would understand and he'd died a week after she married Simon. Sometimes, she thought he'd known he was dying and that's why he'd insisted she marry his friend. Financially, she'd had a secure life, but marriage had not been what she expected. Once she'd tried to talk to her mother about it, but had received a lecture on being grateful for what she had. Although she didn't agree totally, her mother had a point. There were a lot of women with less than she had, so she didn't complain openly anymore.

Wade felt Amanda watching him, but he didn't turn around. He continued to wash his face, letting the chill of the cool water seep into his hot flesh. At some point, he'd had a fever. He remembered thrashing around in his sleep. What day was it? How long had he been out? Just what had he said? His shoulder ached, but not with the earlier raging, burning sensation. Once when Amanda dressed his wound with a clean bandage, he saw the bullet hole. He would always carry the gunman's mark, but she seemed pleased there were no signs of infection.

His head throbbed. When he tried to remember how they had gotten into this canyon, he couldn't. Pain was what he remembered. Amanda Green feeding him, tending his shoulder, examining him with a worried expression in her blue eyes.

"It's about time you woke up." She stood behind him, several feet away.

"That might be well for you to say, but I doubt your head hurts like mine." He continued to wash. The pain eased and he started to feel better. Turning, he glanced at her, and let the water drizzle through his hands.

One button of the light blue cotton shirt she wore was open at the neck. The shirt fell loosely from her shoulders and hinted at the soft curves of her breasts. She'd rolled the long sleeves above her elbows and her skin had a soft golden tan.

He straightened and turned toward her.

She looked a lot like she had the first day he'd seen her. The shirt was tucked neatly beneath the waistband of dark brown trousers, successfully hiding her feminine figure. A pair of black suspenders and black, rugged, well-worn boots finished off her attire. It looked like she'd tried to clean the boots but the desert sand permanently colored them.

His gaze wandered to her face.

She'd tied her hair in a knot on top of her head. All that was missing was the battered hat. She carried it in her right hand.

Wade had an urge to step up to her, unwind her hair and let it drop around her shoulders, pull her close and taste her rosy lips again. Something about her guarded expression told him now wasn't the time. Besides that, his strength had started to slip away. Turning back to the pool, he knelt over, scooping more water into his hands, hoping to regain his strength. He was glad to be alive, even if he did have a few aches and pains.

"You need to be careful not to reopen the wound." She stepped closer.

From his kneeling position, he eased himself to the ground. He dried his hair with the cloth he'd picked up. Dizziness came over him. He wasn't going to make it back by himself. He looked up at her.

Their gazes met.

Normally he wouldn't have asked, but he didn't have another choice. "Can you help me back to bed?"

"I thought you were rushing it." She smiled knowingly.

God, she's beautiful when she smiles.

"If you'd asked, I'd have brought you water to wash." Her voice had grown stern.

Now she sounds like a nurse, givin' orders. Probably better she puts some distance between us like that. He couldn't let his feelings run away while he was in a weakened state of mind and body. "I feel better," he said. "I can't expect you to do everything." His voice sounded gruff. That was all right too. If he started apologizing, she'd start ordering him more. It was better if she thought him angry. Only weak men relied on women. He had his failings, but he didn't have to advertise them. He'd never been dependent before and he didn't intend to stay that way now. Next time he stood, he'd do it on his own.

Amanda plopped the hat on her head, then stepped beside him. Taking his good arm, she draped it over her thin shoulders. The warmth of her soft body seared into his bare skin through her thin shirt. He tried to concentrate on walking rather than the rounded breast pressed against his ribs.

"Lean on me." She tightened her hold on him.

As they moved, he became fully aware of her.

Her swelling breasts rubbed against his chest, creating sensations he had thought he could ignore. He forced himself to stand. "I'm heavy."

"I can handle it." She pulled him to her again.

Another spasm of dizziness hit him. He leaned into her and let her lead him.

"Now, do as I say." Her voice grew gruff, as she efficiently lowered him to the blanket. Wrath flared in her blue eyes. "I know you think you're strong, Sheriff Denton, but right now you aren't. It won't kill you to let a woman help you once in a while."

Anger rose in him. He looked away, rather than get into a sparring match with her. *Damned if she isn't reading my mind.*

A lizard darted into a crevice of a nearby rock and a hummingbird worked on a cholla blossom a few feet away. They didn't notice the confusion in him. He leaned back against the blanket as his equilibrium returned.

Amanda straightened a corner of the pallet they'd rumpled then started to walk away. Stopping at the edge, she turned around. "If you feel the need to wash or do anything else, tell me first. I'll help. With no more than you've had to eat, you're weak." Without waiting for an answer, she pivoted and walked to the fire where she bent and began to stir something.

His loins warmed. The trousers hugging her hips were smooth, her breasts taut against the fabric of the shirt. A memory of her sweet mouth returned. He fought the desire to call her, the longing to kiss her again. "I guess I am weaker than I thought."

"Sometimes having a woman around does come in handy, Sheriff." She turned and her gaze flashed into his eyes defiantly.

"Maybe, I was wrong." His lips curved into a slight smile hoping he could defrost the ice in her blue eyes.

She looked away, stirred the broth, then gazed out over the pool of water.

"How long have I slept?"

She turned slightly. "Five days."

"Five days, I've been asleep." He sat straighter and leaned against the tree.

Five days? Was it Oldham who had shot him? If so, the banker could be anywhere. He'd been hired to catch the thief. For five days, he lay sleeping. He didn't have time to think about injuries or his companion. He needed to concentrate on his job. Glancing toward the rocks where Amanda told him she'd found the prospector, he started to make plans. Tomorrow, he'd be strong enough to investigate.

Six

"Mr. and Mrs. Wade Denton."

The hotel clerk's voice came to Amanda over the sound of wagons, riders, miners and the occasional tinkle of a piano in the street outside. She had just stepped inside the building. Four days before, they'd left the little oasis and Wade had seemed to grow stronger each day. Although they'd met only a few people until they neared Tucson, she didn't think she'd ever been so glad to be in town before.

She moved closer to the counter set the saddle she carried on its horn and leaned it against the wall. She scowled at the Wade, but he ignored her as he wrote something on the register. No way did she plan to share a room with him, or pose as his wife again. Although they had ridden together nearly three weeks, and he'd convinced the soldiers at Fort Bowie he was her husband, they didn't have to duplicate the act in Tucson.

"Wade?" She stepped closer.

He accepted the key and didn't glance at her. "This way, darlin'," he drawled, in an unnatural voice. He bent and picked up his saddle then took her arm. "I told you, you'd love Tucson. The Old Pueblo, fastest growin' town in Arizona. Before you know it, it'll be as cultured as Boston."

Amanda looked around. The hotel clerk watched, as were two men who sat in the lobby. This wasn't the place to make a scene, but she detested the idea Wade was using her, just like Simon had done when he wanted to.

He released her arm as she picked up her saddle.

Together they climbed the stairs.

"Wade?"

He frowned and shook his head, then led her down the hall where he found their room and opened the door.

Seething, Amanda brushed past him. She sat the saddle in the middle of the floor leaning it against the bed then turned on him. "What do you mean, telling them I'm your wife?" Out of the corner of her eye, she saw the huge hand-carved cherry wood four poster bed. "Whose bed is this?" It stood ominously near the middle of the room, covered with a feather stitched double wedding ring quilt made of silk blocks. A good deal of time went into the making. Shipping the bed from New York or St. Louis must have been quite an accomplishment. This didn't look like a normal hotel room. The thought of being alone here with Wade Denton made her edgy.

"It belongs to the hotel." His tanned features flushed slightly. He stepped to the corner and sat his saddle down.

"This is too nice to be a regular hotel room." Amanda nervously moved toward the door.

"It's the only room available." His gaze rested levelly on hers.

She wasn't sure whether she could believe him or not. "I planned to get a room by myself."

A sheepish grin crossed his face. "I had to think fast. There are a lot of miners and cattlemen in town."

"Well, think fast on something else. I have the money to pay for a room, and I intend to have one. There are other hotels." She started to open the door.

His arm shot out, stopping her. "Don't you see?" He turned her toward him, his dark eyes darker pleading for understanding. "Married women are safer. If you had a room by yourself, even if one was available, people would get one idea. You wouldn't be there more than an hour before you'd have company. You may not like being with me, but you're safe. As protected as anyone."

Amanda stared into his dark eyes and saw sincerity she'd noticed several times but chose to ignore. Could he really be concerned for her wellbeing, or did he just want to have control over her? Of course, the folks from Mineral Wells would know by now she'd followed him, if he went back alone he'd have questions to answer. "Who gets the bed?"

"You can sleep on one side, I'll take the other. You don't have to worry about me bothering you." He stared into her eyes without flinching. "I've found rattlesnakes I'd rather sleep with." The words filled the room as if he'd spoken them over a megaphone.

Her mouth dropped open. The heat rose to her cheeks and her eyes stung with hot tears. Blinking to suppress them, she turned away from him. She couldn't let him know how much his words hurt, now or ever.

His boots scuffed on the wood floor. "Here."

She turned slightly.

He stood with his hand on the door handle and tossed her the key.

She grabbed it, mid-air.

"Lock the door on the inside. I'll order you a bath. When I come back, I'll have some clothes that make you look like a woman. These men won't understand a man letting his wife run around looking like one of them." He opened the door and exited without looking back.

Amanda flung her battered hat at the closed door. The sting of what he'd said subsided, but it didn't cool her anger. What did he mean by that statement? Was she really as repulsive as a snake?

Simon had never treated her like a real wife, why should she think a man as virile and attractive, as Wade Denton would consider her other than a troublesome traveling companion? Or was he just trying to keep some space between them? Did she flatter herself with such as thought?

"What have you got that on for?" Wade stood just inside the hotel room door.

"Because it's mine." Amanda stepped toward the open window.

He looked around the room. A tiny hand-carved table matched the bed and stood near the one window. Unbleached muslin curtains blew in the light breeze. A braided rug filled the small space between the bed and the table that held a china water pitcher and matching bowl. Two muslin towels were neatly folded beside the bowl. The only other piece of furniture, a dressing table, had been placed near the door. It also matched the bed. A gold gilt-framed portrait of a young couple graced the middle of the wall. This looked like a room for honeymooners. The thought made his stomach churn.

"You have a dress, and I want you to wear it." He glanced at the unopened package still laid on the bed. "I guess the Chinaman delivered it."

"A tiny man with a long braided pigtail delivered a package. It didn't have my name on it, so I didn't open it. I don't know whether the man was Chinese or not." Huddling against the window she acted like she was trying to keep away from him.

He didn't like the sulky tone in her voice. "I told you I was going to buy you a dress." He stepped further into the room. *Damn, he'd sure messed things up! Nothing about her reminded him of a snake. Why had he said that?*

"How was I supposed to know the package was for me? Like I said, it didn't have my name on it." Her arms were crossed under her breasts and she wore the same determined expression he'd witnessed too many times since he'd met her.

"I thought we'd see Tucson, and if we're going to have dinner at the hotel, you'll need to wear that dress." He sounded angry, but he didn't care. Hadn't she discovered yet the havoc she caused around a bunch of men? Did he have to spell it out for her? It was bad enough what she did to him.

The thought of spending the night in this room with her was about all he could handle. He really should've let her pay for her own room, but if some other man got to her.... What did he care? He hadn't invited her along. She wasn't his responsibility. Of course, she'd saved his life, he owed her something, but she was an adult. If she wanted a room alone, he should have let her have it, no matter what kind of trouble she got into.

Amanda stared at him and stubbornly didn't move toward the dress. "What did the sheriff say?"

"Not much. Didn't know who the miner was. He basically said one dead man was one less to have to worry about. Hasn't seen Oldham and didn't seem to care."

"How long are we staying?"

"A couple of days. I want to get some supplies together."

She still hadn't move away from the window. The package lay unopened on the bed.

"Are you going with me, or not?" He tried to keep the frustration out of his voice, but doubted he succeeded.

"I really would like to see town." Her gaze met his tentatively. "It's been a long time since I wore a dress. I won't have the proper number of petticoats."

"That's the most ridiculous thing I ever heard!" He turned and put his hand on the doorknob. "Why wouldn't you want to wear a dress? I thought you wore trousers because they're comfortable and easier to ride a horse. You won't be riding tonight."

She looked completely serious. "You shouldn't have bought me a dress. We aren't married."

"Are you going to start that again?" He'd had enough of this, he turned to the door.

"My mother wouldn't approve."

"Your mother!" He stopped and swiveled. Now he'd heard everything. "And where is she?"

"Boston."

"Boston! She's never going to know." *Damn, he ought to just go on, but the room was hot and they had a long evening ahead of them.*

"I will. That's almost the same." This was a version of Amanda he hadn't seen before, but she looked very feminine, intriguing in a way she didn't when she fought and scraped, nursed him, and cooked a rabbit she'd killed for their food.

He felt himself start to weaken, but he couldn't. Some things a man just couldn't give in on. "Arguing with you is something I don't have time for. I'm hungry and it gets pretty rowdy around here after sundown. Are you going to wear the dress?"

"No." She turned toward the window.

He wanted to just leave her here, but hesitated. If she stayed here, he'd wonder if she had gotten herself into some kind of trouble that she seemed to have a penchant for doing. "The least you could do is look at the dress." He crossed to the bed and tore the brown wrapping from the package. "Now what's wrong with this?" He held the blue and white checked gingham for her to see.

"Nothing." She glanced at him over her shoulder.

"Then wear it."

"No."

"You're about the most frustratin' woman I ever ran into in my life." He dropped the dress, turned, and walked to the door. "Better lock this."

"All right." She still didn't move.

He stepped out into the hall letting the door slam behind him. *Let her hibernate! She's already tied me into too many knots. I am not going to give in on this one!*

Amanda watched him leave, but felt no regret. The last man had told her what to wear when Simon died. She wanted to impress no one here and she had no intention of being a fawning female who catered to male whims. She'd had plenty of that with Simon but that was over. Why was Wade being so stubborn? Couldn't he see buying her clothes on top of registering at the hotel as Mr. and Mrs. Wade Denton could put them together permanently? What had happened to his thinking?

When she had told him why she'd come to Mineral Wells, he had immediately gone into action and tried to leave town without her. Now he seemed to be trying to keep her with him.

Looking out the window, she saw him enter the cafe across the street. It had been a long time since anyone had told her what to do. Sheriff Wade Denton wasn't going to now.

Moving away from the window, she took her battered hat and plopped it on her head leaving her hair loose. She opened the door and stepped into the hall. Exhilaration flowed through her. She didn't need the sheriff to see the town.

Amanda walked down the stairs, out into the lobby. No one seemed to notice her. She strolled quickly to the front door and stepped onto the boardwalk. The street appeared emptier than a few minutes earlier.

A man in a bowler, tan suit pants and a plaid jacket walked across the street. He tipped his hat, stepped past her and entered the hotel.

Amanda turned east, the direction she and Wade had entered town. She remembered seeing a cafe across the street from where they'd left their horses and the pack mule at the livery. She could eat and check on Pepper.

Strolling toward her destination she took in her surroundings. Most of the buildings were of flat roofed adobe construction with false wooden fronts that appeared to be taller than the building itself. Three or four made of wood were weatherworn, their facades turned gray by the sun. She passed a telegraph office, the assayer office, two cantinas, a general store and another hotel. Across the street, she noted a Chinese laundry, two saloons and a bank, plus the cafe she'd seen Wade enter.

The scent of a food she didn't recognize wafted to her. Men's voices, loud and rowdy came from the saloons filling the evening air only slightly cooler that it had been earlier. Behind her the sun dipped, but it would be awhile before full darkness came. Horsemen on the street glanced at her, then nodded and rode on.

Rather than cross the street to the livery, Amanda stopped at the cafe she'd noticed earlier. The scent of spicy food made her nostrils tingle. She stepped inside.

Wade chewed on the piece of meat, and wondered what he was eating. He'd learned in San Francisco the Chinese could cover up almost any kind of meat in their dishes. He really should have been more selective about where he ate, but Amanda had infuriated him so, he'd gone into the first place he'd seen outside the hotel.

"Is good?" The smiling man asked.

"Yes, it is." Wade finished the food. "Could I have another plate? To take to the hotel?"

"Take hotel?" The man smiled broadly.

"I'll return the plate." Wade tapped the heavy glass in front of him. "Tomorrow."

"Sure." The man nodded, then shuffled away.

The scent of garlic and unfamiliar spices permeated the air. This cafe wasn't that much different than those he'd gone to in San Francisco. A few minutes later, the man returned with the second platter and his ever-present smile. Wade handed him two coins, nodded and took the dish.

He strolled outside and glanced toward their hotel window. Amanda wasn't there. Relieved to see she'd decided to do something other than look out the window, he sauntered around the horse droppings, to the porch and entered the hotel. Maybe they were making progress.

Wade climbed the stairs, wondering whether she would like this food. Since he'd decided it wasn't a good idea to leave her alone long enough to go to another café, he hoped so. While he'd been eating he'd decided to take her to see town, even if she still refused to wear the dress. No point in their to arguing over such a tiny matter.

The sound of his knuckles on the solid pine door echoed throughout the hallway. All else was quiet. Stepping a little closer, he pressed his ear against the door. Maybe she'd gone to sleep. He didn't hear any noise. "Amanda open up!"

Silence.

"Amanda, I brought you some food."

No answer.

Sitting the food on the floor, he turned the knob. The door was locked. *What's she done now? Surely she couldn't sleep that soundly.* Turning away, he walked briskly toward the lobby.

Stopping in front of the counter, he waited for the clerk to notice him. Apprehension gripped him. Where was she? The desk clerk nodded sleepily in a wooden desk chair near the rows of mailboxes behind the counter. All the boxes were empty indicating the rooms must be rented as he'd told Amanda. The clerk didn't awaken. Wade waited a few seconds, then pounded on the counter.

The man jerked. Straightening his half-rimmed glasses he growled, "Yeah, whatcha want?"

"Do you have another key to room two-o-one?"

"Gave you a key." The man stood, stretched, then walked toward the counter.

"I gave it to my wife. She must have fallen asleep. She sleeps soundly."

"Don't have many keys. One to a customer." The clerk frowned. "I'll open the room for ya." Shaking his head, he shuffled across the room to the stairs.

Wade followed.

"Don't know what this world's comin' too," the clerk grumbled. "A man used to keep track of his woman, have control over her. These days a woman can lock ya out and never think a thing 'bout it."

Ignoring the statement, Wade picked up the plate of food.

The man turned the key. The door swung open easily. Stepping inside ahead of Wade, the clerk glanced around the room. He shook his head then his gaze came back to rest critically on Wade. "Looks like the little woman did more than lock ya out. She ain't here."

Wade stepped in and sat the food on the dresser. Anger welled up in him. *He should've known.* Amanda Green wouldn't do anything he told her too. She hadn't since he'd met her, why would she start now? He hated to put himself at the mercy of the clerk any more, but he had to know, "Did you see her leave?"

Scowling at him, the man stared over his spectacles that had slid further down. "Ain't paid to watch over the customers. I rent rooms and give out keys." He started to walk away.

"But did you see her leave?"

"Can't say that I did." He stopped in the doorway. "Course, I was a nappin'. People come and go all the time. A body has to rest when he can."

"Relock the door." Wade stepped around the clerk, into the hall.

The man pulled the door shut behind them. "I will, but don't 'spect me to open it for ya later."

"I won't." Wade turned on a heel and walked down the hall. *Where the hell is she?* His boots echoed on the plain board wooden floor. *Where should I look for her?* Knowing Amanda, she wouldn't make it easy for him to find her.

* * *

Amanda walked away from the stable. Pepper seemed to be doing fine as were Wade's horse and the pack mule. When the sun slipped below the horizon and the western sky glowed an iridescent gold that faded into a light pink gradually turning to mauve above her. Further to the east the sky turned into the daytime azure and finally indigo.

She liked Arizona and especially Tucson. If things didn't work out for her in Mineral Wells, she'd consider moving here. Already she'd made a friend in Mrs. Garcia and she liked her food too.

Mamma Garcia had made her promise she'd stop by the cafe again before she left town. Glancing down the street, she realized she wasn't tired, nor was she anxious to go back to the hotel. Sheriff Denton would probably be angry because she didn't stay in the room. She wasn't in the mood to argue with him.

Staying together was bound to cause trouble, especially for her. Although he said sleeping with her was akin to napping with a rattlesnake, she didn't believe he felt that way. If he had, would he have kissed her, not once, but twice? She hadn't just imagined a fire between them, had she? No, she didn't think so.

He didn't seem to notice the discomfort she experienced around him at bedtime. Her thoughts shifted to his kisses, the heady feelings he stirred. Had it been her imagination, or did he watch her comb her hair every night? He could just be angry. They'd both be better off if she didn't return until time to sleep. Instead of turning toward the hotel, she walked the opposite direction toward the edge of town.

A warm breeze ruffled through her hair, cooling her. She lifted the hat and pulled the strands back. The temperature was too hot to wear it loose. In the future, she'd braid it. The darkening sky surrounded her, making her feel alone and vulnerable.

To her right, the mountains, tan and parched in full sunlight of the day, took on a soft lavender hue. The crevices and shadows colored a deeper amethyst beckoned to her. She missed the familiarity of home, but where was that? Boston? No, she'd left there much too long ago. Springfield? Did she really have a reason to return there? No.

Near the end of the street, she saw a sign above a building reading 'Cantina.' The sound of men's voices, glasses clinking and rambunctious laughter inside filtered onto the street. She started to walk past. When she stepped near the entrance, two men rode up. They started to dismount, but hesitated watching her.

"Well, look at that." The tall man near her spoke.

His hair, long and matted, hung loosely around his head, his graying beard, colored with tobacco juice, fell to his chest.

"A white woman, as sure as I'm standin' here."

"Whatcha' mean?" The other man asked.

He was clean-shaven his braided long hair fell in two ropes behind his shoulders.

"A white woman in front o' the cantina. Been months since I've seen one."

Amanda's stomach rolled. She stepped away from the door, pivoted and started back toward the hotel.

"Not so fast, sister."

She recognized the first man's voice.

"I wanta look at your perty yellow hair."

Amanda ran, but she wasn't fast enough to escape his long strides.

He grasped her arm forcing her to stop. "All I wanted to do was look at your hair." The grizzled man turned her toward him. With a toothless grin he snarled at her.

A whiff of his filthy breath bruised her nostrils. Her stomach constricted. She suppressed nausea that nearly overcame her.

"Since you don't seem willin', maybe now I'm a wantin' more." He rubbed his bristled face against hers.

The dirty beard scratched her tender cheek.

Revulsion filled her. Suddenly, her carefree evening ended. Glancing down the street, she saw that she and these two men were alone. The night grew dark fast. Fear gripped her, but she didn't let it show. "Release me!"

"I will." The bearded man spat a stream of brown tobacco juice into the street, then chuckled. "When, I'm good and ready."

The clean-shaven man joined them. "Let me look at her too, boss."

Panic rose in Amanda, but she ignored it. Now wasn't the time to lose her head.

Noise from inside the cantina changed. Laughter stopped, voices grew louder. More men than Amanda had time to count rushed out on the boardwalk.

"My, ain't she perty?" The second man touched Amanda's hair, pulling until it hurt. "Haven't seen hair like that in years."

The first man slapped his friend's hand away then grasped her hair and ran his rough fingers through it again. "She's mine,

Blaisdale, I seen her first." He drew his gun and pointed it at the other man.

"All right, boss, all right." Blaisdale stepped back. "I just wanted ta look."

Fear rippled through Amanda when she heard other men joining them. No way could she fight off a dozen men. With all the power she had, she stomped the grizzly man's arch.

"Ouch!" He loosened his grip on her hair and jumped around in the street.

Laughter filled the air.

Amanda tried to step away.

Blaisdale had moved into his friend's place. He grabbed her, and pulled her to him. "So that's the way it's goin' to be, huh?" He clutched at her hair, pulled her head back and tried to kiss her.

With all the force in her, Amanda drove her knee into his groin.

"The hell with you!" He dropped her hair and bent to grasp his crotch.

She stepped back and looked around. The crowd had quieted. With angry scowls, the two men stood in the middle of the street watching her. A chill ran down her spine. Obviously, neither of them liked being humiliated. She had wounded their pride severely. She was in trouble. "I need to find my husband."

"Did ya hear that, boss?" Blaisdale looked at the other man. "She's got herself a husband."

"Yeah, then where is he?" The leader stepped toward her.

"Right here!" Wade Denton's voice rang out above the crowd.

The man stopped in the middle of the street and looked at him. "Sorry, sir," Blaisdale said, "I didn't think she had a husband. Most men wouldn't let their wife be out in town alone this time of night especially wearin' pants."

"I don't either, usually." Wade stepped off the boardwalk toward Amanda. "She wanted to take a walk - alone. If you fellas will excuse me, we've got a full night planned." He took her arm and guided her through the crowd past the cantina.

Amanda was relieved that Wade had come to her rescue, but he didn't have to manhandle her. "You don't have to drag me." She hissed through clinched teeth, as he hustled her toward the hotel.

"Oh, yes I do. You just angered and humiliated two tough men. They'd all have been on you, if I hadn't arrived. If they think I'm as tough as they are, they'll leave us alone." Without slowing his pace, he guided her through the hotel door, up the stairs and to their room. "May I have the key?"

She dipped into her pocket, retrieved the thin piece of metal, and handed it to him.

He unlocked the door, then stepped back for her to enter.

She glanced at him, but couldn't read the expression on his face. Lifting her chin slightly, she stepped across the threshold ahead of him. She didn't think she'd done so badly defending herself. Strolling across the room, she gazed out the open window. A slight breeze filtered in, but not enough to cool her in the stifling heat. She tried to concentrate on the street, but could only think of the man in the room with her.

Wade had stopped to light the oil lantern. Even if the room hadn't been so hot, it felt close and small with him so near. Amanda's arm still seared where he'd touched her as they walked to the hotel.

"Now!"

She stared at him.

He stepped away from the dresser, and stood just inside the door.

She didn't like his authoritative expression. Her nerves were on edge and she didn't plan to listen to a lecture.

"Just what did you think you were doing?"

She turned back to the window. In the street, she saw her two attackers. They went into a cantina across the street. "Maybe I should be careful. I didn't intend to cause trouble. I'll be more careful in the future." Who was he to question her? She looked at him.

He'd taken his hat off and hung it on the peg by the door. His sandy colored hair curled slightly where his hat had been making him look young and almost vulnerable.

"I got something to eat. I wanted to see the town. Everything was fine, until I walked past the cantina."

Their gazes collided across the space of the room.

She felt herself warm, but this time it was from the intimate expression in his eyes, not the heat. For a moment he seemed to be looking into her heart seeing the very depths of her.

"You handled yourself well, I'll admit, but one of these times...." His expression had softened. "Someday, you're going to get yourself into something you can't get out of." He ran his right hand through his hair.

"Would you really care?" That would be something new. Simon had cared, especially about what she could do for him. Never had he considered how she felt about anything.

He stood looking at her for a moment like he didn't know what to say.

She should have known better than to ask a question like that. So far, the only thing he'd done was try to get rid of her. Even saving his life hadn't changed that. "I'm sorry, Wade, I just couldn't stay here." She turned away. She couldn't look him in the eye knowing he'd meant what he said earlier. At least he'd verbalized it then.

"I brought you dinner, since you were too stubborn to go with me. I told you to stay in the room because these men are rough. A lot of them will do anything to get a woman, especially a white woman."

The magnitude of what could have happened came to her. "You told me that earlier, but I couldn't believe it. Now I do." She turned toward him.

He closed the distance between them.

"You've got to listen to me, sometime, woman." His voice had grown husky. He placed his hands on her shoulders. His dark eyed gaze seared into hers.

Her hands grew moist and her stomach fell fluttery.

"Don't you know how beautiful you are?" His right hand slipped to her neck. He continued to look down at her.

"Oh, yeah, I've been told that before, especially when someone wanted something." Her heart beat faster and her anger had disappeared. She liked the warmth of his hand on her neck.

His left hand moved to her chin and he gently tipped it so he could look directly into her eyes. "You're beautiful, Amanda, and yes, I'd care if something happened to you." He stared intensely down at her then bent as he pulled her to him.

Their lips touched tentatively.

Warmth crept through her. She leaned into him.

The kiss intensified as he hungry mouth devoured hers.

Amanda melted into him, slipped her arms around his neck and held him close.

Groaning low in his throat, his arms slid down around her waist. His warm moist tongue touched her lips.

They opened instinctively to allow him entrance.

She breathed in the scent of his male muskiness mingled with a faint hint of tobacco. They gave her a heady feeling she hadn't experienced before.

He plundered her mouth, then slowly pulled away as he gazed down at her. "Don't you see, Amanda?" His voice shook. "Every one of those men wants to do this to you, and more."

"I've been around a lot of men, and this never happened before." She stared up at him defiantly, but her heart still raced from their embrace.

He let his hands drop away from her waist and stepped back. Strolling to the opposite side of the bed he turned back toward her. "When a man comes out here, sometimes, it's years before he sees a white woman. That's why I checked us in as a married couple. You're not safe any other way. I'm not even sure you're safe here." Anguish, filled his voice. Staring at her, across the bed, he didn't speak for several minutes.

Amanda saw emotions on his face she didn't understand.

"Please do what I say, the rest of the time we're in Tucson." He let out a tired sigh.

"I will." She turned around. What did all this mean? Her heart hammered. She tried to think of Simon, her father, the reason she'd followed Sheriff Denton, but all she could focus on was the kiss he'd given her and how she hadn't wanted him to stop.

Wade sat on the edge of the bed, and looked at the wall. *This isn't going to work. No way, after that kiss, can I sleep in the same bed with her. I'll have a hard enough time sleeping in the same room. What possessed me to do that?* He took the pillow and tossed it in the floor, then tore the quilt off and folded it, laying it beside the pillow.

"I can sleep there." Amanda's voice came to him from near the window where she'd stationed herself again.

"No you won't." His voice was raspy as he sat down.

"But, I caused this."

"A woman shouldn't sleep on the floor." He pulled his boots off lay back and closed his eyes. A few moments later, he heard the bed creek and turned his back to it. In the morning, he'd get the supplies they needed together. They had to get out of town, the sooner the better. He didn't know how long he could keep up this charade without proving himself a liar. He'd told her he didn't want anything from her, but that wasn't true. For the first time in three years, he wanted a woman, no not just a woman – Amanda Green.

Seven

Someone knocked at the door.

"Who is it?" Amanda glanced at the wrinkled toes of the men's boots curling up at her. They looked terrible with the blue gingham dress Wade had bought, but she didn't have anything else.

"Wade Denton."

She sighed, relieved that he had returned. She'd awaken to find his pillow on the bed beside her and the quilt he'd used neatly folded at the foot. Glancing at herself in the mirror she let the smile slip through in spite of her determination not to let it.

Walking to the door, she opened it wide. "Morning, Sheriff." Her stomach fluttered. She liked the startled expression on his face.

"Mornin', Amanda." He took a step back, slipped the hat off and stood in the hallway staring at her an appreciative expression on his face.

"Do come in." She moved back.

His gaze swept her then came back to rest on her face. He stepped inside.

"Do you like it?" Nervously, she swirled around to put some space between them and to interrupt his concentration.

"That's why I bought it." The glimmer of his eyes betrayed his harsh voice. He closed the door.

Amanda took a deep breath, to regain her equilibrium. Never before had any man, made her feel the way he did. She stopped in the middle of the room and turned toward him. "Where have you been?"

"Ordering supplies." He scowled.

"Then, we're leaving?"

"I planned to right after breakfast, but they won't be ready until this afternoon and my horse needs new shoes. The blacksmith's busy. We're here for the day."

"Is that so bad?"

"No, but I wanted to move on." He twirled his hat like he didn't know what to do with his hands. "I'm not sure what we'll do with ourselves."

Her blood boiled, remembering their kiss from the night before. The one thing they couldn't do was spend the day in this room, then an idea hit her. "I know what we can do."

"Do I dare ask what?" A wry smile lifted his lips slightly.

"Oh, it's nothing bad. Mrs. Garcia told me about a mission just outside of town. She said it's beautiful. I'm not Catholic, but I'd love to see it."

"And, who is Mrs. Garcia?" He tossed the hat on the bed and lifted an eyebrow.

Amanda knew what had happened the night before and other things since she'd been riding with him made him leery of doing anything she suggested. "She's the woman who runs the restaurant where I ate last night. I had tamales. She wanted me to come back again before I leave town."

"I might have guessed. You do make friends easily." He sighed and eyed her suspiciously. "We aren't travelers on holiday. We're looking for a thief, in case you've forgotten."

"So?" She smiled letting her excitement increase. It had been a very long time since she'd done anything just for the fun of it. "We have nothing to do but see Tucson. This is a few miles from town. We could even look for Oldham. If we stay in town, we know he's not here. Besides, everyone deserves a day off now and then." She took a step closer. "We could have the tavern prepare a basket for us. I'll bet there's someplace by the mission we could have a picnic."

Their gazes caught.

She sensed him getting caught up in her enthusiasm.

"Oh, all right, let's have breakfast. I'll order a wagon from the livery." He picked up his hat and slid it on, although she still sensed his reservations.

"There it is." Wade pointed toward the horizon.

Among the saguaros, cholla and prickly pear cacti, Amanda saw the stark white of a building, still a couple of miles away.

"That's got to be it. It's the only building out here." He slapped the reins and the rented horses trotted a little faster.

The wagon rolled slowly down a road barely wide enough to allow passage. Saguaro cacti lined each side their huge arms lifting gracefully toward the heavens. Mesquite and palo verde trees made a tangle between the cacti. A tiny lizard darted across the road.

"Do all missions look like that?" She could now see a domed roof and two steeples above the plants.

"I don't know. Can't say I've seen many. A couple in San Francisco." He kept his attention on the road ahead.

"San Francisco?"

"Yes, 'Frisco. I came to Arizona territory by way of San Francisco."

"That's a lot of traveling for a man who served in the war."

"I didn't stick around after it ended."

"Why?"

"Our plantation was destroyed. Mother moved into New Orleans. No reason to stay." His voice had grown harsh almost angry again, like she'd gotten used to hearing it.

Even though Amanda sensed he hinted that he didn't want to talk about what had happened, she asked, "How did you get there?"

"Where?"

"San Francisco. Did you travel in a wagon train, or what?"

"I took a ship. New Orleans around the Gulf of Mexico picking up passengers past Florida then Cape Horn and South America."

"What an adventure!" She gasped. "I'd have loved to do something like that. Simon promised me he'd take me to England, but...he was busy with the bank. Then when the rebellion...."

"I didn't travel for the fun of it. I got away." He slapped the reins again. "I worked to pay for my passage. Scrubbed the deck, hoisted sails and emptied slop jars. Not adventurous, if you ask me."

Amanda smiled. She couldn't imagine Wade Denton emptying a slop jar. "Get away from what?"

He pulled on the reins. "Whoa!"

The horses stopped.

Wade tied the reins to the wagon, then turned toward her. "Did anyone ever tell you that you ask too many questions?"

"My father told me that I'd never learn anything if I didn't ask questions." She smiled.

He seemed to relax a bit as he looked out over the desert.

Why was he so tense?

"If you want to continue on this trip, quit asking questions." He pulled a cigarette paper from his shirt pocket, rolled a smoke and continued to gaze at the desert.

"All right." Maybe she was being too nosey. Her Pa would say so. "Why'd we stop?"

"I saw something ahead I didn't like. I thought I'd give it some time to cross the road."

"What?"

"A gila monster, I believe it's called, a big black and red lizard. It crossed the road. They're poisonous. I understand that once they start biting, they don't know when to quit. Don't want to replace a rented horse."

"Agreed." Amanda squinted, into the bush, but saw nothing. Swiveling on the seat she looked behind them. No town was in sight.

Wade watched Amanda lick the remaining tamale grease from her fingers. *Wonder what her mother would think of that?* Licking fingers probably wasn't considered civilized back in Boston.

"Delicious." She broke the silence and smiled at him.

Whether he wanted to admit it or not, he found her attractive and the shade of this mesquite tree made a perfect picnic spot. Nearby, the monastery stood tall and regal among the saguaros, prickly pear, cholla, and mesquite trees.

Amanda began to gather Mrs. Garcia's plates and dishtowels.

"Yes, the food was better than I expected." He straightened out on the quilt and rested his head against a boulder. Covering his face with his hat he felt like taking a nap. To keep from falling asleep, he sat up abruptly and stretched. "I saw a well over by the mission. I'll go see if there's water."

"We have this." Amanda lifted the canteen then stowed the remains of their picnic in a basket.

"I know." He slipped his hat on, then stood. "But we might need it before we get back to Tucson, besides fresh water would taste better."

"I agree." Amanda stood and picked up the basket.

He took it from her, walked to the wagon and placed it behind the seat. Pivoting, he found her watching him.

She brushed her hands together. "I'm ready to explore."

Suddenly, he became cautious. He needed to watch her or, she'd get them into trouble. "We came to see the mission. We've seen it. You're not expecting more, I hope."

"No." She laughed low in her throat. "I just want to see it closer." She stepped toward him looking absolutely feminine and fine in the blue gingham.

His heart made a crazy leap, but he tried to relax. "Would you like to join me?" He bowed slightly and pointed toward the well. Another time, he might have thought this a silly thing to do, but at this moment he felt light-hearted and it seemed the appropriate action.

"Yes." She stepped beside him and placed her tiny, warm hand in his.

He didn't think he'd ever felt such a small hand that also felt strong and confident. The warmth seemed to transfer to him, fusing them together.

They strolled across the mission grounds toward the well. He fought the urge to pull her close, kiss her again, but he'd been doing too much of that lately and they were a long way from people. He glimpsed her out of the corner of his eye. She concentrated on something ahead. Did she feel this pull?

He looked away from her to the mission. The pristine walls jutted from the desert floor rising through the fauna like a great white dove. The gold edging of the two steeples and alabaster domed roof spoke of the higher purpose for the building.

"Oh!" Amanda stopped several feet away.

"What's the matter?" Wade glanced at her, then at their hands. He released her hand.

"Nothing." She sighed. Her blue eyes sparked with awe. "It's just...I don't think I've ever seen anything as beautiful."

He looked at the building. It was impressive, but not compared to her. He turned toward her and their gazes intermingled. For a moment he thought he'd kiss her in spite of himself, but instead, he said, "I have."

She smiled an intimate light in her eyes.

For a moment, he thought his heart was going to jump from his chest, then she turned toward the monastery.

"It's so quiet." She took several steps toward the building breaking the spell that seemed to have overcome them.

"A mission is supposed to be a place to contemplate the higher powers of life. It should be quiet." He followed. Although the moment of intimacy had passed, he felt like a magnet from her pulled him. He no longer wanted to resist.

"I wonder if there's anyone here."

"Didn't Mrs. Garcia tell you?"

"I didn't ask." She paused at the entrance. Hand carved doors reached from the tiled walk to the roof.

He strolled past her to the well using his thirst as a reason to put some space between them before he lost his head completely. "Somebody lives here," he said, seeing a rope and bucket in the well.

"Yes, sir, that's true." The man's voice startled him.

Amanda turned away from the church entrance to see who spoke.

A man, about her height, stood in a grove of palo verde trees near the well.

"I hope we aren't interrupting anything." Wade stood a few feet from him and the well.

"No, of course not." The man stepped away from the trees, toward them. Dressed in a robe of unbleached muslin with a metal cross hanging from a leather thong around his neck, he looked humble and reverent. "It's rare when anyone visits."

"Do you get lonely?" She stepped away from the building to get a better look at the man.

"I talk to *Him*." He pointed toward the sky.

"Mrs. Garcia from the cafe in town told us of this place." She moved closer to the well and Wade. Although she wasn't frightened, she'd never seen a monk before.

His white hair gaped in the front, making his tanned bald head glow in the sunlight. "And what brings you here?"

"We came to Tucson looking for two men who shot Sheriff Denton." Amanda motioned toward Wade. "We're also looking for a man who has tried to bankrupt the residents of Mineral Wells. When our supplies are ready, we'll be off again."

"Is that right?" The priest stepped closer and looked at Wade. "You're a sheriff?"

"Yes, of Mineral Wells." Wade moved away from the well extending his hand to shake.

The priest took it as moisture accumulated in his gray eyes.

"I've been praying for a lawman to come." He smiled wanly.

"Why?" Wade dropped his hand and the priest stepped back.

A frown crossed his unflawed face. "Come inside." He walked
slowly toward the building. "She's called Mission San Xavier de
Bac. Built almost two hundred years ago. Father Kino, started it.
Many of us have ministered here." The door squeaked when he
opened it and stepped inside holding it for them. Walking to a
small basin, he paused briefly, dipped his hand in and made the
sign of a cross over his heart. He pointed toward the side of the
building. "This way."

Excitement filled Amanda as they walked through an archway.
Terra cotta tiled floors echoed beneath their feet. Cool, undisturbed
air relieved them of the heat. She wanted to ask questions about the
building, but the man's serious expression told her to wait.

Halfway down the corridor, he stopped and opened another
door. "This is where we live in the summer."

She and Wade stepped through.

"He's over here." He pointed to a dark corner.

Amanda squinted. A cot came into view. At first she couldn't
see the slim figure laying on it, but as her eyes adjusted to the
darkness she saw a person covered with a light blanket.

They crossed the room.

The man lay staring, but not seeing the ceiling.

"It happened about three months ago." The priest leaned over
his friend. "I've been praying for someone to come. Peppie?" He
touched the silent figure's shoulder. "We have visitors."

The man didn't move.

The priest turned toward them, an expression of desperation on
his face.

"What happened to him?" Wade asked.

"Early one morning Peppie went to the well for water." He
paused and leaned closer to his friend. "Peppie, do you hear me?"

Again, the man did not move.

"I'm not sure what happened. I heard shots. When I found him,
Peppie was tied to a tree riddled with bullet holes all around him. I
could show you. Peppie," he sobbed, "was like this. I saw two men
ride away, toward Mexico. I brought him in. Have been praying
ever since."

"Do you have an idea who it was?" Wade spoke with
compassion Amanda hadn't heard in his voice before.

"No. A few days earlier, two men had stopped for water. We
gave them bread too. Always do. I suspect those men, but I'm not
sure."

"Can you describe them?"

For the next few minutes, the priest told them as much as he could about the men.

Amanda knew from the priest's description one of the attackers could be Oldham, but could also be someone else.

"Why didn't you report them?" Wade asked.

"And leave Peppie?"

Amanda's heart wrenched at the expression in his sad eyes. She'd seen his friend's condition before. During the war they called it wounds of the mind. Perfectly healthy men couldn't talk, walk or feed themselves. She turned away when memories of wounded soldiers she couldn't help returned. She couldn't do anything for this man either.

"I don't know if I can help or not," she heard Wade say. "We're returning to Mineral Wells. I'm hoping the man we're looking for has reappeared. The sheriff hasn't seen anyone fitting our thief's description in Tucson, but I'll report what's happened here."

"Thank you, sir. I appreciate that." Hope filled his voice.

For several minutes he and Wade talked then Amanda and Wade left.

As they walked toward the door, Amanda's thoughts raced. "Could it be Oldham?"

"It was three months ago, Amanda."

"Yes, but I think one of them is Oldham. The Mexican wouldn't be, but the white man could." She couldn't keep the excitement from her voice.

"Don't get any ideas. We're headed straight east when we leave tomorrow morning. I'm going back to Mineral Wells to see if anyone has seen Oldham while we've been away."

They stopped at the well and quenched their thirsts.

Strolling toward the wagon, Amanda insisted, "But, this might be him."

"It might, but it also might not."

A slight desert breeze rippled through the trees and bushes. She felt cool and rejuvenated. "Send a telegraph."

"No, I'm going back." He helped her into the wagon, then watered the horses.

Her thoughts churned. He hadn't wanted her with him anyway. He'd made that clear, more than once. If she decided to continue searching for Oldham he couldn't stop her. She saw no alternative,

if he insisted on returning to Mineral Wells in the morning, she and
Wade Denton would part company.

Wade swung into the saddle, took the reins leading to the pack
mule from the saddle-horn, then turned the animals east. He'd only
ridden a few feet when he realized he was alone. He stopped and
turned around.

Amanda rode away from him.

"Where are you going?" He called.

She kept riding.

Hadn't she'd heard? *Let her go.* The last two nights had been a
trial, sleeping in the same room and not touching her. He'd done it,
but he couldn't forever. Last night, they'd slept in the same bed.
He'd kept to his side, but had gotten little sleep.

If she wanted to leave, he didn't owe her anything. Turning his
horse toward Mineral Wells, he spurred it, and jerked on the reins
to the mule. The animals jolted forward. Wade rode for several
hundred yards. *She'd saved your life. She's a woman in danger.*

Was she really in danger? The person traveling with her seemed
to suffer more harms than she. He hadn't been lonely since she'd
joined him. Stopping, he turned around. She and Pepper were
near the other edge of town.

Turning his horse, he clicked and pulled the mule's reins. At
least he should ask what she intended to do.

Dust billowed around them as they rode down the main street.
People stopped and looked, but he ignored them. When he reached
Amanda, he slowed the animals to match her pace. "Where are you
going?"

"South."

"I told you, I'm returning to Mineral Wells."

She stopped. Determination filled her face like he hadn't seen
before. "I didn't ask you to come along, Sheriff."

"No you didn't, but I'm responsible for you."

Her blue eyes grew dark. Her cheeks flushed. "No one is
responsible for me, Sheriff Denton, except me. I'm looking for
Maurice Oldham."

"So am I."

"You are, but you're looking, hoping not to find him. I'm
searching, knowing I will." She clicked to Pepper, spurred the
horse and they rode away.

"Damn!" He should've known better than to let her ride with him. Spurring his horse, he rode up behind her again. "The priest didn't say it was Oldham."

"I know, but the description sounded like him." She'd stopped and turned toward him. "What's it too you, Sheriff? You didn't want me to ride with you. Now, you've got what you want."

Her words stung. He had told her that to begin with, but lately.... *Yeah, lately, what, Denton?* He shook his head. He didn't know. His gaze met her blue eyed stare.

"I suspect you've tried to get rid of me every time we've stopped. Well, now you are." She clicked to Pepper, spurred her and they galloped away.

Let her go, an inner voice said. He watched her turn left at the edge of town the way they'd ridden the day before.

Maybe she was right. What if the man was Oldham? She actually knew him. He followed.

Eight

"There's a small town around here." Wade rode up to Amanda.

She nodded. Lines of fatigue marked the fine features of her face.

He wanted to help her from the saddle and let her sleep until the line disappeared and she felt better, but he couldn't. They'd made this decision, now they had to follow it through – with no water around they didn't have much time.

She swayed in the saddle and didn't reply.

Pink rays of early morning sunshine marked the horizon. It'd be another hot day and they needed water before nightfall. He thought they were near the Mexican border.

Since leaving Tucson they'd resumed an aloof, but somewhat more strained, partnership. That had been seven days ago. The heat slowed their travel. They had tried to sleep during the day and move only early in the morning and right before sunset until the horses couldn't see any longer. He felt the fatigue too.

"This town is in Mexico." He scrutinized her, hoping she wouldn't argue with him. "Will you wait here?" The place he'd picked was an outcropping of rocks surrounded by mesquite and palo verde trees. There was little fauna to hide behind and no water, but he didn't know what he'd come across in Mexico. She'd be better off here.

"I'll wait, Wade." She slid from Pepper, removed the saddle and placed it near a saguaro.

Wade tethered her horse and the mule.

"My saddle sores have saddle sores." She groaned and stretched then sat on the blanket she'd laid beside the saddle.

He considered joining her, but feared they wouldn't accomplish their task. "I know what you mean." He looked at his horse. The thing he didn't want to do was climb back into the saddle. "I'm still skeptical we have reason to think we'll find Oldham out here."

"I know. I'm glad you're with me and this was all my idea. If you don't find him where you're looking, we can return to Mineral Wells."

A few days before, he'd have felt some joy at her words, but now, he didn't. For the first time since he'd met her, he heard rare humbleness in her voice, but he also saw the weariness on her face. At least she wasn't trying to hide her fatigue anymore.

He sympathized with her. Once, he'd chided her for not being willing to give up. She still hadn't. A lesser person would have-- days ago. He admired her determination and a whole lot of other things about her, but thinking about them wasn't getting the job done. "If Oldham hasn't been seen here, we'll need to decide whether to continue. He could be anywhere by now."

"Yes, he could." She smiled, the gesture barely moving her lips. "I'm not one to complain, but I haven't had good sleep since we left Tucson."

"Nor have I. I'll be back as soon as I can."

"I'll be here." She stretched out and closed her eyes.

Turning his horse toward where he thought the town would be he let his mind wander to the last few days. Sleeping in the daylight wasn't the only reason he couldn't rest. Heat from the sun was minor, when compared to his thoughts of Amanda. He found himself watching her sleep constantly. He'd begun to wonder why he had wanted to keep away from her. His failures seemed less with her around.

Of course, lately he hadn't had a real test. She was as self-sufficient as any man, but if he told her that they'd be in for another fight for which he didn't have time nor the energy. Spurring his horse, he pushed away the niggling thought that he shouldn't have left her alone.

As he rode, Wade mulled over again her reasons for being here. He'd put her in the proper place in his thoughts. She obviously had more reason than Simon's memory and a few depositors to find Oldham and she mentioned her father frequently. He and she seemed to have been very close. There were many unanswered questions about her, but he'd come to the conclusion she'd saved his life for a purpose. She'd let him protect her while she sought Oldham, then she'd leave once they found him. He suspected she and Oldham were plotting together. All he had was her word Simon gave Oldham money. He didn't even know there was a

Simon or any of those people she was supposed to be helping back in Illinois. The whole story could be a way to keep him off-guard.

When she'd arrived in town, she'd made a point of telling him if he'd lead her to Oldham, she'd have a place to stay. Since Oldham wasn't there he'd directed her to the stable.

If Oldham had been there, would she have moved in with him? Why hadn't he thought of this before?

Amanda woke with a start and a sense of danger. The horse and mule were gone. Looking around, she saw a few scrub bushes, sand, and rocks that made up a small mountain range. Not a living creature was in sight. Fear gripped her along with the sense of self-preservation.

Where were the animals?

Reaching for the gun she'd carried from Springfield, but rarely used, she started to stand. A bullet zinged past her right ear. Crouching, she grabbed the rifle and slid behind a nearby rock.

Another bullet ricocheted close by – very near.

Fear seized her. How many assailants were there? Without horses, food or water, she wouldn't last long, even if she didn't get shot.

Moving behind a boulder, she knelt low and waited several minutes.

No shots.

She continued to wait.

"Maybe we got him, Jose." Maurice Oldham's familiar voice floated across the desert.

Joy spread through her. She'd finally found him, but the elation quickly subsided as common sense reigned. She'd found Oldham, but she wasn't in a position to capture him.

"No, Amigo, I don't think so. I saw him slip behind those rocks." The Spanish accent floated up to her.

A chill ran through her as she sensed them watching her hiding place.

They were close, not more than twenty feet away and spoke in low tones, but their voices echoed.

"We have his horse and mule," Oldham replied.

"But he's not alone. I saw another man ride away."

"He's alone now. Let's get him before his partner returns."

Panic gripped Amanda, but she hadn't survived by running every time she came up against an obstacle. Looking overhead and behind her, she saw a small cave. She holstered the pistol and picked up the rifle. Easing herself away from one rock, she dashed to another. As she climbed, she could see her surroundings better.

Wade rode toward the Mexican border trying to ignore the uncomfortable feelings he'd had all morning. He couldn't shake the thought that Amanda might be in trouble.

I should have left her in Tucson. He spurred his horse and urged him on. Glancing at the horizon, he saw heat ripples radiate across the sand. His skin felt gritty and his beard generated heat. He'd come to the conclusion he was spending too much time thinking about Amanda. Getting back to town would give him other diversions and he needed it--soon.

He came to a wash that might be the border. Crossing it he continued to ride in a southeasterly direction. Nothing looked like a road, there was no evidence of a town.

The further he rode, the more apprehensive he became.

"Damn!" He pulled up on the reins. "I should've known better." He rode to a small rise, several hundred yards away and crested a hill and still saw no sign of town.

This was no use. He couldn't keep his mind off Amanda long enough to search for hoof prints or other signs of the banker. Turning his horse around, Wade spurred it, and pointed it toward the hills where he'd left her.

In the distance, Amanda saw the two horses plus Pepper and the pack mule. They were tied to a tree. Somewhat relieved to see her animals so near, she continued to climb toward the cave. A few boulders later, she came in clear view of her sanctuary, but Wade's warning, 'everything bites, stings or sticks,' stopped her. As hot as the air outside was, that cave would provide a cool refuge for a snake. Knowing this would give her location away she picked up a good sized stone and tossed it into the cave.

No rattles, no snakes.

Behind and beneath her, the Mexican ask, "Did you hear that, Boss?"

"What?" Oldham growled

"Rocks, up in them hills."

Amanda slid into the cave and breathed easier.

"Sneak up on those rocks from the other side." Oldham ordered.

Several feet beneath her, the two men's hats bobbed above the rocks.

"I'll come from this side." Oldham whispered loudly. "One man with no horses and water can't last long."

"*Si, Senor.*"

The men disappeared.

Taking the opportunity, Amanda eased herself from the cave. Skirting the rocks hiding it, she started climbing again. Moments later, she slid behind a small tree and paused. Her pulse raced, perspiration trickled between her breasts. She took a deep breath and relaxed slightly while she listened.

A man spoke, very near and directly beneath her, but she couldn't understand what he said.

Peeking around the tree, she saw his black head. She pointed the pistol at him.

He turned, but didn't look up. Instead, he walked to the cave she had just vacated. A moment later, he reappeared and stepped to the edge of the rocks. He cupped his hands around his mouth and shouted, "He's not here, Boss!"

Fear gripped Amanda. She'd never shot a man before. She didn't want to start now. He was close enough she saw a peppering of white hairs on his dark head. Camouflaged by rocks and bushes she'd be safe as long as she didn't make any noise.

"He couldn't have gotten far!" Oldham called.

"Gone as far as I'm goin'," the man replied.

"I told you to find him, Jose."

"Boss, I wanta live to return to Mexico."

"Should've done it myself, can't count on anyone," Oldham grumbled. He climbed toward his partner.

Amanda's heart pounded loud enough she wondered if the man could hear. Her palms grew moist. The pistol weighed heavy in her hand, but she didn't move. If she stayed here, she'd be safe.

Looking at the tied horses, she considered trying to go to them, but they were too far away to reach safely. Her gaze caught the sight of smoke or dust on the horizon.

Wade?

The rider was definitely headed toward the hills.

Oldham said, "I should've known not to trust a Mexican."

Amanda looked from the rider to the men.

"I did the best I could, Boss."

"I should've let you go home when you wanted to." Oldham sounded closer.

Although she couldn't see him, Amanda continued to point the gun at the Mexican. The man disappeared. Dust rose beneath her. Sounds of flesh against flesh were very close. She realized this might be her only opportunity to escape. Scanning the desert floor again, she saw the rider had almost reached the rocks. She focused on the horseman, but couldn't be sure it was Wade.

A different fear filled her. If the rider weren't Wade, would she have a chance against three men? She couldn't dwell on the thought. Pushing it aside, she refocused on the fighting men.

The scuffling had stopped. They breathed hard, but she saw no dust.

Silence filled the hills, then Oldham's head popped out above the rocks again. "Now, you've done it, Jose! I should shoot you for what you've done to us. Someone's coming."

"All we have to do is hide." The Mexican's labored voice sought the banker's approval.

"You fool," Oldham said. "We left the horses in plain sight. If he's with this man, he'll know something's wrong when he sees all the animals."

Amanda didn't hear the Mexican's reply. Her gaze traveled to the approaching man – Wade? He rode to the rocks, and jumped off his mount. Using the horse for a shield, he edged his way toward the tethered animals, then she couldn't see him. Next, she saw him moving their mounts.

"He's takin' our horses, Boss!" Jose cried.

"He's not goin' far," Oldham replied.

Amanda was relieved to have Wade close enough to help.

"We're above him," Oldham said. "We can see him and he can't see us."

"Where's he now?" Jose asked.

"Just shut up, Jose! Shut up and get over there. Watch for him." Oldham's voice was hushed.

He must be hiding very close, beneath her.

Apprehension gripped Wade as he moved the horses. Where was Amanda? Had they already killed her? He couldn't think of that. Guiding the horses away from the scrawny mesquite where they'd been tied, he didn't intend for them to be ridden unless he knew who rode them. Several yards away, he tethered them. He pulled a box of shells from his saddlebag and checked his pistol then turned toward the rocks.

He'd climbed a few steps when a bullet zinged past and hit a nearby rock. He stopped, caught his breath and waited for the next shot. The loose rocks moved precariously under him, but the shot didn't come. Hastily, he looked around.

If he could make it a few feet further, several boulders would obstruct his attackers' vision. Slipping off his hat, he peeked above the rocks. He could see only the tip of a gun, several feet above him. Where was Amanda? Picking up a rock, he threw it in the opposite direction.

A shot rang out, followed by another.

He darted toward the boulders. Like a man driven, he climbed. A few moments later, he stopped to catch his breath.

Beneath him he saw Amanda and several feet lower, two men watched the spot where the rock had landed. The sight pleased, but frightened him. Amanda pointed her gun at one man, but if she shot him, the other would surely kill her before she could shoot again. Wade slid down the rocks toward her.

"We shoulda went down, Boss," the Mexican said. "He's got our horses. We're in trouble."

"Maybe that's the man we'd thought we trapped," Oldham growled.

"Cain't be. We were shootin' at him a few minutes ago."

"He could've gotten away," Oldham insisted.

Amanda's hand felt numb from gripping the gun. She didn't dare take a deep breath. Fear seized her again. Maybe she'd been wrong. Maybe the rider wasn't Wade. A new thought made her blood run cold. *What if Wade was in cahoots with Oldham?* She heard a scuffle. The men had climbed further up and were in full view.

"Stop!" she ordered. Her heart pounded wildly.

They faced her.

"Well, if it ain't a woman," Oldham chuckled, taking a step closer. He dropped his hands to his sides, and rested his right near his gun handle.

"You heard the lady." Wade Denton's strong, reassuring voice penetrated the silence. "That's far enough."

The Mexican moved behind Oldham.

"I wouldn't do that if I were you," Wade cautioned.

"Si, Senor." The man stepped into full view.

"Throw your weapons over there." Wade motioned with the barrel of his revolver toward a sandy spot a few yards away then stepped closer.

Oldham stared at Wade, then pulled his pistol and tossed it into the sand.

"Now, you." Wade pointed to the Mexican.

"No gun."

"The knife."

"No speak English."

"You won't be speakin' anything if you don't get rid of that knife." Wade's firm voice boomed over the desert.

Watching him warily, the Mexican pulled a long thin knife from his boot and tossed it to Oldham's gun.

How had Wade known about the knife? Amanda began to relax and let him take control.

"We haven't done anything," Oldham said.

"Amanda Green will determine that." Wade nodded toward her.

"Amanda Green?" Oldham scrutinized her.

"Yes, Amanda Green, Maurice all the way from Illinois. I came to get Simon's money." Her gaze met his cold stare.

"The citizens of Mineral Wells want to know what happened to their money too." Wade stepped closer to the captives.

"I haven't done anything." Oldham brushed at his dirt encrusted clothes. "Tried to make a life for myself in these godforsaken hills."

Wade stepped up and kicked the weapons further away. "Unless I miss my guess, I have a souvenir from you too."

"I told you we didn't kill him," the Mexican screeched.

"Shut up!" Oldham scowled.

"Pick up their hardware, Amanda."

"Sure, Sheriff." She lowered her gun, climbed from the rocks, and picked up the weapons as relief washed over her. She'd been wrong about the sheriff and somehow that thought along with the realization she'd finally caught up with Maurice Oldham made her happy in a way she hadn't been in years.

Relieved to see Amanda retrieving the weapons, Wade fought the desire to pull her into his arms and tell her how glad he was that she was alive. In a memory that lasted only a second, he saw himself walking down the street in New Orleans, tromping on dried, wilted roses meant for Sarah Jean Sturdyvent. The pain he felt that day long ago revived as well, but it wasn't as strong. Amanda had needed him and he'd gotten there in time. He couldn't remove his former failures, but he could build on what had started today.

He stepped forward and pointed in the direction Oldham and his accomplice should move. "Start walkin'."

Once they reached their horses, he tied the thieves' hands to the saddle-horns and knotted the rope in such a way that if the men tried to escape they'd be dragged.

Strolling to Amanda, who worked adjusting the stirrups on her saddle he smiled one of the few she'd seen since she'd met him.

Taking a deep breath, he said, "I think we should ride until dark, then start again early in the morning."

She straightened gazing deep into his eyes. "Thank you for saving me, Wade." Her voice was husky with emotion.

He moved closer. All resolve, not to get too close disappeared. He touched her face. It felt soft and delicate, oh, so feminine. His rough skin tingled. Sliding his hand to the back of her neck, he pulled her to him. The prisoners seemed miles away. He and this woman, were the only people alive. "I'm glad you're safe, Amanda." He didn't try to hide the emotion in his voice.

She looked vulnerable. A tear formed at the corner of one eye.

"I should never have left you alone."

"I survived." She blinked the wayward tear away.

He bent to kiss her.

"Well, if that ain't cute," Oldham's harsh voice interrupted. "The little wife and the sheriff."

Amanda pulled away, glaring at the thief. "I'm no longer a wife. Simon died during the war."

"Too bad, too bad." Maurice snarled exposing dirty tobacco stained teeth.

Wade fought the urge to pull the man off the horse and beat him senseless. *If he'd hurt Amanda!* The thought was more than Wade could handle at the moment he forced it away and glanced at the prisoner again.

"A man free with his money." Oldham's laugh rang out across the desert. "That Simon was plenty trusting, a good businessman."

Wade stepped away from Amanda. It was probably better the intimacy was broken anyway. This wasn't the time to be thinking about a woman and emotional things involving her. Turning away from Oldham, he looked down at her. "Are you ready?"

"Yes."

Their gazes tangled momentarily, but he sensed she'd distanced herself. He helped her onto Pepper.

"Thanks." She looked down at him, an expression he couldn't read in her blue eyes.

"You're welcome." He turned away, his face warming as he strolled to his horse. Did she feel guilt over Simon's death? He didn't see a reason she should.

Why had he helped her onto the horse? He'd never done it before. If he had she'd probably have slapped him. Had something between them changed? What had come over him lately? Why couldn't he stay away from her? He'd never had any trouble distancing himself from women, some more attractive than Amanda.

But she was different whether he wanted to admit it or not-- dangerous and different. He walked to his red roan and mounted. He needed to be careful or she'd have him jumping through more hoops than Sarah Jean Sturdyvent ever had.

Wade fed the rope through the horse's bits, then dallied it about his saddle-horn. He spurred his horse and pulled the leads to the horses carrying the prisoners. They moved docilely forward. The sooner they returned to Mineral Wells and other people, the better.

Nine

Wade led them into a deep ravine. The fortress-like walls of sand and rocks on either side held little of nature except an occasional cactus or mesquite protruding from beneath the rocks. Pepper's hooves clunked against the pebbly creek bottom, as did those of the other horses and the pungent scent of dampness came to Amanda, but she didn't see any water.

Even on horseback, the ravine hid them by several feet from anyone riding across the land above. Ahead, a bobcat darted out of a small cave and dashed away, but his presence didn't seem to affect Wade, although he did pause to look inside the opening as they passed.

After riding several hundred yards into the arroyo Wade stopped. "We'll camp here tonight. I don't think there's any danger of rain washing us away this time of year." In the last few hours he'd rarely spoken. Once they'd stopped at a small stream, watered their horses and refilled the water bags and canteens, otherwise, he'd pushed them to keep riding.

Amanda sensed, now they'd found Oldham, Wade couldn't return to Mineral Wells soon enough. Sliding from Pepper, she stretched her legs and twisted her back to relieve the tired muscles, then she scanned the place he'd decided to stop. She admired his survival skills. Picking this place gave only two directions from which they might be attacked, making it easier for one man to defend.

He tied Oldham and Jose to a mesquite tree protruding from an outcropping of boulders. Securing the rope tightly he glanced at her then quickly looked away as he walked to his horse.

She shivered although she wasn't sure why. With the sun hidden by the top of the arroyo the air had taken on a chill she was no longer used to, but not enough to make her tremble. "I'll gather wood."

"Sheriff, you tryin' to starve us?" Jose whined.

"Enough of that," Wade growled, taking the saddle off his horse. "You'll get fed soon enough."

With one foot, the horse dug at the pebbles nervously.

"There boy." Wade gave the animal a comforting pat on the neck.

Ever since they'd captured Oldham, Amanda had sensed Wade distancing himself and she hadn't been willing to interrupt his self-imposed solitude. She'd ridden with him long enough to know when he was concentrating on their surroundings and felt sure he was again looking for Apaches or other possible attackers.

He strode away from the horse and began picking up stones that he arranged into a circle. "Oldham doesn't look like a man to be trusted to me," he finally said, after he'd placed the stones the way he wanted them.

"I know. If he'd been as shabby as he is now, Simon wouldn't have loaned him a penny." Amanda dropped a bundle of driftwood, limbs and twigs to the ground and looked at the prisoners. "The Maurice Oldham I knew in Illinois was well groomed and immaculately dressed." This man wore ragged trousers and a soiled shirt that would never be blue again. His unkept hair frizzed wildly around his long dirty beard and his brown eyes no longer held a mischievous sparkle. Disgust spread over her.

"Simon must've been quite a man for you to ride fifteen-hundred miles to clear his name." Wade picked up his saddle and deposited it near the middle of the pebbly floor, then turned toward her as if he expected some kind of answer.

"Simon was a good man." She took the coffee pot from her saddlebags, added water and coffee grounds then bent placing the pot on a large flat rock in the fire. She felt Wade's eyes on her, but didn't look at him for fear he'd ask more questions she wasn't prepared to answer about her life with Simon.

The fire popped and sizzled. Her nostrils filled with the scent of mesquite burning and coffee starting to boil. She wrapped her arms around herself trying to stave off the chill and thoughts of Simon that always made her feel inadequate.

"So far, that's all I've heard you say about your husband." Wade squatted beside her and she sensed she couldn't leave his questions unanswered tonight. "Why would a beautiful woman, like you, chance her life to ride across wild barren country for a dead man?"

Amanda looked at him.

His gaze demanded an answer, but she couldn't open her mouth to tell of their unfulfilled marriage.

What good would it do? She'd always heard, 'if you can't say something good, don't say anything at all'. Life with Simon hadn't been all bad, but their marriage hadn't been what she'd dreamed it should be.

Forcing her gaze away from him to the darkening night she couldn't fight the questions her own mind asked. "Why do you continue to ask these questions? What does it matter why I came west? What do you care what my relationship with Simon was?" She stood and walked to Pepper to remove some of the tension building in her and to put some distance between them. Taking her saddle, she carried it back to the camp placing it directly across the fire from Wade.

"Maybe...maybe, I care about you." The words seemed to be wrenched from him. He reached into his pocket for another cigarette paper as he watched every move she made.

"I didn't come here just for him," she said finally, trying to ignore the lump that had formed in her stomach, but his words 'maybe I care for you' came back. What was happening to them? She felt out of control and alive in a way she never had before.

His features blended into the darkness and she couldn't see his expression. Only the red tip of his cigarette and the outline of his taut features in the light of the fire made him visible.

"I came to Arizona Territory for myself and others who need the bank's money. I had no reason to stay in Springfield."

He moved closer, but stood several feet away. "You're a beautiful woman, Amanda." He tossed the remains of his cigarette into the burning logs.

It flamed instantly, then disappeared.

"People used to tell me that a lot." She looked up at him.

"People?"

"Yes, people. Men - who wanted Simon to loan them money. I didn't believe it then, and I don't now." She didn't try to temper the tone. She didn't like the memory and she wanted to be sure she didn't find herself in that situation again. "I was used enough by Simon and his friends, to last a lifetime."

"Used?" He moved closer. "In what way?"

She stared into the fire not wanting to talk about it, but by his insistence she knew he wouldn't stop until she told the whole story. "As a part of the furniture. Someone to entertain, dress up and impress the clients with what a happy home Simon had and what a wonderful businessman he was. I hated it and sometimes him for making me do it."

He touched her shoulder, then slowly turned her toward him as his gaze burned into her.

A lump formed in her throat.

With his right hand he lifted her chin gently to where she had to look into his eyes. His callused palms cradled her cheeks, warming them, making her feel safe and his serious expression reassured her. "Too bad. No one should use someone as pretty and brave as you, Amanda, for anything."

She leaned toward him, in spite of warning bells. "I don't think Simon meant to use me, but business came first."

"Then he missed the most important part." He pulled her to him, covering her lips with a feather-light kiss that rocked the ground where she stood.

Leaning into his embrace, she savored the masculine taste of his lips. Her head spun, her heart pounded and all thoughts of Simon, what had once been disappeared.

Wade folded her to him, his warmth driving her chills away. Her skin tingled where his beard grazed her cheek. For the first time since leaving her father's home, she began to trust a man.

With anguish on his rugged features he unexpectedly pushed her away. "We'd have both been better off if you'd never come to Mineral Wells."

"Why?" She fought to control the emotions she couldn't name.

He turned away and took a step.

She touched his broad back. "Why?"

Glancing at her over his shoulder, a mask seemed to have covered his features. "It's a long story. One I can't talk about right now." He walked toward the prisoners.

Feeling almost as stricken as the day he'd said she resembled a rattlesnake, Amanda swiveled away. He couldn't toy with her this way. She wouldn't accept it, but he stepped around the fire and stopped in her path.

"I can't seem to stay away from you, Amanda Green." His voice sounded husky and harsh. "I vowed, I'd never get involved with another woman." His eyes looked sad and seemed to plead for understanding. "That includes you."

"We're not involved, Wade." She forced the words from her although each clutched at her stomach. "I had a reason for coming to Arizona Territory. I've reached part of my goal. As soon as I get the money, I'll be leaving."

"Yeah, I know. You're strong, too, like a woman who's done things she didn't want to." His intense stare cut into her, as if he saw something she didn't want him or anyone else to see. "You remind me of a kitten who's been kicked around, friendly until someone gets too close, then you hide."

"I'm a woman who does what she has to." She walked away, needing desperately to put some distance between them.

Wade watched her sink to the ground and sip a cup of coffee. She wanted to be away from him. He couldn't blame her after what he'd done, kiss her then walk away. He really should tell her why he couldn't commit himself to her or anyone else. Instead, he said what he knew could do only one thing, make her angrier. "Is that all, Amanda? Is that really all? Some women are driven by greed. Are you like that?"

"You make me sound mercenarial. I'm not driven by money, but I'm a practical person." Her eyes had grown stormier than he'd ever seen them and the anger was directed at him.

That's what he deserved even though it hurt. He couldn't get too close although that's exactly what one part of him wanted.

"I know what I can and what I can't do," she said with conviction in her voice. "I have to support myself. Union widows get pensions--eight dollars a month. How could I take that when Opal Worthington needs it so much?"

Oh no, now he had pushed too far. He should have known though. Amanda, a woman who would nurse during the war wouldn't take when others were in need.

He looked at the stars twinkling down on them and wished he could just disappear. The fire crackled and a horse snorted. He didn't move as he sought words to make what he'd said right.

"Opal can't help it if her husband felt loyal to the Confederacy. Eight dollars will barely help her. It won't touch what she needs for those seven children. If Simon hadn't taken their money...." She sounded angry and tense. "I've had enough criticism to last a lifetime. You don't need to think you can join the ranks. My mother and Simon knew what I should do and didn't hesitate to tell me. Simon can't tell me surviving is wrong anymore, and Mother, she's too far away. I'll do what I have to, and do it well, no matter what anyone thinks."

"I'm sorry. I didn't really mean anything. I'm just trying to understand." His voice sounded lame and he felt like kicking himself. "Most widows marry again, as soon as they can."

The pleasant night had disappeared and he wished he hadn't started this conversation.

She met his gaze boldly. "I'm not inclined, Sheriff, to marry just to be taken care of. Simon was good to me, but our marriage was merely a business deal. I've had enough deals." She took her blanket, whipped the wrinkles out, then spread it on the ground across from him, then laid down and closed her eyes. Occasionally, she glanced toward the prisoners, but ignored him.

He sat beside the fire and tried to put their tense conversation out his mind, but he had trouble. He couldn't keep his eyes from her. The light of the campfire danced on her feminine form beneath those trousers and shirt that didn't seem so baggy now, drawn taut around her soft curves. Taking a cigarette paper, he didn't roll a smoke, but toyed with it, folding it and unfolding it. Finally, he wadded the paper and tossed it into the fire. The paper ignited and flamed bright for a moment, then just as quickly disappeared.

Just like love, he thought. *Bright and hot when it's there, then gone in a flash.*

What would it be like to sleep beside her and hold her every night? She was all woman, one he couldn't stay away from.

Pepper stumbled slightly beneath Amanda.

"It's all right, girl." She patted the horse's neck, urging her forward.

Her mouth felt as dry as a cotton-ball, her eyes burned and her muscles ached. They'd had little water for themselves or the animals in the last two days, but Wade rode on anyway.

This had been the most grueling trip she'd ever made. They stopped for short periods of time, but Wade insisted he couldn't be comfortable until Oldham and Jose were behind bars. He'd proved it by pushing the men and horses almost beyond endurance.

Determined not to be a liability, Amanda found herself drifting to sleep in the saddle. A couple of times he'd caught her nodding but hadn't said anything. She assumed he ignored her weariness to keep their prisoners from knowing they weren't being guarded well. With this in mind, she tried harder to stay awake.

She approached Mineral Wells with mixed emotions. Since the night after catching Oldham and Jose Wade hadn't questioned her anymore about Simon. In fact, he'd only spoken to her when he needed something done, but when they reached town they'd see each other regularly. She couldn't imagine living in the same town with him. A part of her had come to realize she felt more for him than she had any man she'd ever known, but she hadn't analyzed the feelings for fear she might be falling in love with him.

All reasons for travel had disappeared with the capture of Oldham. She'd planned to make a home in Arizona, but could she? That plan had taken a turn when she saw Wade ride away and decided to follow him that morning several weeks before. Now they had found the banker she had no reason to stay, but could she leave?

"Well, look at that, Mineral Wells," Oldham's voice interrupted her thoughts as they climbed a tiny rise in the horizon. "Measley little town. What's it goin' to be like to be livin' in a town near that little woman, Sheriff?"

Amanda caught a glimpse of Wade riding a few feet away.

He seemed to wince at the question. "That's no concern of yours, Oldham."

"Maybe not, but I've seen you eyein' the little widda. 'Pears to me one or both of you might have to move on or do somethin' 'bout it." He laughed, a course ugly sound echoing out over the hill.

She looked at Wade to see how he reacted to Oldham's statement. He sat tall in the saddle, ramrod straight, his head moved slowly back and forth as he surveyed the landscape around them like he hadn't heard a thing. At the moment, she couldn't imagine his lips on hers, passionate and possessive, but she sensed he held his emotions under a tight rein. Maybe he felt this was a crucial time when they could be in danger of losing their prisoners.

A crudely branded sign listed limply in the late morning breeze. The leather thong once holding it to the post now lay on the ground nearly covered with dust.

Amanda looked away from the dangling sign to the sheriff. Staring straight ahead, he seemed to see Mineral Wells for the first time.

A fly buzzed around her head and perspiration ran between her breasts. Desert fragrances she couldn't recognize floated to her as a lump formed in the pit of her stomach. They'd arrived new decisions would need to be made.

Wade moved his horse closer to hers then stopped. He gazed out over the valley like he anticipated a welcome then he turned to her, a wry smile curving his lips. "I hate to admit it, but I couldn't have done this without your help."

She met his look without moving as anger welled up inside. *Of course, you couldn't have done it without me you'd have been dead.* By the prideful set of his chin, she knew he'd come as close to admitting how much he really needed her as he probably ever would. "I think we're even, Wade," she replied. Her voice clipped and terse. That was best. "Don't get sentimental on me, Sheriff."

"I wouldn't think of it." His short statement matched hers in tone.

"We're in town now." She met his blank stare with hers. "You don't need my services anymore." Slapping Pepper's flanks, she kicked the startled horse and they galloped away.

Wade watched her ride toward town, somewhat bewildered by her reaction. He'd tried to thank her for helping, let her know he really appreciated her saving his life, but that didn't seem to be enough.

"Looks like you offended the little woman." Oldham's surly voice interrupted the silence around them. The prisoner chuckled, a sound Wade had already grown to hate.

He suppressed the urge to smash his fist into Oldham's dirty face. "Don't concern yourself. Ride straight ahead and don't waver. My trigger finger might get nervous."

"Want everyone to see what a prize you have, huh?"

"Just move." Riding toward the main street of Mineral Wells, Wade caught a flash of Amanda as she stopped in front of the livery stable. Walt Brauns came out and took the horse's reins and they talked for a few moments, then without glancing back she marched across the street to the hotel.

He shrugged. He had obviously angered her, but that was probably for the best. Now they were in town, the more distance they kept between themselves, the better off they'd both be. As it was, he wasn't sure the town was big enough for both of them.

People stopped to watch him and the prisoners.

Walt Brauns held Pepper's reins in one hand and blocked the sun with the other. "Looks like you caught them, Sheriff."

Wade nodded.

Boyce Stewart rearranged buckets and picks in front of the general store. Although he didn't look up from his task, Wade sensed the storekeeper knew every move.

When they neared the hotel, Gladys Richardson stepped out on the porch. A woman in her early sixties, Gladys wore a bright yellow dress. Her snowy hair flew around her plump, smiling face. She waved and shouted, "Good work, Sheriff."

Delbert Deans, owner of the saloon called, "Got a good rope handy, Sheriff?"

Rosemarie Hernandez, who worked for Deans, smiled, clapped her hands then threw Wade a sultry kiss. He continued to ride toward his office. If he'd known he'd have this kind of reception he'd have waited until dark to ride into town. He didn't like advertising his successes especially when the job wasn't done and it wouldn't be done until they knew where the money was.

Amanda stepped from the hotel door behind Gladys and watched Wade's unflappable profile as he rode toward the jail. Cold, undisturbed by all the attention he drew, she'd been right little phased him when he was on the job. She looked up and down the street, quite a crowd for such a tiny place. At the general store, directly across from her, the owner stopped moving barrels to watch Wade and the prisoners. Two chickens pecking at the dusty soil cleared a path for the riders. The sound of a piano tinkling stopped as people gathered in front of the saloon. To her left, the boarded up old bank looked empty and weather-beaten. Across from it Walt Brauns led Pepper inside the stable.

Beyond the sheriff's office covered wagons formed a circle. Horses and oxen tied to fresh built hitching posts indicated new settlers. Children played around the wagons their joyous voices filling the air.

The town didn't look like much, but for now it was home. A whiff of fried potatoes floated from the open hotel window filling her nostrils. Her stomach growled. "Looks like we've had a population increase since we left."

Gladys looked at her, a scowl on her face. "Nesters. Been here almost a week." The scowl changed to a happy, conspiratorial sparkle. "But, there's a parson."

"That's nice," Amanda replied. She didn't know Gladys was religious, but she hadn't had much time to get to know the other woman. Her stomach growled again. "Is it too late for breakfast?"

"Not for you and the sheriff, it ain't."   She stepped around
Amanda and opened the hotel door. "Come on in. He'll be back in
a few minutes."

Amanda followed.   The hotel seemed dark after the bright
sunshine, but the room felt cool and for the first time in months, she
began to relax. The thought of a soothing leisurely bath sounded
glorious – it'd been years since she'd had that kind of luxury.

Gladys motioned her toward the dining room. "Have a seat. I'll
get some coffee." She disappeared through double doors.

Taking a seat, Amanda scanned the yellow flocked floral
wallpaper and matching lace curtains that blew gently away from
the windows. The room was distinctly feminine. A smooth oak
table and chairs shined to a high gloss would have been fitting for a
royal visit.   Obviously, the owner's personality reflected in the
room, but she felt a bit uneasy after all the months roaming around
in the wild.

Slipping her hat off, she tossed it in the chair beside her and
thoughts of what the future held invaded her mind again. What
would she do? Would they expect her to wear a dress because she
was in town? She purposely didn't let her thoughts stray to the
sheriff. Later, she'd think about him.

Behind her the door squeaked and Gladys pushed through
carrying a silver serving tray and China cups which she placed in
the middle of the table. Pulling out a chair, she sat across from
Amanda. "As soon as the sheriff returns, I'll take your orders. I've
requested you a bath too. Should be ready by the time you're done
eatin'."

Amanda smiled, but again felt a bit uneasy. Had it really been
that long since she'd been around another, or were there
undercurrents here she didn't understand?

Gladys poured the coffee into a cup and handed it to Amanda.

"A bath sounds wonderful." Amanda leaned against the chair
trying to feel at home in this pretty room much like where she'd
grown up. "It's been a long time."

"Yes. We have a lot to celebrate." Gladys poured another cup of
coffee.

"I'm sure everyone wondered if we'd ever return."   Amanda
sipped the coffee. She agreed, they had a lot to celebrate, but she
wasn't sure bringing Oldham in without the money was enough to
justify use of Gladys' silver service and best China.

* * *

The metal key squeaked in the lock when Wade removed it from the cell. He scrutinized the prisoners who smelled of sweat, horse dung and dirt. They needed a bath - soon. Slipping the key into his trousers, he turned to Del Deans, who had followed them.

"That's Oldham?" Deans hooked his thumbs in the tiny pockets of his tan vest and moved closer to the cell eyeing the prisoners with interest.

"Amanda says that's who he is." Wade watched the saloon owner with caution. The content of a conversation he'd once had with Gladys returned. She'd implied Dean's could cause trouble, but until now Wade hadn't had any problems with him.

"Looks different." Deans continued to scrutinize the prisoners as he paced around the room. His brown suit looked new and boots a shade darker sparkled beneath his trouser legs. His business was as prosperous and his clothing showed the owner's penchant for finery.

"That's what happens when a man lives a rough life." Wade crossed the room to his desk and wondered what the saloonkeeper really wanted. He had no intentions of being pushed around by anyone and he hoped Deans didn't plan to try.

"What's next, Sheriff?" Deans turned away from the cell, a malicious gleam flashing in his hazel eyes.

"I'm going to wire the marshal in Prescott. I plan to give the prisoners a fair trial." Wade pulled out his chair and sat. Picking up a slip of paper and lead pencil, he started composing the message.

Dean's friendly expression disappeared and his face reddened as he stepped to the cells again. "Who needs a trial?"

"There will be a fair trial, or I'll know the reason why." Wade finished the note and slipped it in his shirt pocket then stood and walked to the cell and stood between Deans and the prisoners.

The saloon-keeper's eyes grew darker, his nostrils flared, and he didn't budge.

"I came here to keep the law," Wade said. "A vigilante group will not ride rough shod over justice. I have work to do. There's the door!" He pointed toward the exit.

Deans muttered something Wade couldn't understand, turned and marched away

Wade glanced at the prisoners who appeared to be settling in as they'd each taken a bunk.

The door slammed and a window pane rattled then the room grew silent except for sounds of the prisoners flopping on their cots as they settled down.

Wade sighed. The first crisis had passed. If Deans didn't return with more avenging townsfolk, maybe he could keep Oldham and Jose behind bars until a judge arrived. He stepped away from the cell and crossed the room then went out on the porch.

Deans had reached the boardwalk. He turned and glared at Wade.

"My prisoners will be safe for a few minutes, won't they, Deans?" Wade closed the door.

"Now, Sheriff, I wouldn't think of getting in the way of the law." Deans pulled his suit coat closed, lifted his chin, and stepped inside the saloon.

"I want to keep it that way," Wade muttered as he strolled toward the hotel.

Amanda yawned and stretched. Glancing out the window she saw Wade Denton walking toward the hotel. Automatically, her heart began to pound louder. His long strides oozed confidence. This was his town and he was in control. Her thoughts returned to how abruptly she'd left him earlier. Why had he angered her so? Why had she reacted the way she had? She hadn't planned to ride away, it had just happened.

Savoring the coffee, his compliment returned, but she'd had enough of his thanks. If he said it again, she'd scream. But what exactly did she want? To be kissed, held, and told how beautiful she was, then have him prove it? Her cheeks warmed, she squirmed uncomfortably, then gulped the coffee. He wasn't like Simon. Anyone married to him would be a wife in every way.

His boots clunked in the hallway outside the dining room then he stood in the doorway looking at her.

The full beard covered the fatigue lines of his weatherworn face, but his dark eyes looked tired. Crossing the room, he rubbed his forehead with his right hand. He sauntered to the rack and removed his hat, then moved to the table and pulled out a chair opposite Amanda. Sinking into it, he sighed.

"Got them locked up?"

"Yeah." He glanced at his hands and rubbed them on his trousers.

Amanda understood. For weeks they'd traveled together, but now she felt grimy and dirty. They seemed out of place in this sunny room.

"Had my first run in with someone who doesn't want to wait for the judge." He reached for a cup.

"Deans?"

"How'd you know?" He poured a cup, then sipped the coffee as his gaze met hers.

"I saw you talking to him."

He smiled. "I'll have to be cautious with you around. You don't miss much."

"I wouldn't have survived to get here alone, if I hadn't noticed what was happening around me."

"I guess you wouldn't at that."

For a fleeting moment, she thought she saw admiration and maybe something else – affection - in his eyes, but no, not from this hardcore sheriff.

Ten

Gladys bustled in, giving Wade her full attention. "It's good to have you two back in town, Sheriff. I'm so glad you caught Oldham. Whatever you have this morning is on the house." Excitement sparkled in her blue eyes.

"That's good of you, Gladys. Trail food wasn't bad, but I sure missed your cookin'." He glanced warily at Amanda, hoping his statement didn't rile her. Since the morning when he'd made the greasy gravy, she'd done the cooking and an admirable job with limited supplies.

Amanda smiled.

He breathed easier. Apparently he hadn't offended her.

"Well, I'm glad to hear that," Gladys smiled. "What'll you have?"

"Whatever you've got, a bath, a shave, and a haircut."

"The water's heatin', 'nough for both of ya." She beamed. "I'll send Sadie after Abe. Ya both need to look your best for what we've got planned."

"What might that be?" An uneasy feeling passed over him. He'd never seen Gladys happier. He felt good too. He'd finally accomplished what he'd come to town for. Besides that, he'd succeeded twice in a row with what needed to be done.

Gladys bustled from the room.

Wade looked at Amanda. "What's up?"

She shrugged. "I don't know either."

He wasn't sure he liked being on the outside of the secret, but he and Amanda were heroes at the moment. They'd have to go along with whatever celebration the residents had planned.

Amanda finished the two eggs, a stack of flapjacks, sausage, a large portion of potatoes and washed it all down with three cups of coffee. She'd eaten like a half-starved person, but like Wade, she had to admit, Gladys' food did taste better than what she'd cooked on the trail. She glanced across the table at him.

He pushed away from the empty plate having eaten even more than she and laid the cloth napkin beside his plate. "That's sure fine food, Gladys." He took a final sip of coffee.

"I'm glad you enjoyed it." The older woman smiled from a chair she'd placed at the end of the table. "How'd you catch them?"

Wade took several minutes to explain their trip and their final run-in with Oldham.

"Did you find any money?"

"Not yet."

"We accomplished something," Amanda interrupted. "But until we find the money or know it's gone permanently, I don't intend to rest. I plan to talk to Oldham now that he's behind bars."

"Amanda." Wade leaned back in his chair and stretched. "The law is going to take care of this situation."

Their gazes met and locked. Tension filled the room that hadn't been there a few minutes before.

She didn't like the authoritative expression in his voice and she hadn't heard it since the beginning of their ride together. Did he think she would get in his way? After all these weeks together he should know she wouldn't do anything to cause more problems. Then she remembered, sitting in the nest of ants, losing their animals, and nearly causing an uprising in Tucson. Maybe he didn't know she wouldn't cause problems.

Amanda started to say she wouldn't get in the way, but the expression on his face told her he wouldn't believe her, at least now. Silently, she vowed, even though she wanted to know everything she could about the money, she wasn't going to put herself or Wade into jeopardy to find it.

The chair squeaked under his weight as he stifled a yawn. He leaned forward and placed his elbows on the table. His eyes had grown serious and he stared directly into hers. "I'm going to have to watch Deans. He's ready to get the ropes out and string up Oldham and Jose. I don't expect to have to watch you, too." He slid back in his chair without looking away. "The judge may well sentence them to hang, but if they're dead before then, they won't be any help to us."

Now that they were back Amanda knew he expected her to follow his orders. She wasn't sure she could or would, but for the moment, things might go smoother if she acted like she'd listen. "I have no intentions of causing you trouble, Sheriff." She didn't try to hide the sarcasm in her voice. "As I've told you before, my priority is getting Simon's money back."

"Now, don't you two start fightin'." Gladys, who'd been quietly listening to their discussion, stood and pushed back her chair. "It wouldn't be right, everything considered and all." She walked to the kitchen door. "Is that hot water ready yet, Sadie?"

"Yes'am."

"Then bring it in. The sheriff and his lady are ready for baths."

Amanda warmed. She glanced at Wade, but couldn't read his expression as embarrassment bombarded her. Why was Gladys connecting them so intimately?

Moments later, Gladys scurried back into the room. "Amanda, Sadie's takin' your bath to the second room at the head of the stairs. You, Sheriff, can use the bathroom. I'll see that Abe is here to give you a shave and haircut before you finish."

"Thanks, Gladys'." Wade stood, took his hat off the rack, nodded to Amanda, and strolled away.

Again, Amanda wondered what the townsfolk had planned for them. She glanced at Gladys but saw no hint of the celebration in the hotel owner's blue eyes. Pushing away from the table, she stood, retrieved her ragged hat, and plopped it on her head then stepped toward the older woman. "You've got a wrong impression," she said, as they walked through the door into the hallway.

"I don't know what you mean." Gladys smiled the same glowing expression she'd been using ever since they returned. She stepped aside and motioned for Amanda to precede her up the stairs.

"You called me Wade's lady." Amanda passed her, but walked slowly. She had to get this situation under control before it became a real problem.

"Oh, don't worry about that. Some men are hard to convince. My Bernard, he was." Gladys chuckled. "Once he got used to the idea, he didn't mind. Neither did I." Gladys' dress rustled as they reached the landing.

Amanda sensed her friend hadn't heard a word she'd said. A chill of anticipation gripped her as she looked at the closed door. Exactly what did Gladys and Bernard have to do with her and Wade? She had no time to ask. The hotel keeper ushered her into a tiny room holding only a double bed, a bathtub, and one straight chair.

Flocked paper filled with irises covered the walls. A silk bedspread in a shade of lavender matching the flowers covered the bed. The scent of lilacs floated to her nostrils from the steaming tub. Her heart thumped and again she felt nervous about her situation. Amanda glanced at Gladys.

"It's our guest room. When Bernard and I built the hotel, we thought we'd have family come visit from out East. They never came, but I've always kept the room for special occasions." Her face glowed with warmth and pride.

Maybe I'm wrong to be suspicious, Amanda thought stepping further into the room. She looked down at her dusty worn clothes. She certainly did need something else to wear.

"We'll take care of them. Now, you soak. I'll have clean clothes ready when you're done." She turned and walked out.

Suddenly, Amanda felt tired. She sat in the chair and tugged off her boots. Slipping from her dirty clothes, she stepped into the water. Slowly, she sank into the suds, letting the soothing warm water caress her tired, overworked muscles.

She relaxed, leaned her head against the tub and closed her eyes. Whatever Gladys planned, she'd deal with later, right now the water felt heavenly.

Wade rested in the copper tub as Abe Martin trimmed his hair short, then shaved off the beard. Most of the time, Abe made a living cutting hair. Occasionally he was called on to patch up someone who'd been shot and when the need arose, he buried those who didn't survive.

"That sure feels good, Abe." Wade closed his eyes and leaned his head against the high tub back.

"The least I can do for you, Sheriff."

Barely tall enough to reach Wade's throat over the headrest without cutting him Abe had come to Mineral Wells shortly after Wade. They'd rarely had cause to get to talk, but right now, he was as close to a friend as Wade had. "Gladys mentioned that there's something in store for me and Mrs. Green. You wouldn't know what it is, would you?"

The barber stopped shaving him and gazed down at him, annoyance on his face. "You wouldn't want me to tell the whole town's secret, would you?" He chuckled, then started shaving again. "You'll find out soon 'nough."

Wade suddenly became alert and more than a little apprehensive. What did the town have planned?

Clean clothes were laid out on a settee across the room and he didn't like the looks of the boiled white shirt, black coat and trousers along with a celluloid collar. They weren't his and he rarely wore a suit. Although he hadn't expected anyone to ride out to his ranch a mile and a half south of town to get his clothes, couldn't they have given him something a little more like he was used to wearing?

Amanda walked down the stairs in the pink and white gingham dress that had been left for her. When she woke, this and the crispy white drawers she now wore were all the clothes left in the room. They felt clean, if a bit scratchy on her soft skin.

She had combed her blond hair and let it hang freely down her back. She'd hardly recognized her reflection a few minutes before in the mirror by the tub. The clump of her well-worn men's boots on the stairs proved she was the same person who had ridden into town less than two hours before, no matter how she questioned it.

Boots scuffed on the hallway at the bottom of the stairs and Wade stepped into view.

Their gazes met for a moment, then his moved away, taking in the dress.

He wore a suit with short sleeves and the legs that left his boot tops visible. His discomfort marred his handsome rugged face now clearly visible with the beard gone.

A lump rose to her throat and her stomach quivered as she stepped onto the lowest stair. "I...I see they dressed you too."

"Yeah! Why didn't they ride out to the ranch and get me something comfortable to wear. It's been years. I hate suits and white shirts and a fake collar." He tapped the strip of white buttoned around his neck.

Amanda would have snickered he looked so funny, if she hadn't felt something serious was about to happen. "They mean well," she said, although her apprehension grew. She'd anticipated a greeting, but this appeared to be well planned and extreme. She stepped onto the floor beside him.

Together, they walked toward the parlor.

The door burst open and Gladys, now wearing a blue silk dress announced, "Here they are, everyone." She glowed with pleasure as she ushered them inside.

The excitement within might have been contagious, if Amanda hadn't been so nervous.

Delbert Deans, Abe, Sadie, Gladys, and a young man Amanda didn't recognize stood smiling at them. Three women, wearing black dresses buttoned to their chins, and a man dressed in a suit much like Wade's, except that it fit, stared at them like they would someone who had just committed a horrible crime.

Amanda noticed the man carried a Bible. "Oh!" She took a step back.

"What is this?" Wade asked.

"I'm Reverend Wilbur Jones." The man with the Bible moved forward. "Here to do what's right by you." Nearly as tall as Wade, the man's angular features could only be described as plain. His black hair, parted in the middle, had a cowlick in the back making him look messy although he'd obviously tried to comb his unruly locks down with liberal use of bear grease. He reached inside his coat and pulled out spectacles.

"What are you saying?" Panic engulfed Amanda.

"I'm here to marry you." His angular jaw was set firmly and he didn't smile.

The women beside him, just as sober as he, nodded.

"What makes you think we wanted to get married?" Amanda couldn't believe her ears. Her palms grew damp and her heart pounded like the boom of cannons she'd heard during the war.

"It's not a matter of wanting to or not." His dark gaze condemned.

Instantly, she disliked the beady-eyed man and the accusation he implied. She glanced at Gladys. Someone had to help.

Her friend smiled, but didn't move to rescue her. Amanda clenched her hands together. This couldn't be happening! She couldn't, wouldn't marry another man who didn't love her! Her hands grew clammy, desperation swept over her. She glanced at Wade - her only hope.

Despite the frown creasing his brow, he seemed unaffected. "I think you're mistaken, Parson," he said. "Mrs. Green and I--"

"I know all about you and Mrs. Green, Sheriff," the parson interrupted. "Sinners, that's what ya are, and that's just the reason I'm here. Been livin' in sin for weeks, I've heard. Traipsin' across the desert together, just the two o' ya. Went to Ft. Bowie and told the storekeeper ya were man and wife. Went to Tucson and told the hotel manager. People like to talk. We won't have sinners livin' in Mineral Wells, even if ya are the sheriff unless yourn married. We've got to set an example for the rest of Arizona Territory. No, people like you are the reason I'm here. It's my God given duty to see ya do what's right." The man slapped his Bible and took a step closer.

Amanda stepped back and looked at Wade again.

His frown had disappeared. He didn't seem quite as collected as he had a few moments before. "Well, Preacher Jones, since Mrs. Green and I weren't expecting this, I'm sure you can understand our need to have a few minutes alone."

The man clasped the Bible over his heart, rocked back and forth on his feet, then sighed. "If you must, but we need to hurry, there's a revival tonight."

Amanda felt the pressure of Wade's hand on her arm.

"If you'll excuse us."

They turned and walked back into the hallway.

"Don't get any ideas about leavin' without gettin' this done. We're stayin' right here." The parson's voice echoed behind them.

The doors closed quietly.

Amanda turned on Wade. "I told you." Her voice was stony.

He winced under her stare. "It won't be that bad, Amanda."

"That's easy enough for you to say." She stopped speaking, before she blurted out all the sordid details of her non-relationship with Simon. Now wasn't the time, especially with all these prying ears.

"If we don't, Amanda, one or both of us will have to leave town. You heard Preacher Jones. He's come here to clean up the territory and he's starting with us."

Leave town, the words echoed through Amanda's mind. If they left town, they'd never know if Oldham was convicted, never have an opportunity to find the money.

Speechless, she stared at Wade.

He smiled slightly, but she sensed he was as nervous as she. "We have no choice. They obviously know more about us than we do ourselves." He took her hand and pulled her closer. It felt comfortingly warm, strong and reassuring. Maybe he was right and what choice did they have?

Together they turned and stepped back into the homey parlor and their anxious crowd although Amanda couldn't believe this was happening.

She tried to pull her hand away, but Wade wouldn't release it. She glanced at Gladys again. The older woman beamed back at her, offering no help. *Her friend?* At the moment, Amanda wondered.

"Stand over here." The preacher directed the young man to move beside Wade.

The man smiled.

Wade nodded.

Did they know each other?

"You're in luck, Sheriff," the preacher said. "Having an old friend come to town in time to be a witness at the most important event of your life."

"It's good to see you, Harvey." Wade offered his free hand to the man who grasped it momentarily then stepped beside him. Wade turned toward Amanda. "This is a friend of mine, Harvey Griggs. We fought together during the war."

Amanda nodded.

His red hair reached to his shoulders, the handlebar mustache bounced on his clean-shaven face. He wasn't as young as Amanda had thought at first, but he was obviously younger than Wade.

He smiled and nodded. "Glad to meet ya Ma'am."

Her mind screamed, but no one listened. "Wait!" she cried.

"Gladys, you stand by her." Parson Jones motioned where she should stand. "We'll get this taken care of. Someone needs to be watchin' those prisoners."

"I just checked them," Harvey Griggs said. "They're hollerin' for food, but otherwise, they look all right."

"Dearly beloved." The preacher's words silenced the rustle of voices that had filled the room.

Amanda looked at Wade.

A red streak marked his face where the barber had shaved him too close. His skin looked white after being covered with a beard so long, or had it turned white at what was happening to him? His expression was stern as he listened to the parson. His hand felt warm on her cool one. He squeezed it, then she heard him start to repeat the words the preacher said.

Wade slipped out of the ill-fitting coat and hung it across the back of the crudely built chair. Across the room, he heard the faint rustle of Amanda's skirt as she moved near the bed.

"What are we going to do?" she asked.

He looked at her. "For now, we're married. I don't want it any more than you do, but we didn't have much choice. I wired the marshal at Prescott, he'll send the judge as soon as he can get here."

Shaking his head, he scrutinized the cabin. Everything appeared to be the same as it had before he left to search for Oldham, but now it seemed smaller, much smaller. He'd never known one woman could take up so much room. "I expect the judge can help us out of our legal problem as well as try the prisoners. In the meantime, you can sleep on the bed, I'll stay in the barn."

"But, that isn't fair. This is your home. You haven't had a good night's sleep in weeks."

"I know, but there's not much I can do about that either." Actually, sleeping away from her might give him more rest anyway. He sure hadn't had any lately.

"Well, there's something I can do." She stared at him with that stubborn expression in her eyes he'd seen more times than he wanted to count. "We'll put a divider in the bed, just like we did in Tucson. Tomorrow, I'll work on making a cot for myself." She walked over to the fireplace and began to rustle the pans around. "You've got to have some sleep, Wade. We've only partially completed what we started. You said yourself there are more people involved than just Oldham and his Mexican friend. If you can't sleep well, we'll never be able to determine who the rest are."

"What makes you think I'm going to sleep well, anyway?" If he hadn't been so tired, he would have closed the distance between them and showed her exactly what he meant.

"You're tired enough to sleep and I don't think Deans' whiskey did anything good for you. Now come on, I'll pull your boots off." Amanda took him by the arm and guided him toward the bed.

He looked down at her, felt his head pounding, and fought the urge to pull her to him. She was right. He felt terrible. He felt the pressure of her small hands on his shoulders.

"Sit."

He did.

She pushed him back against the bed.

He didn't protest, nor did he say anything when he felt her remove one boot then the other. In the morning, he'd straighten this out he'd correct everything. He closed his eyes and thought of Harvey Griggs. At least the prisoners were in safe keeping tonight.

Amanda laid awake for a long time listening to Wade's smooth breathing. Occasionally, she glanced at him, trying to get the fact he was now her husband through her stunned brain. Over and over, she planned what she would say when he woke. She'd never intended to become his wife or anyone else's without them telling her they loved her. He certainly hadn't done that.

In the morning, she'd tell him. Meanwhile, she had to decide what she'd do next. With the added complication of being married, she realized what she'd planned might not work, but she intended to move toward it anyway.

Her thoughts drifted to her brother Jed back in Springfield. Before she'd left, he'd finally relented a bit. Although she'd been adamant she wouldn't need his help, he'd insisted if she did, he'd expect to hear from her. She'd write him and see if he could finance a new bank until she and the sheriff found the money they thought was still in town.

Rolling over, she closed her eyes. That wouldn't take care of her immediate needs. Although she and the sheriff were married, she had no intentions of being dependent upon him. He could give her a place to stay, which would soothe the minds of the residents. Like he'd said, as soon as the judge arrived, they'd get their legal entanglement straightened out.

Somehow, that thought hurt. She realized in the weeks they'd been together the sheriff had come to mean something to her, more than she wanted anyone to. At the moment, she didn't want to, couldn't think about the feelings she had for him.

She had to get the money back, open a new bank. While they waited for the judge, she'd get a job. Her thoughts honed in on the general store and her father's back in Boston. Besides banking, this was the only type of business she knew anything about.

One glance at Stewart's General Store told of the need for a woman's touch, but would he hire her? He'd glared at her when she rode into town. He seemed to be the only resident not present for the wedding, but from what Gladys said, he'd been the person who knew about her and Wade posing as a married couple.

He might be hard to convince, but she'd do it. She couldn't stay out on this tiny ranch, even if there was enough work to keep her busy as long as someone other than Maurice Oldham might have taken Simon's money.

Wade opened his eyes and tried to focus, but what he saw was blurred. Closing them again, he turned, trying to ignore the pain in his head. He was in bed, not out in the desert. He opened his eyes again, and looked at the wall beside him. It looked familiar--his cabin. How had he gotten here?

Then he remembered. He studied the boards for a few moments as the memories returned. Glancing at his chest, he saw the unfamiliar white shirt. No, it hadn't been a dream. Sitting up slightly, his gaze ran the length of his body. He still wore the ill-fitting black pants, but his feet were bare.

A sound came from the other side of the room. He turned slowly, moving his throbbing head carefully to control the pain. At first he saw the coat that matched his trousers, then Amanda Green bending over the coals in the fireplace.

Not Amanda Green anymore. He'd married her early yesterday afternoon. Sinking back into the bed, he closed his eyes again. At the time, marrying her seemed to be the best solution to a problem he didn't know how to resolve. Now he wasn't too sure. He'd married a Yankee woman, a stubborn one at that who once thought he might be involved with a bank robber. He groaned softly.

"Are you awake?" She stood and turned toward him.

"Yeah." He opened his eyes and sat up. Somehow, he had to face this day, and this woman. He was a married man. He had fought being involved with women for the last three years. Now....

"I made you some coffee. That whiskey of Deans was pretty strong. Thought you might need it to clear your head." She crossed the room and handed him a chipped china cup he'd found in the cabin when he'd bought the place. The steaming brew would have smelled good if his head hadn't hurt so.

Her blond hair hung loosely around her shoulders the tiny waves giving her a soft femininity he'd tried to ignore for weeks. He liked her hair loose. "Thanks." Taking the cup he sipped it as he watched her cautiously. What would she expect? She'd been married once, would she take over his cabin? He took another sip of coffee and his tongue burned, but he didn't react to the pain.

"It's hot." She stood a few feet away watching him and he felt self-conscious.

"I found out."

She'd strolled back to the fireplace, bent over and stirred something.

Probably mush. He'd come to like the mixture she seemed to prefer for breakfast. In fact, there weren't many foods she cooked he didn't like. Having her along had saved him from having to eat his own cooking. That alone might make this marriage more feasible, but how could he survive at night? It had been almost more than he could take trying to keep his hands off her those nights in Tucson, but for now he had prisoners, and a reason to spend most of his time in Mineral Wells.

"I have a plan." She turned away from the fireplace an expression that told him she'd made up her mind about something, probably something he wouldn't like. "I've written my brother Jed a letter asking him for the money to finance the bank. In the meantime, I'll get a job."

By the firm set of her jaw, Wade knew he'd have trouble convincing her she shouldn't be traipsing around trying to get a job. "That's not a wise idea." He slid to the edge of the bed.

"And why not?" She placed her hands on her hips and met his gaze, determination on her face. She again wore the trousers and shirt, the pink gingham dress hung on a nail just inside the door along with the blue one he'd bought in Tucson.

"Because we're married now, Amanda. People will think it's strange if I let my wife work." He slipped his feet to the floor and let the feel of smooth solid wood help him get his perspective back. If Del Deans' whiskey always did this to him, he'd be better off to stay away from it.

A rolled up quilt fell into a heap beside his bare feet. He recognized the barrier she'd placed between them like she'd done in Tucson. At least he didn't have to deal with her trying to make a real marriage out of this situation. Maybe he should let her work.

"You said you think someone else in town is involved with Oldham. In the months you've lived here, you haven't been able to determine who it is. If I'm in town observing too, maybe between us, we can figure out who it is." She took the boiling pot off the fire. "Mush's ready." She walked to the table, placed the pot on it then sat down.

He stood and walked to the table, taking the seat opposite her. Never before had he thought much about the crude furnishings in his cabin, but this morning the roughly hewn table and benches he used for seats looked like they needed work. They were certainly a long way from Gladys' parlor, good enough for him, but not much to offer a woman.

Amanda had covered the table with a piece of cloth he used to dry dishes. *She's already begun to make changes.* Would his life ever be the same again? He looked at the bowl of mush. No, his life had changed the day he'd tackled her in the desert.

"I still plan to look for the money, Wade. And, I have no intentions of being dependent upon you. You didn't even want to marry me. Like you said last night, as soon as the judge gets here, we'll get this legal entanglement straightened out." She dipped a couple of spoonfuls of sugar and added them to the mush. "In the meantime, I need to support myself. I'd like to eventually open the bank, whether we ever find the money or not."

Her reasoning was sound, although he hated to think of the noise people in town would make, and he wasn't sure she could get a job. But maybe if he let her work, the townsfolk would realize they'd made a mistake forcing the marriage.

When the judge came they'd get an annulment or divorce. People would see the marriage couldn't be forced, no matter what Parson Jones thought.

Eleven

"You want me to what?" Amanda stared at the storekeeper not believing what he'd just said.

"I want you to go for water." Boyce Stewart's beady black eyes stared through her. His matching handlebar mustache twitched above his lips and his baldhead glared under the lantern light.

This had been a rough day for Amanda, arranging cans and buckets on the shelves, but he didn't need to think he could get rid of her that easily. When she'd finally convinced him she could do the work, he hadn't hesitated to give her something to do, heavy tasks with the light.

"I thought you had a well."

"I've had five dug, but there's no water on this side of the street." He'd begun to bring merchandise in from the porch in anticipation of closing.

"Why don't you use Gladys' water?"

"That woman! She wants me to pay, and I won't." His eyebrows lifted disgustedly and he bit a hunk of tobacco.

"Well, I think she's nice." Amanda stubbornly defended her friend.

"If you want to work for me, the less said about her the better." He spit at the spittoon near the counter, but missed, then walked toward the door to bring more buckets inside. "Now are you going for water, or am I firing you?"

"You'd like that, wouldn't you?" She met his stare without flinching. "Where are the barrels?"

"There are six on the wagon. Once they're filled and brought to town you can leave. I get water from the pool on the creek two miles north of town. I won't expect you to unload them." He went out.

"Thanks." She muttered, walking through the storeroom toward the backdoor. She was tired and had other things she wanted to do like make dinner for Wade, but she couldn't chance losing the job.

Wade came out of the jail and mounted his red roan. It had been a long day. He'd overseen the bathing up of the prisoners and tried to interrogate them. The Mexican hadn't been too hard to deal with although he'd come to the conclusion Jose didn't know anything about the money.

Oldham had said little, and what he had told Wade didn't relate to the case. As the day wore on, he found himself thinking more and more of going home with Amanda. Harvey Griggs agreed to watch the prisoners until midnight, then he'd take a shift. He wasn't sure why he had insisted on taking the midnight shift tonight, but the thought of Amanda in his house seemed to draw him to it.

He glanced toward the general store where a light glowed in the window. Was she still there? He'd seen her arranging buckets and picks earlier. Why had Stewart hired her? Even though her father had a general store back in Boston, Stewart still didn't have to hire her. Knowing Amanda though she'd probably persuaded enough even the storekeeper couldn't ignore her.

In the setting sun, this place had been peaceful and pretty with the last rays shimmering silver on the deep still pool of water nestled among the bushes and reeds that grew nearby, but now Amanda felt lonely and she couldn't get away fast enough. Blisters and scratches made her hands sting. Her back hurt and her damp, torn clothes clung to her body. Angry tears streamed down her face as she forced her weary legs up on the wagon one last time. She knew more about a general store than anything else, but Boyce Stewart didn't have to take advantage. She had come to the conclusion there was reason to be suspicious of him. He was the only person in town who had made no comments about Oldham and his Mexican accomplice and she found that unusual.

Sitting on the rough wagon seat, she reached for the reins then heard horses moving in the bushes. She reached for her gun.

"I wouldn't do that, if I was you," the gravelly voice said.

She moved her hand away from the firearm.

"Awww, why don't you just leave him alone. He ain't doin' nothin'." A more youthful voice came from the edge of the bushes.

"What did I tell you about thinkin', boy?" the first man demanded. "If'in you don't learn to keep your mouth shut, I'm goin' to show you what I do to people who talk out o' turn with me."

"Yeah." A third man added.

A short woolly haired man with a beard stepped to the side of the wagon. "We might even drop you off in town. I'll bet that sheriff in Mineral Wells would like to get a look at ya." He snickered.

A young boy followed a few feet behind him.

The two crossed the short distance to the wagon.

The grizzled man glared up at Amanda. "Get down!"

"No!" She tried to make her voice as male-like as she could and didn't move.

"I said get down!" He grabbed her leg and jerked.

"I'm just getting water for people in town. I don't mean you any harm." Fear gripped Amanda. Willing the terror away, she tried to slap the reins, but the man grabbed her arm and tugged.

"I said get down and I mean get down!"

She fell with a jarring thud. "Ouch!" Pain ripped through her body, but she scrambled to her feet.

"Didya hear that, Boss?"

"Did I hear what, Dingy?" The leader, who still hadn't come into view, asked. "All I can hear is you two talkin' all the time. This youngin's tellin' me what I'm doin' wrong and you're talkin' 'bout the next whore you can get. How can a man hear anything with you two yammerin' all the time?"

The man he called Dingy stood over her, snarling. "This here's a woman." He touched her arm. The smells of sweat, stale tobacco, garlic, and bear grease filled her nostrils and made her stomach roll. Moving around her like a lion stalking its prey, he glanced at the boy. "Light the lantern. I want to see what we've got."

"But...but," the boy didn't move.

"Don't *but* me boy. When he hit the ground that wasn't a man's voice sayin 'ouch'. No siree, that was a woman."

The boy scurried away.

"Dingy, you've got women comin' out of your brain," the third man grumbled. "Check the wagon. See if there's any money. He's from town and travelin' light. Someone'll be lookin' for him soon."

Amanda cringed hoping Dingy would do as he was told and leave her alone.

But, Dingy ignored the instructions and ran a grimy hand down her back while he held her tight with the other. His hand was rough, hurtful, bruising through the shirt.

The boy returned with the lantern.

"Light it, boy," Dingy ordered.

She slapped at his filthy hand but he pushed her hands away as he fondled her. The memory of her encounter in Tucson returned, this time no one was around to help. She kicked at the man who crouched above her and screamed.

A rough hard hand covered her mouth.

Dingy pulled at her shirt and she heard the fabric rip, then cool air hit her making her shiver. She tried to curl into a ball, but Dingy grappled with her clothes, then pulled her hat off and tossed it aside. Hair pens fell away and he ground her head into the sandy soil.

"See, I told ya, Boss. We's got us a woman on our hands. She's a little mite, but she's a woman, just the same." He laughed.

He rolled Amanda over on her back and the younger man grabbed her hands pulling them above her head. She spat at Dingy and tried to aim for his groin with her knee, but he grabbed her legs and forced them against the ground with his.

"Ain't had me a woman in a long time." He grabbed the waistband of her trousers and pulled.

Buttons popped and the thin leather belt stretched then broke. She felt her warm skin rubbing against the cold grass and sand beneath her. She watched the three men and knew exactly what they had in mind. *They wouldn't get me easily*, she vowed.

"Let's flip a coin." The third man had climbed in the wagon, but now seemed as interested as the others.

"Can I have a turn?" The younger man salivated above her.

"I'm first," Dingy proclaimed. "I found her." Holding her legs with his, he laughed, exposing decaying brown teeth with dark holes between, then he pulled his trousers exposing his engorged member. He bent forward as if to kiss her.

She twisted her head to the right and he missed her mouth, plowing his face into the grass and sand.

"Hurry, Dingy, I want my turn." The younger man gripped her wrists tighter.

"When I'm done." Dingy gasped pushing himself back on top of her. "She thinks she's cute doin' something' like that. I'll show her."

Horror gripped her as he plunged toward her. She wanted to kick but couldn't move her legs. She twisted to bite at the hands restraining her, but couldn't reach them.

Dingy laughed. "You're goin' to like it."

Bang!

His heavy body fell on her, but she felt nothing else. She shuddered as she tried to push him away.

The leader shouted, "Run!"

Amanda heard movement, but her hands were free. With all her might she pushed at the dead weight.

Dingy breathed. The shot had hit him in the back.

Who had done it? A shiver of fear ran through her as she reached for what was left of her clothes.

"It's all right, Amanda." Wade's soothing voice came through the darkness.

Relief replaced fear. She pushed at the frightful man. This time his body moved enough for her to slide out from underneath him. She turned and pulled at her shirt and trousers, but they didn't near cover her.

"Here." Wade handed her a blanket.

"Stewart said he'd fire me if I didn't get the water."

"I know. He won't do that again." His stern voice filled the night air. He examined the man's wound, then turned him over to look into his face. "I think he'll live. We'll take him back to town and have Abe patch him up."

Looking at the filthy man, Amanda tried to stifle the image of him over her. If Wade had been a few seconds later...?

"I wondered when you'd be ending your day," his voice trailed off.

She didn't need him to complete the sentence. She knew the rest of the story. If he hadn't gone to check with Stewart, Dingy would've raped her. Pulling the blanket closer, the wool scratched her skin, but couldn't stop the shivers.

The full moon, hidden by clouds earlier, reappeared. She stared into Wade's eyes. At first she thought she saw anger on his face as humiliation washed over her, then she realized what she saw was something akin to sympathy.

His expression was her undoing. The seriousness of what had almost happened to her unleashed emotions she had held in check throughout the ordeal. Tears sprung to her eyes and sobs wracked her body.   She glanced at the wounded man and shivering uncontrollably.

Wade's arms slipped around her and pulled her close.

She felt safe never so cared for. They stood there for several minutes and she wanted to never move, but knew she had to. Stepping away from him, she inched her way toward the stream. Earlier, she had been ready to be done with water, now she needed to feel it around her - the coolness, the cleanliness.

Amanda sobbed again, this time, cleansing tears running down her face. At the water's edge, she knelt. Cupping her hands, she brought them to her face and let the cool water trail down her scalding skin. How could she ever look Wade in the face again? Glancing over her shoulder, she saw him standing where she'd left him, an expression she couldn't read on his face. Then she knew she could face him, he seemed to bear the same anguish.

Wade loaded the wounded man in the wagon, tying him behind the barrels of water so he couldn't escape, then he secured the man's horse and his.

Amanda continued to kneel near the water.

This was about as awkward a situation as he had ever experienced. He sensed her pain, wanted to comfort her, wished he could tell her he recognized the wounded man as one on a poster in his office. Slowly, he walked toward her. Obviously, although she had traveled by herself and helped him capture Oldham and Jose, she wasn't really prepared to defend herself. Of course, anyone would have trouble fighting off three men. He hoped she'd learned not to put herself in that kind of situation and he'd do anything to see it didn't happen again.

The water splashed gently against the boulder as he stepped closer. The night was too dark to search for the attackers and thunder rumbled in the distance.   In the morning, he and Harvey could look, but by then they'd probably be miles away.

As long as they stayed away from Amanda, he wouldn't bother. He couldn't identify them. If they didn't stay away, they'd have to reckon with him.

She turned away from the water and pulled the blanket tight.

He realized he would kill for her. It'd been a long time since he felt this kind of responsibility, that time, the person he'd needed to help had died. The fact he'd succeeded now frightened him a little, but also gave him confidence. If anyone tried to harm Amanda again, they'd have to get him first. "Can I help?"

Her sobs had subsided somewhat. She didn't look up at him, nor did she stand.

What should I do? He took another step.

"I'm all right," she sobbed, through another rush of tears.

He reached out to touch her.

She jumped, skittish as a newborn colt.

Anger filled him again. Nothing he'd ever done in his life had prepared him for this situation. He wanted to help her, bring that spunky Amanda he knew back, but at the same time, she had to know she shouldn't come out into the desert alone at night.

He knelt beside her. "It'll be all right. That man was a criminal, I'm sure I have a poster on him." Reaching inside his shirt pocket, he pulled out a cigarette paper. He definitely needed a smoke.

Amanda turned slightly toward him.

He gazed into her horror filled eyes.

She grimaced. "I shouldn't have come out here by myself, even if Stewart did insist."

"I know." His hands trembled as he lit the cigarette. "If you're dead, you're not going to be able to help me find that money."

"You're right. I've learned a lesson." Her tear-stained gaze met his in the moonlight.

He felt a rush of uneasiness. She was his wife now, whether either of them wanted it or not. Part of him wanted to protect her. He might not be able to keep her from working or insisting she help him find the money, but he intended to see she didn't put herself into harm's way again.

She stood and moved a few feet away, looking out over the river. She looked forlorn, lonely and very lovely as the moonlight created a silver sheen upon the loose strands of her golden head.

Tossing the cigarette butt into the pool of water, Wade watched the red tip of it disappear into the depths. "I'm glad you now know how dangerous it is, although I'd rather it not have been like this." His voice sounded harsher than he wanted. Rising, he stepped closer and placed his hands on her shoulders, shaking her gently. He'd never felt so frustrated.

"I can't go back to town like this." She pulled the blanket tighter and stepped closer to the river. "What will people think?"

A wave of sympathy flowed through him.

She looked pathetic, standing there.

He wanted to take her in his arms and remove all the pain and agony. Rage welled again. It was a wonder he hadn't killed Dingy.

Peering up at him, her eyes looked puffy.

He imagined they were red, still streaked with tears.

Her hair was matted against her head. "Let me take a minute to wash up. I feel so...filthy."

"I'll turn my back." He moved a few feet away. Moments later, he heard the quiet lapping of water.

Amanda slipped into the dress Wade had bought in Tucson, then tried to comb her hair. The strands were tangled and she couldn't move the comb through the mass. Their ride to town and then to his ranch had been slow and wet when a thunderstorm hit as they reached the edge of town. This had helped in one way, Amanda didn't have to face townsfolk who might wonder what had happened.

But she had begun to question where Wade had gone. He'd told her he would draw a bath, but that had been almost an hour before and he still hadn't come into the cabin.

The door squeaked behind her.

"Is it all right to come in?" He stuck his head inside.

"Sure, I'm dressed and everything." She finished pouring the cornbread mixture into a heavy iron skillet then pushed it into the fire.

"What's that I smell?" He sounded almost lighthearted as he walked further into the room.

"Beans, I started them on the coals this morning. They're ready to eat. I'm baking the cornbread now." She moved away from the fireplace to a pan of water where she rinsed and dried the bowl she'd used.

"Good." He strolled to the table and sat on the bench, a thoughtful expression on his face. "You're a very resourceful woman, Amanda."

"Thanks." She felt herself warm at his perusal. "I learned it during the war."

"What was that you said earlier about Stewart?" He leaned forward, his elbows on the table giving her his full attention.

She stepped toward the fireplace, trying to keep her nervousness in check. Somehow, Wade seemed more direct now than he had before her encounter with Dingy. "Oh, you mean that I think he's the one?" She wiped her hands dry on the towel, not understanding why she felt uncomfortable with him right now.

They'd traveled together for weeks, but she hadn't felt this self-conscious before.

"One?" His left eyebrow rose with the question.

"Yes, the one who's working with Oldham." She folded the towel and laid it on the table, then walked to the fireplace although she felt his gaze on her back.

"How did you come up with an idea like that?"

She bent to check the cornbread. I should've known. He's questioned everything I felt strongly about. But she had to tell him her suspicions, no matter how foolhardy he thought they were. She peeked at the cornbread that was cooking nicely, but still had several minutes to bake before it would be ready to eat. Replacing the lid, she turned toward him. "Well, he's the only one who didn't seem interested in the prisoners, didn't attend the wedding. Doesn't want me to work for him. Clearly wants money. I think he knows something."

"Maybe he's just not interested."

"Too uninterested to suit me," she insisted, "and besides, he was interested enough in us he told Pastor Jones we were traveling together."

"How'd you learn that?"

"Gladys. She and I are friends. While everyone was enjoying Del Deans' whiskey we were talking." She thought she saw his face color slightly, but she didn't want to embarrass him more, so she turned back to the food. "Give me a few days."

"I've got water heating and it may take an hour or more to heat. Damp wood isn't easy to burn. Looks like it might rain all night."

She didn't like the sudden change of conversation and sensed he disagreed with her analysis of Stewart's actions. "I didn't think it was supposed to rain here much."

"Sometimes, depends upon the time of the year. Late summer rains are called monsoons." He stretched his long legs seemingly relaxed, but she wondered. This evening hadn't been anymore normal for him than it had for her as again she felt his gaze on her back, but didn't turn as self-consciousness again returned. Did he think she'd invited Dingy's attack? She probably shouldn't have gone to the stream that late in the evening, but who'd have thought? After all, she'd traveled across the country without problems. "Was Dingy on one of your wanted posters?" She turned slowly. They couldn't live in the same house without looking at each other and talking about the situation.

Their gazes seemed riveted together. Tension became as thick as the cornbread batter.

Her stomach quivered and her hand shook slightly as she reached for the pan.

"I didn't take time to look at the posters. Harvey said Dingy's a thief from Santa Fe believed to have killed a family of nesters in New Mexico Territory."

Amanda shivered. If Dingy had killed a whole family, he could have killed her too. Tonight Wade had saved her life and more. Could she ever repay him? He didn't appear to expect payment anymore than she had. With the thought she began to relax slightly.

"After we eat, I'll set the water up for your bath. I've made a cot for myself in the barn." His voice sounded calculated, his motivation well thought. "Under the circumstances, I thought, you might feel better alone."

Again her stomach felt queasy, but her impressions of him vanished forever. She'd thought him cold and unfeeling, but he'd proved to be thoughtful and considerate. "Thanks, I appreciate that."

Amanda had placed the copper bathtub in the middle of the floor. Wade added hot water then went back for some to cool it. All the while, he tried to force himself to think of something other than her bathing in his house. As soon as the water was the right temperature, he strolled to the door where he paused. "I'll use the rest of the water to clean up myself. Give me a holler when you're done."

"Sure, Wade. And, thanks again."

"Think nothin' of it." He exited before he let his thoughts get him in any deeper.

In the barn, he set the kettle of hot water in the middle of the floor then added cold water until it was just right. Stripping, he slipped in trying to block the image of Amanda doing the same from his mind. He rolled a cigarette and leaned back.

This isn't going to work. No way can I live here and stay away from her. But, she didn't act like them living together bothered her at all. Somehow, that thought disturbed him. He'd fought hard not to become emotionally involved again and to do so with a woman who barely acknowledged his existence made him angry at himself.

Inhaling he groaned then drown the cigarette and tossed the damp butt away. He dunked himself. *Maybe I can wash these feelings away.*

Amanda combed through her hair and let it fall around her shoulders then she slipped on the drawers Gladys had given her. Another glance in the mirror told her she'd done everything she could to remove signs of Dingy. Stepping to the door, she opened it and peered out, but couldn't see Wade. "Wade, I'm done."

"I'll empty it now," he replied from the shadows where she saw the red glow of a cigarette tip, near the tiny corral.

The damp air hit her hair making it feeling cold against her skin. Her stomach knotted. How long had he been standing there? It had quit raining and the air had a fresh-washed scent mingled with the sweet smell of creosote bushes.

Stepping back, she held the door open wider.

He stepped in and crossed to the tub.

She followed. "Wade?"

"Yes." He bent to pick up the tub, but waited.

"Do...do you feel I've been dirtied?"

He looked at her, an expression she couldn't read on his strong handsome features. "And why would I feel that way?"

"Well, some men, when...when something like what happened tonight happens.... You couldn't seem to get out of the cabin fast enough, so I wondered." She twisted her hands in front of her. "Anyway, I just wanted to again say, thanks."

He straightened, cleared his throat, and took a step toward her. His stare held her in place and he didn't move. The silence in the cabin was almost deafening. "Once I told you thanks, Amanda. You told me not to be melodramatic. I give you the same advice."

"But--"

"No buts." He stepped closer, pinning her with his gaze. "I don't know what's going to happen between us. I've never had such experiences in my life until that day I tackled you in the desert. If you know what's good for you, you'd better let me empty this tub and sleep in the barn."

"Is that where you want to sleep?"

His dark eyes flashed. "No, but considering what's happened, I think that's where I'd better stay, unless you're afraid of being by yourself."

"No, of course not." The words seemed to fall between them.

"I didn't think so. Someone as brave as you wouldn't let a little thing like almost getting raped affect her, would they?" He turned, picked up the tub and carried it toward the door, but before he left, he turned slightly. "Humor me, Amanda. Lock the door."

"All right."

Twelve

Amanda dusted the shelves behind the metal containers of lead shot and smiled inwardly then glanced around the general store. Even though Boyce Stewart never said a word, the shop appeared cleaner and neater since she started working for him.

Barrels of sugar, flour and meal filled the middle of the room. Picks, shovels, tack and mining tools hung along the wall with no window. Buckets in different shapes and sizes sat under the front display window. Boyce kept them there so he could easily move some of them out onto the porch each morning.

The shelves where Amanda worked were stacked with canned goods, dusty from lack of sales. She squinted and picked up a tin of peaches. One dollar! Setting it back down, she examined a can of pears, then one of applesauce. The same price. No wonder dust had accumulated a regular settler couldn't afford them.

Glancing again at a can of peaches, an idea began to develop. For weeks, since she and Wade had brought the prisoners in, she'd tried to decide how to get in the jail to question Oldham. She began to hum as she dusted. Maybe, just maybe, her idea would work. For now, she put the thought on hold. She would wait for an appropriate time before the judge arrived.

Boyce kept the fourth wall bare to display posters and advertisements for different kinds of mining equipment. Except for these signs of the west, Amanda could almost forget she worked for Stewart in Arizona Territory rather than her father's store in Boston.

Climbing on a tiny ladder, she cleaned the shelves behind the counter. The untreated wood glowed under the lemon oil in the rag she used.

The three weeks she worked for him had passed quickly. She liked living near a town and she'd started to become accustomed to living with Wade Denton, even though she saw little of him.

Although he hadn't wanted her to search for Oldham with him, he now seemed to accept the fact she lived in his house. Obviously he liked her cooking meals and she found she enjoyed talking to him even though they saw little of each other. Most of his time was spent at the office watching the prisoners, although he'd now officially deputized Harvey Griggs.

The front door squeaked. Someone had come into the store. Stepping off the ladder, she looked toward the sound. Boyce Stewart entered. Lately, he trusted her enough to leave her in charge for a short time each day, when he took a walk and he wasn't as opposed to having her work as he'd been at first. "Did you have a good walk, Mr. Stewart?"

"Yes." He strolled into the room, around the counter and placed his bowler on the shelf beneath. "Still using that lemon oil, huh?"

"Yes, I am. I purchased it with my earnings. The cabin looks and smells good when I use it. I didn't think you'd mind me using it here too."

"Just as long as I don't have to pay for it." He opened the money box and thumbed through the contents. He always counted the money before he left, then again when he returned.

Amanda had grown used to the fact he'd never trust her completely.

"Did we have any customers while I was gone?"

"Mrs. Jones came in, but she didn't like that blue fabric you had, so she wouldn't buy it. I think you should order some gingham. That way you'd get more female customers." Amanda walked to the furthest wall where she rearranged the fabric Mrs. Jones had left in disarray. Black wool, linsey-woolsey, and navy blue, no wonder Mrs. Jones did not want a dress made of it. In the desert heat, any clothes made from wool would be very uncomfortable.

"I have no intentions of purchasing gingham, Mrs. Denton," Stewart snorted, closing the lid on the metal moneybox, then slid it under the counter. "I didn't plan to satisfy female customers when I opened the store and I have no intentions of changing my mind now. Miners, that's why I'm here. They bring in good money, not a few cents like those sniveling nesters."

Amanda ignored his statement. They'd had this discussion before. She didn't particularly like her boss and she suspected he might be involved with Oldham, but in the few weeks she worked for him, she had grown to sympathize with him somewhat. He'd told her keeping a general store in Mineral Wells wasn't the profitable endeavor he'd planned when he had moved from Virginia.

Even though the thought kept coming back to her and she had gone over and over in her mind who Oldham's accomplices might be she had to stretch her imagination to the limit to include her boss as a suspect. Looking at the balding storekeeper as he lit his pipe, she couldn't imagine him involved with Oldham. She reminded herself one never knew for sure, but nothing the storekeeper had done made him look like a culprit. She could be wrong about him.

"Could I take my lunch break now?" All the bolts of cloth had been rearranged.

"Yeah, and you don't have to come back either." His dark scowl met her gaze.

She walked toward the counter and smiled, although she saw the earnestness in his dark eyes. "Now, Mr. Stewart, we've talked about this before. Even you have to admit, I've helped a lot."

"Not that I asked for it," he reminded her. "Where are ya eatin'? 'Cross the street at that woman's?"

"Yes, Gladys is my friend." Amanda raised her chin a little higher and stepped behind the counter to retrieve the reticule Gladys had given her. Stewart aggravated her when he tried to tear Gladys down. "She cooks the only good meals in town."

"Didn't realize I was payin' you enough to eat there all the time." His beady eyes glared into her.

Amanda walked to the front door where she stopped. Pivoting slowly, she met his gaze without wavering. "Mr. Stewart, it may surprise you, but I'm not entirely dependent upon the salary I receive here." She opened the door slightly, then added. "I'll be back in twenty minutes."

She slipped out and walked across the porch, taking care not to catch the blue gingham dress Wade had bought her on the dry building splinters. Sadie, Glady's servant, was making her a couple more dresses. For now, though, all she had was this and the yellow one she'd worn to be married. She needed to preserve them for work.

Glancing over her shoulder she looked at the window. Boyce Stewart stood inside watching her. At first, this had bothered her, but not anymore although she still hadn't decided what about him didn't ring true? He'd flat told her he didn't want her to work for him, but he'd hired her with very little insistence. At times she sensed his scrutiny of her as much as she observed him. He hadn't sent her for water again, and she sensed Wade was the reason why, but otherwise, he treated her no more courteously than the first day and routinely told her she didn't need to return.

Wade had just sat down when Amanda stepped into the hotel dining room. He looked at her, and couldn't suppress the smile.

Wearing the dress I bought in Tucson again today. She looks beautiful. Her blond hair hung carefreely around her face inviting a man to run his fingers through it. She'd worn the dresses a lot lately. Having a job must be the reason.

She returned his smile.

Instantly, his body warmed. No doubt about it, he wanted her, but he suppressed the impulse which kept getting more frequent and intense. Best keep those thoughts under control because once a man let them out who know what could happen next.

Strolling across the room, she took the chair opposite him.

"How's it going?" he asked.

"The usual, Boyce just told me I didn't have to come back. Then I see him watching me walk cross the street. I tell you, Wade, I think he's watching me as much as I'm watching him." Her blue gaze tangled with his.

His gaze dropped to her red lips. He wanted to taste them again in spite of his resolve not to. His mouth grew dry and his resolve to stay away faded. In the last three weeks, he'd done pretty well by her, but what would he do when the judge came? He wouldn't have the excuse of watching prisoners to stay away from her. Of course, they'd agreed to end their situation. The mere thought caused a whole array of conflicting emotions in him. Leaning forward, he propped his elbows on the table. "I sent a wire back to Virginia like you suggested. Got an answer this morning. Nothing on Stewart."

Amanda's smile faded. "Did you ever ask Gladys what he has against her?"

"No, I didn't know he did." *Damn, leave it to her to learn something about the storekeeper he didn't know.* Sometimes it really got under his skin when she learned more about people around town than he. Maybe it shouldn't, but there was just something about his wife knowing more. *His wife? When had he come to think of her as that?* He looked at her.

Her blue eyes sparkled with enthusiasm. "That's why he won't buy water from Gladys. He doesn't really want me eating here either."

"Who doesn't want you eatin' here?" Gladys Richardson stepped into the room. The large tray she carried held several plates, a half a dozen cups, and a pot of coffee.

"Boyce Stewart," Amanda replied. "I never did ask you why he dislikes you so."

"Oh, that." Gladys sat the dishes on the table then pulled out the chair beside Amanda. Her blue watery eyes seemed to grow darker as their cheery paleness disappeared. "I haven't talked about it, because it's unimportant. At least that's what everyone told me." She looked sad.

Wade sat up straighter, waiting.

"All it did was cause trouble, for me and stir the town up, so I finally shut my mouth."

"About what?" He listened intently having never seen her like this before.

"My Bernard's death." Gladys closed her eyes for a moment. When she opened them again, her gaze met his fully. All of cheeriness he'd grown used to in the hotel owner was gone. "I guess I should've told you this before, Sheriff, but I have to live and make a living in this town. It wasn't easy after Bernard died. I didn't have the money to go back east, no reason either. This hotel is all I have. Bernard and I built it. We were the first people to settle in Mineral Wells. Shortly afterward though, Del Deans came."

She took a deep breath, placed cups in front of Wade and Amanda, then herself. Picking up the coffee pot, she poured each of them a cup. "We had been here a couple of years when Boyce came. He and my Bernard, they hit it off very well. I think Bernard felt toward Boyce almost like he would a son. Bernard helped him build the general store, staked him for the first merchandise he bought."

Taking a long swig of coffee, Gladys cleared her throat. "One day, Boyce seemed to change. He'd paid all the money Bernard loaned him back, and didn't come to the hotel anymore. We hit some hard times." Her gaze was reflective. "The mines weren't doin' well and a lot of the prospectors had left. Business was slow for everyone, except Boyce and Delbert. Well, Bernard got to drinkin' more than normal. I think he was worried about us loosin' everything."

She glanced at Wade and his sympathy went out to her. Never before had she looked so vulnerable.

"One night, Bernard didn't come home." She paused. Tears filled her eyes. "The next morning, I found him layin' behind the general store." She pulled a handkerchief from her apron pocket and dabbed at her eyes. Sliding the cloth away, she took a deep breath and looked at him again.

"I accused Boyce of killin' Bernard. He'd been drinkin' with them too and I thought he was angry at Bernard, the way he paid him off so sudden and all. But Del and Maurice Oldham, who had started up the bank by then, swore they'd seen my Bernard drinkin' two fifths of tequila the night before. Probably alcohol poisonin' they said. There wasn't anything else I could do. I had to make a livin' here. But Stewart, he never forgave me for accusin' him. I guess he still hasn't."

A bell on the front door jingled. Gladys stood. "Well, that's the story. I still ain't too sure Boyce didn't have something to do with Bernard's death, but I don't have a way to prove it." She walked toward the hallway door. Stopping in the middle she turned back to them. "Keep this under your hat, the two of you. I don't want anymore trouble because I'm accusin' someone."

"We will," they replied.

Gladys nodded then scurried away.

He glanced at Amanda.

"Sounds like she's afraid of him."

"I noticed." He took a drink of coffee as Gladys' story soaked in. Did this mean something, or was it coincidental?

Wade ran the cloth across his boots again. He'd gotten mud on them the night Amanda had been attacked and hadn't been able to get them cleaned well since. He glanced at his reflection in the mirror, above the cot at the back of the jail. Would Amanda have supper ready?

He'd been working a lot lately, but after having lunch with her, he couldn't resist the need to see her again. All afternoon, he'd thought about having dinner with her. As soon as Harvey Griggs returned, he'd go home.

"The sheriff must be plannin' to impress the little wife," Maurice Oldham mocked.

"Nothing for you to concern yourself about." Wade glanced at the former banker and his cellmates. They seemed to have taken to being in jail well, ate all the food given them and slept the rest of the time.

"How is she, Sheriff? I always did think Simon was lettin' it go to waste." Maurice leered.

Wade stopped shining his boots and looked at the prisoner. Just what did Oldham mean by a statement like that? He had no idea, but he didn't intend to give the man the satisfaction of asking. Amanda had told him her marriage wasn't perfect, apparently Maurice thought he knew something Wade didn't.

Before the banker could agitate further, the door opened and Harvey strode in.

Dropping the cloth, Wade straightened and looked at his old friend. "He's feelin' it tonight."

"Don't worry about a thing." Harvey walked jauntily across the room. "I could use a little challenge tonight. Where ya goin', out to see the little wife?" He smiled and sat, putting his feet up on the desk.

Wade nodded. He'd told his friend there wasn't anything between him and Amanda, but he wasn't sure Harvey believed him. By the grin on the younger man's face, Wade was almost positive he hadn't. "It's Saturday night. Since she worked until only two this afternoon, maybe she's got something good cooked for supper."

"Yeah, feed me that," Harvey laughed. "Better take advantage of me bein' willin' to stay with these critters tonight. That Rosemarie, if she wasn't workin'....."

Wade looked at his friend who spent most of his spare time at Delbert Deans' lately. He hoped the barmaid didn't distract Harvey too much. "Just don't forget you're on duty." He stood and stretched.

"Don't worry about me, Wade. You know me better than that." Harvey twirled his mustache between two fingers bending the ends of the handlebar to keep it in place.

At the open barn door, Amanda brushed the final mats and debris out of Pepper's coat, and stepped back. Since she had been working, she hadn't given the mare the kind of attention she needed. Today, she'd decided to give the filly a thorough bath she deserved.

As she worked, Amanda let her thoughts drift to Wade. There wasn't any point in expecting him home early. He usually spent most of the night in town, eating at Gladys' then going back to the office. Late at night, he'd slip into the cabin after he thought she'd been asleep for hours.

She'd gotten used to the routine. Sometimes, she did go to sleep before he came in, but she always woke up. She attributed her light sleeping to the years she'd spent as a nurse and the need to get to injured soldiers quickly, but she couldn't be sure. The one thing she knew was, Wade Denton meant more to her than any man she'd ever known, although she tried not to think about her growing feelings for him.

In the weeks they'd been married, she'd had ample time to analyze her feelings. She hadn't been able to come up with definitive conclusions and tried not to think she might be falling in love with him. She also avoided thinking about how much care he took to avoid her.

After the judge came and they got their legal entanglement straightened out, she'd have to decide whether to take the money Jed would send her and reopen the bank or use it to return to Springfield. She didn't think she could live in Mineral Wells with the humiliation of an annulment or divorce.

She stepped away from Pepper and picked up a bucket of water then walked back to her. Pouring the water to rinse the soap away, Pepper caught her off-guard, turned and nudged the bucket. Cold water gushed over Amanda soaking her.

"Oh!" She gasped, as she began to laugh. She should have known better. Pepper had never been fond of bathing. She shivered, gooseflesh popped out on her arms in spite of the heat. She stepped away as a light breeze rippled through the barn caressing her wet skin. She started unbuttoning the shirt.

Wade stopped at the edge of the corral when movement near the barn caught his attention. *Amanda and Pepper.* She wore her usual trousers and shirt, but the sunlight touched her golden tresses of hair reminding him of the day he'd seen her bathing in the lake. It glowed like a halo in the late afternoon sunshine.

He started to ride up to them, then she picked up the bucket and moved toward Pepper. He watched in wonder as the horse turned and pushed the bucket until, covered with water, Amanda stepped away. The lilt of her laughter filled the ranch yard. His heart hammered and a pang of loneliness hit him. He wanted to join the fun. What's more, he wanted to be part of her. She looked beautiful her head thrown back, unaware of anything except herself and the horse. She sat the bucket on the ground and stepped out into the sunlight.

Pulling her shirt free of the trousers, she unbuttoned it and removed it, showing creamy white skin above a pristine chemise, very wet and clinging to her full round breasts. Without pausing she unhooked the trousers and slipped from them, then she stood in front of the barn, with drawers pasted to her smooth curves.

He'd never seen a more gorgeous sight. *Turn around, Denton and go back to town. She hasn't seen you yet.* But his thoughts were wasted. He couldn't leave, no, not this time. He spurred the horse and rode closer.

A startled expression came to her face as he approached.

"Wade, what are you doing here?" She started to search for her clothes.

He smiled and slid from his horse. Standing inches from her, he said, "I live here, in case you've forgotten."

"Oh, yeah, I know. It's just that...I...I wasn't expecting you tonight, at least not until later."

"I thought I'd come home early. Hoped you'd have something good cooked to eat." He took a step and dropped the reins.

"I didn't cook tonight." She looked up at him, a defiant light in her eyes. "You've been eating at Gladys', so I didn't bother."

"Well, I wasn't that hungry anyway."

Get out of here, Denton, an inner voice said, but Wade ignored it.

Their gazes met and he saw the same desire in her eyes he felt.

The surprise had disappeared from her face. She smiled a soft intimate expression that told him she couldn't resist anymore than he could.

He bent forward. Only their lips met, but the flame couldn't be quenched with one kiss. He slipped his right arm around her, then his left and pulled her to him. Her arms slid around his neck and the scent of her, damp and clean the smell of soap and woman seeped into him. Too many times he'd ignored the sensations she produced, but not now.

His warmth penetrated the chill of Amanda's wet drawers. Where they'd been cool a few moments before now his heat singed her. He kissed her lips, her face, her neck. Lifting her gently his strong arms cradled her close then he lifted her and walked toward the cabin.

Her head whirled and her heart pounded uncontrollably as they crossed the distance to the cabin. She should stop him. They were legally married, but they'd agreed....

He slowed long enough to open the door, then he kissed her again. Raising his head, he smiled into her eyes. Stepping across the threshold, he said, his voice husky, "Welcome home, my bride." His lips covered hers again.

His male muskiness mingled with a hint of tobacco filled her nostrils and she knew this is where she belonged, at least for the moment.

He trailed kisses down her neck making her skin tingle, her body ache for more. Deep within he groaned. She removed his hat and tossed it on the table. He kissed her bare shoulder and nuzzled the breast beneath it, searching for its quivering tip as he carried her across the room.

This time no quilt separated them, only one thin layer of fabric that his hands burned through kept them apart. He laid her gently against the feather mattress, then stepped away, gazing down at her. "I've tried not to do this, but I can't stop myself." His voice was hushed, almost reverent, his eyes dark with emotion. He bent and kissed her again gently at first then with increasing urgency. Then he paused and pulled away as if to move.

She took his hand and placed it on her breast. Their skin seemed to sear together. "Don't stop, Wade."

Their gazes suspended in time then he leaned forward and skillfully pulled the damp chemise from her shoulders and replacing it with gentle kisses. "Amanda, Amanda," he breathed. He trailed kisses down her right shoulder to he rise in her breast then finally rested on the firm taut tip.

The need within grew as her body came awake to a stirring ache she'd never had before. She groaned and loosened his shirt, wanting desperately to feel his warm smooth strong skin next to hers. The blond hairs of his chest made her hands tingle as she removed the shirt and explored the contours of his body.

His lips returned to hers. Warm strong hands roamed freely over her breasts, her throat, and her chin. The pressure of his chest against her breasts sent delicious chills throughout her body as she arched toward him. Every nerve ending came alive. She ran her hands over his chest, gently touched the wounded shoulder, the taut muscles of his back tangled in the mass of curls caressing her. He pulled away long enough to slip off his boots and trousers.

His strong torso in the dim light of the cabin glowed with vitality and Amanda had never seen a more beautiful sight. He turned toward her and gazed down letting his eyes travel the length of her, then he leaned forward and again claimed her lips. The heat of his manhood brushed against the inside of her leg, singeing her skin through the drawers, inviting her closeness. With one swift movement, he slipped his hand into the drawers and removed them. His lips covered hers, and his hand slid to the V of her womanhood caressing, heating her, and sending delicious quivers of anticipation through her.

"Amanda, oh God, you're beautiful."

He caressed her buttocks, causing ripples of pleasure then, moved to her thighs, and gently stroked them.

She writhed toward his touch and thought she'd explode with her wanting.

His hand moved to the mound of dark hair between her legs again and he caressed her most sensitive spot.

"Oh!"

He stroked her until she thought she'd faint then gently he separated her legs and moved between them. She felt his thrust, his heat and a slight discomfort as the tender membrane gave way, then the pleasure of his entry erased everything except the sensations created by his loving her.

Amanda breathed quietly beside him on the bed. The room felt cool. They had let the fire die completely. The tip of his cigarette glowed red at the end of his fingertips in the dark cabin.

What had he done?

Now he knew why Oldham made that remark, why Amanda had told him she hadn't had an ideal marriage. Even if he hadn't felt that slight resistance from her body, a faint bloodstain would be on the quilt in the light of the morning, he was sure of that.

How could he have been so naive as to love a virgin?

But she'd been married. Who would have thought?

Snuffing the cigarette out in a can he kept close by he thought about going back to the office. Harvey said he could handle things tonight, and he realized he didn't want to leave her now - maybe never.

He thought of Sarah Jean Sturdyvent. He'd never loved her like this. But he didn't love Amanda Green Denton, did he? This marriage was a farce something forced on them by the citizens of

Mineral Wells. A problem they would straighten out when the judge came from Prescott.

Turning toward her, he touched her silky hair. She moaned low, deep within her. He bent toward her and kissed her cheek. She opened her eyes, sleepily. "Wade?"

"Yes, Amanda." He kissed her, then he was lost again.

Amanda opened her eyes slightly as an unfamiliar coolness touched her body. Realizing she didn't wear any clothes she moved her right hand to her waist as the memories swept over her. Wade had made precious, ravishing love to her. He wasn't repulsed like Simon he'd taken not only her body, but her heart, no matter what happened now. She belonged to him in every way. Fully opening her eyes she turned her head to the pillow where he'd slept.

He wasn't there.

Across the room, she heard logs hitting the grate in the fireplace. Looking toward the sound, she saw flames flicker to life and Wade kneeling by the hearth wearing only his trousers. He stared into the fire, deep in thought. The taut muscles of his back, strong and sinewy, glistened beneath his smooth skin in the faint light of daybreak. She wanted to feel them again, touch them, kiss them, but by the way he'd hunched his shoulders, she knew he'd drawn away again.

Did he regret what had happened? No, they'd made love twice. If he regretted the first time, he surely wouldn't have done it again, would he? She wasn't sure. Never before had she felt so alive, so awakened. She wanted to think he needed her as much as she did him, but as the light caressed his hard back, she couldn't put her doubts aside. "Good morning." She kept her voice light and cheery.

He turned slowly and stood.

For a moment, she thought she saw the raw passion on his face like she'd seen there the night before. Would he join her on the bed?

He didn't take a step toward her. Instead, a mask seemed to fall across his face. "I'm glad you're awake."

"So am I." She forced cheerfulness although she didn't feel it.

"I built up the fire. It's time I got back to the office. Harvey will be wondering what happened to me." He reached for his shirt and slipped it on, then picked up his boots and socks and walked to the bench by the table where he put them on.

"Will you be back for supper?" Amanda hesitated to call the cabin home - their relationship was much too tentative for that.

He strolled to the door, took his hat and slipped it on. "I don't know." He didn't look directly at her. "But, I'll plan on eating at Gladys'. You don't have to fix anything special." He stopped for a moment and looked at her. For a second she thought he would come to her, but instead, he said, "About last night."

"We'll get the legal matters settled when the judge arrives," she replied, suppressing the pain that ripped through her with the words.

"Yes." He opened the door and stepped out.

She turned away and squeezed her eyes shut tight stifling the sobs that threatened to escape for fear he might return and see how hurt she was. How long she lay this way, she didn't know. Finally, she rolled over and took a deep breath. This morning he seemed to be running from her, but he'd called her his bride, said he was bringing her home. What should she believe?

Slowly, she rose and let the sheet fall to her waist. Glancing down at her body, she saw no changes, but she'd never be the same again, a part of her would always belong to her husband, Wade Denton, whether he wanted to believe it or not.

The fire crackled, she heard the clop of hooves outside and knew he'd ridden away. She looked around the cabin – their home? Would it ever really be that? Sliding to the edge of the bed, she put her bare feet on the floor. She didn't know, but she was sure of one thing, she'd never be the same because she knew for sure now that she was in love with Wade Denton.

Thirteen

The front door bell of the store jangled again, for what seemed like the thousandth time that morning. Amanda didn't bother to look away from the notepad where she wrote the price of a bucket, pick and shovel.

It had been an unusual morning. Delbert Deans came in three times to talk to Boyce and a gold strike just north of town had everyone purchasing new picks and shovels.

"Mrs. Denton?" A young male voice interrupted her concentration.

It took a few seconds for Amanda to realize he was talking to her. "Yes?" She looked up and recognized Billy Swanson, the delivery boy from Miller's Freight Depot and Telegraph Office. She smiled.

His cheeks turned crimson as he gripped his well-worn cap self-consciously. "I have a wire for you."

Suddenly, excitement filled her. *Could it be from Jed?* Stepping around the counter, she took the envelope he held out to her. "Thank you, William." She'd once heard him tell Gladys he preferred his real name to Billy although that's what most people called him.

"Will there be anything else, miss?" He seemed anxious to depart.

"No, nothing."

"Good!" He beamed. "You're my last delivery and I'm headin' for the mines like everyone else. How about sellin' me a pick and a bucket?" He grabbed one of each, then plopped them on the counter.

Amanda laid her telegram down while she completed the sale.

"Thanks, Ma'am." He dashed out.

She smiled at his youthful excitement and reached for the telegram again. The bell jingled and she glanced up. Wade entered, looking tall and professional with his gun on his hip, his badge over his heart. The strange excitement she always felt in his presence gripped her.

He smiled slightly as he sauntered across the room.

She willed her heart to slow although it didn't seem to be listening. Her palms grew damp and suddenly the store seemed tiny. *Has he come to right things between us?* Her heart pounded wildly at the thought.

He hadn't returned to the ranch until very late the night before and he slept in the barn, only coming inside for coffee and a day old biscuit this morning.

Putting his hands on the counter, he leaned forward slightly. "Is Stewart here?"

"No, he rode away about thirty minutes ago, said he had to take care of an errand." She tried to keep the disappointment that his visit was official rather than personal out of her voice.

Straightening he scanned the room like this was the first time he'd been there. "Anything unusual happened here this morning?" He turned back to her, but she sensed he hardly saw her.

"You must be joking," she chuckled. "I've sold more buckets, picks and shovels this morning than I have in the month I've worked here."

"I mean, anything involving Stewart?" His gaze turned dark with concern.

"Well." She hesitated. Boyce's business was his own and she might be wrong about him. All he did that she could see was keep the store and take a daily walk.

"Well what, Amanda?" Wade stared at her, impatience on his face.

"Delbert Deans has been here three times and I've never seen him here before."

"Just what I thought." He tilted his hat back. "Did you hear their conversation?"

"No, they went in the back room each time and I was so busy, but...I did think it strange."

"Why?"

"Boyce usually counts the money before he leaves me alone with it. He didn't count it once. What's happening?"

"I'm just suspicious, I don't know." He sounded evasive.

"Everyone's crazy about the new strike." Amanda smiled having enjoyed all the excitement herself.

"So I noticed."

She warmed as his gaze traveled from her face to the envelope in her hand. "What's that?"

"Not sure. A telegram from my brother Jed, I think." She looked at it then at Wade. "I asked him to stake me to reopen the bank until we find the money."

His gaze darkened.

She couldn't read the expression, but she sensed disapproval. Raising her chin slightly, she met his gaze without wavering.

"Is that a good idea?"

"I'm not sure." She turned the envelope over and slid her finger under the flap. "All I know is, I have to make a living and I intend to do it." Pulling a paper from the envelope she started to read. The light scuff of boots on the wooden floor and jingling bell told her he'd left.

Wade pushed thoughts of Amanda reopening the bank from his mind as he stood on the general store porch and surveyed Mineral Wells. He didn't want his wife in a position to be robbed and shot at daily. *My wife?* That thought kept coming back regularly lately and life hadn't been easy since Saturday night. He wanted her in the worst way and she looked absolutely lovely in that dress they'd gotten married in standing there behind that counter.

Stepping closer to the edge of the porch he looked down the street. Earlier it had been full of horses, wagons, burros, mules and miners carrying mining equipment in all shapes and sizes. Now it seemed deserted with only two men entering the saloon. This made him uneasy. Deans was up to something, he was as sure of it, but right now all he could do was wait and see what might be next.

Could Harvey be wrong? Maybe Rosemarie had only thought she overhead Deans planning to break the prisoners from jail? Too bad Judge Tucker hadn't arrived. Deans had had plenty of time to gather men and develop a legitimate complaint.

Glancing at his pocket watch, Wade noted it was a quarter to twelve, almost time for lunch. Stepping off the porch, he sauntered across the street to Glady's.

At the hotel Walt Brauns rushed out. "Good day." The livery owner smiled. His dark brown eyes flashed with excitement and the whites seemed to pop out of his brown skin.

"Hello." Wade didn't think he'd every seen the other man so fired up before.

"You're just the man I wanted to see." Brauns stepped closer.

Wade waited.

"I just told Miss Gladys, I think we got more than a new mine on our hands." Walt let the hotel door close and looked toward his stable. "I've shoed four horses this morning, more than I normally do in a week. Deans and Stewart were a talkin' and I haven't seen that since Gladys' Bernard was found dead. I heard talk too." His eyes sparkled with energy.

Wade wished he'd hurry and tell the story, but if one rushed Walt, he might forget what he wanted to say.

Amanda looked at the grandfather clock near the front door. *Five to twelve.*

Stewart had told her if he didn't return by lunch time to put the sign saying she'd back in a few minutes in the window then to go eat. This statement seemed unusual and now, after Wade's visit, she was sure of it.

Counting the money, she wrote the amount down like Stewart did every time he left, then placed the box under the counter. Putting the sign in the window she stepped outside and looked both ways. The street was empty. Maybe there would be no customers while she was away long enough to eat and talk to Gladys.

Jed's telegram told her he would send her money to reopen the bank and she wanted to discuss leasing the building with her friend.

She strolled across the street, and stepped up on the hotel porch. The scent of steak and fried potatoes tantalized her nostrils. She opened the door, stepped inside and closed it quietly behind her. Starting to walk into the dining room she hesitated when she heard Wade and Harvey Griggs talking.

"Walt says he thinks this gold strike is a diversion," Wade was saying. "He thinks Deans is tired of waiting for the judge and overheard something about a necktie party when he walked past the saloon last night. He saw Stewart ride out of town going north a little while ago then a few minutes later Deans left going south."

"What are we going to do?" It was Harvey's voice.

"We should move the prisoners, but we don't have anything as secure as our own jail and it's not very safe. There's just the two of us, Walt will watch the north, but I can tell by the look on his face, he's more involved now than he'd like to be. You ride south. If you see anything come to the office, I'll need reinforcements."

"Sure."   Harvey's spurs jingled.   Amanda turned abruptly, slipped out the door and darted across the street. In the general store, she closed the door and caught her breath. Turning slowly, she looked out the window.

Wade and Harvey came out of the hotel and walked toward the office.

She moved across the room to stand behind the counter, all thoughts of lunch gone, but she couldn't ignore the fact Wade and Harvey were preparing for some kind of attack. Sitting on a small stool, Amanda glanced beneath the counter. Her gaze fell on the pistol lying there. Stewart had told her to always keep it handy in case a customer decided not to pay. She had her rifle in the backroom. If Wade, Harvey and Walt were up against an army led by Deans and Stewart, they didn't have a chance, but maybe she could help. Wade had probably left her out on purpose, but that had never stopped her before. She walked through the backroom, grabbed the rifle, and opened the door.

Outside she passed the six water barrels Stewart had made her fill and his small corral and barn. The street was still quiet, unnaturally so. Looking away from the store, she noted that a stairway was built along the north side of the saloon leading to the upstairs living quarters. The roof slanted close to a landing near the stairs and overlooked the sheriff's office at the front.

With the rifle, she slipped across the empty lots, climbed the stairs then slid onto the roof. Crouching low, she wished she'd been wearing pants. The skirt fabric tangled around her legs as she climbed, but she unwound herself and continued until she reached a good vantage point above the saloon entrance. Looking toward the sheriff's office she would have an excellent view of it and hotel. She laid the gun down, picked up the tail of her dress and surveyed the street again.

All was quiet.

Noontime heat beat down on her and she started to perspire. With the agility of a cat, she climbed from the roof and walked across the lots. The effort might be wasted, but if something did happen, she'd be ready to help. After a few moments, she caught her breath. Since no customers had come into the store she again left, crossed the street, and entered the hotel.

* * *

Wade intently watched from the jail window. The street was empty in the late afternoon heat. Even Gladys' chickens had found somewhere else to look for bugs and worms.

Walt Brauns appeared to be falling asleep in front of the stable. That wasn't unusual for Walt in the afternoon, but Wade hoped he wouldn't sleep too soundly. They might need whatever signal the blacksmith could give.

At least, he didn't have to worry about Amanda. She had crossed the street and gone into the hotel, stayed long enough to eat, then returned to the general store. He hadn't found it easy to ignore the plea in her eyes when he'd questioned her about Stewart, but she had to learn there were situations where she shouldn't get involved.

He thought about the telegram. Would her brother stake her bank? Maybe he should have stayed until she read it. *Would she tell him its contents?* She still hadn't told him how much money Simon loaned Oldham. By leaving before she read the message, he'd saved them the embarrassment of his desire to know the contents and her determination not to tell.

Glancing over his shoulder he saw Oldham lying on the cell cot. *Was there any money left? If so, where was it?* Amanda wouldn't quit looking until she knew what happened to it, but would she ever know? This kind of mystery might never be solved.

There were other things Amanda ought to realize. She meant something to him. He hadn't examined his feelings thoroughly and he'd been avoiding thoughts of her as much as possible, but it wasn't easy. One day, he'd need to put Amanda Green Denton in her right place in his life and right now, he wasn't exactly sure where that was. He seemed to thinking of her as his wife, more and more and in actuality, she'd become that a few days before. She was very important to him, maybe more than anyone he'd ever known. Could he be a husband? Would she leave if they found the money?

Looking south, he saw Harvey Griggs' horse tied to a mesquite and knew his deputy had hidden in the rocks and shade. Turning toward the livery he saw Walt Brauns stand, remove a red handkerchief from his back pocket and wave it frantically, then blow his nose. Wade opened the door and stepped out, shotgun in hand, Colt Peacemaker strapped to his waist in the gunbelt.

* * *

Amanda sat on the general store porch letting the slight breeze cool her. It had been a long afternoon and occasionally, she found herself getting drowsy and wondering what Wade was doing. She hadn't had a single customer since she'd returned from the hotel. Glancing toward the livery, she saw Walt disappear inside, then she heard horse hooves approaching. Suddenly alert, she looked toward the north. At first, she didn't see anything, then men shouting to each other, drowned out the sound of hooves. Approximately thirty men led by Boyce Stewart and Delbert Deans galloped past her.

As soon as they passed, she jumped up, ran inside, placed the closed sign in the window and darted out the back door. Running across the empty lots she bounded up the stairs beside the saloon taking two at a time. One of Deans' girls stood on the landing. "Excuse me." Amanda pushed past, gathered her skirt in her left hand, and climbed to the spot where she'd left the rifle.

With gun in hand, she looked at the street. Wade stood in front of the sheriff's office, a shotgun pointed at Deans.

Foreboding filled her. Even if Wade shot the saloonkeeper, he couldn't hold off thirty men alone.

She saw Walt Brauns leave the livery and run behind the saloon, then caught a flash of movement from the south. Harvey Griggs galloped toward the jail.

Three men against thirty? Not nearly enough. She crouched where she could see the street, but not be seen. Pointing the rifle toward the crowd, she waited.

"That'll be far enough, Deans." Wade's voice rang out across the heat ripples.

He sounded confident, but Amanda couldn't relax. She moved her aim slightly to point at Deans'.

"Now, Sheriff," Deans said, "we don't mean any harm. We just think it's time justice was done. We been feedin' them prisoners long enough. I'm in favor of a trial now. There are plenty of men here for a jury. One of us can be the judge." He motioned to Stewart who rode beside him.

"None of us have the authority to try a prisoner. You know that, Deans." Wade raised the gun higher.

Only a slight breeze interrupted the tension beneath her. Amanda's brow grew damp her hand shook slightly. Her trigger finger felt stiff from holding it still. She continued to aim at Deans.

"You can't keep us from doin' what's right to protect ourselves," Deans drawled, but he didn't move closer.

"I'm doing what's best to protect everyone in town." Wade moved forward on the boardwalk.

"By lettin' us feed them, keepin' them safe in jail?"

"That's what we're supposed to do. I'm a sheriff, Deans, that's why you hired me."

Amanda's heart thumped in her ears as she watched Wade stand before the men, tall and brave. Any doubts she'd ever had about his ability to handle a crucial situation disappeared.

"I want justice now!" Deans roared, spurring his horse.

"I said halt!" Wade raised the gun higher.

"And, I said, we are going to try those men, aren't we men?" Deans glanced around him.

"Yes!" The cry filled the air.

"Half on this side, half on that." Deans pointed toward the jail.

"I don't think so." Brauns' heavily accented voice boomed, above the rustle of hooves, at the side of the saloon. He stood in the middle of the street, an iron pole in his hands, his huge muscles flexed, ready for action.

"It's going to take more than the sheriff and a blacksmith to keep us from those prisoners," Stewart bellowed.

"Yeah!" the crowd echoed.

"You heard them." Harvey Griggs spoke from the side of the jail.

"We can't let three men stop us, can we?" Deans yelled.

"No!"

Deans started to move toward Wade.

Amanda pulled the trigger.

The shot landed near Dean's horse's left forefoot.

The animal reared, dumping Deans on the dusty street.

Other horses bucked and reared. General mayhem filled the area until the riders regained control over their animals.

When the dust settled, one man shouted, "I didn't think we were going to be surrounded. Count me out. I'm willin' to wait for the judge."

"Me too," another added.

As fast as they'd ridden into town, the men began to disappear.

Only Deans and Stewart faced Wade, Walt and Harvey.

Amanda smiled, slid away from her post, down the roof and stairs and crossed the empty lots, entering the store where she'd been not long before. She hastily placed the rifle in the corner where she kept it and went into the other room where she removed the closed sign.

In the distance, she saw Boyce Stewart riding toward the store.

Wade watched the men disappear as he continued to point his gun at Deans. Glancing toward the saloon roof, he thought he saw movement and was glad someone had been there. He was pretty sure they had seen the last of the vigilante party. Deans obviously wasn't happy about the humiliation he suffered and Stewart had ridden off without comment.

"Have you had enough, Deans?" Wade asked.

"Yes."

"You know I could lock you up, for obstructing justice, don't you?"

"Yes." Deans looked humble.

"Do I have your word you'll leave the prisoners alone?"

"Yes."

"Then, I'll let you go, on your word. But, be sure, if anything happens to these men, you'll be the first person I look for."

"I understand." Deans led his horse to the saloon and tied the reins to the hitching post. Glancing at Wade once more, he disappeared inside.

Wade lowered his gun, sighed, then turned and strolled into the jail.

Harvey followed, smiling from ear to ear. "Who did it, Wade?"

"I don't know." Sliding his hat off, Wade hung it on the peg near the door. "I saw someone move on the saloon roof, but I didn't see who it was."

"I couldn't either. I thought maybe you'd found someone else to help."

"No, I didn't, but we needed it." He sat in the chair behind the desk and pulled out a sheet of paper, trying to put the thought that kept popping into his head out of his mind. *Could Amanda have been the unseen gunman?* He pushed the idea away as he wrote a report of exactly what had happened in case he ever needed to refer to it again.

"Would you mind if I left a few minutes early today?" Amanda asked Stewart who had counted the money and checked her transaction notations.

"This store is open until six o'clock. I told you that when you insisted I hire you. I expect you to work until then, not one minute less." His dark eyes glared into hers. His handlebar mustache drooped on the right side and he seemed flustered since his return.

She'd asked who was shooting up town.

He'd mumbled something under his breath, then went into the storeroom. Now he walked around the room, examining the merchandise as if he were taking a mental inventory.

"You'll see each missing item written in the log. I was quite busy while you were away earlier." She'd been a little nervous since returning wondering if anyone had seen her. As the afternoon passed, each minute without someone pointing her out gave her confidence that no one except Dean's girl had and maybe she wouldn't talk.

Stewart stopped near the front door and turned toward her. "Why did you want to leave early, Mrs. Denton?"

"I have an appointment to examine the old bank building. I received a telegram from my brother. He will stake me so I can reopen it, as long as the property hasn't deteriorated."

He glared at her. "We've survived without a bank."

"Oh, I know. But with miners finding new color in the mountains close by, I'm sure they'll feel much safer knowing we have somewhere to put their gold. Dust isn't easy to spend. Some will want to keep their treasure safe."

"You told me your father owned a store." He strolled to the counter apparently satisfied she'd recorded all of the items.

"Oh, he was. My husband, my first husband," she amended, "was a banker. He's the reason I came to Arizona Territory. He's the one who gave Maurice Oldham money to start the bank here. It's imperative, Mr. Stewart that I either retrieve the money or work at something where I can make a living of my own."

"But, you're married to the sheriff now."

"Yes, I am." She looked him directly in the eye. "It seems someone convinced Parson Jones that since the sheriff and I had traveled together for several weeks, we should marry. I'm sure when Judge Tucker arrives, that problem can be solved. You wouldn't have any idea who instigated that little bit of morality on this town, would you, Mr. Stewart?"

He smoothed the hair on the back of his head. "No, I wouldn't."

"You wouldn't have any idea what Oldham did with the money, either would you, Mr. Stewart?" She was pushing and knew it, but if he were involved, maybe he'd give something away.

"Of course, not, Mrs. Denton." He glanced at the clock.

Amanda looked too.

The hands pointed to quarter to six.

"Since you were here alone for several hours today, and there aren't any customers, you may leave early."

"Thank you, Mr. Stewart. I assure you, I'll work the extra fifteen minutes tomorrow." She didn't try to hide the mockery in her voice.

"Good day, Mrs. Denton."

"See you tomorrow, Mr. Stewart."

Wade strolled toward the hotel. It was nearly seven o'clock and he wanted to go home, but he hadn't told Amanda he would be there for supper, so he decided he should eat first. Since he hadn't been keeping regular hours, she hadn't been cooking much. As he stepped up on the boardwalk she and Gladys exited the backdoor of the bank building.

That could mean only one thing. The telegram was from her brother and he would help her finance the bank. Wade was uncomfortable with that thought, but hadn't had time to examine the reasons why. Glancing toward the general store, he saw it was dark and the closed sign was in the window. Apparently, Stewart had had enough for one day too. He hadn't figured out what the storekeepers' involvement with Deans was either, but he intended to keep his eye on him.

Moving to the hotel door, he saw Amanda and Gladys turn toward him, but they were deep in conversation and didn't notice. Strolling into the dining room he slipped his hat off and slid a chair away from the table. He didn't have a right to say anything to Amanda about what she did with her life. Like she'd said Sunday morning, as soon as Judge Tucker arrived, they'd put an end to their legal entanglement, but a pang of regret hit him when he thought of that.

Sitting in the chair, he stretched out his legs, unable to pull his thoughts away from her. He should be happy she wanted to support herself, be independent. What was the matter with him? She'd intruded on his life more than anyone in the last three years, ruined his plans to search for Oldham alone, caused more trouble than three men in a posse would have and she'd continue to do it.

Why, someday, if she stayed around he'd probably wind up spilling his guts and telling her all about how he hadn't been able to save his brother from his drowning or his best friend Fred Bessler from dying of a gunshot wound. She had a way of getting him to talk about things he normally didn't. He could even envision himself telling her about Sarah Jean Sturdyvent and their ill-fated engagement. For a reason he didn't understand she didn't anger him like she once had.

Did she interrupt the near insurrection this afternoon? Whoever it was had done a damn good job! No way could he, Harvey and Walt have stood off thirty men.

Sadie, Gladys' cook came into the room and poured his coffee. He ordered the special. A few moments later, he heard the front door and Gladys' and Amanda's muffled voices.

"Well, hello, Sheriff." Gladys stood in the doorway.

He turned toward her. "Hello."

"I've just made a deal with your wife. We're going to have us a bank in this town again soon." She beamed from ear to ear.

"Is that right?"

"Yes, it is." Amanda stepped in the doorway behind the hotelkeeper. "Gladys has agreed to lease me the bank until we find the money Oldham took. Jed is sending me a stake from Springfield. He's not sure how long it'll take to get here, but I'll start cleaning soon. I'd like to open when the money arrives." Her eyes sparked with enthusiasm.

Wade had trouble joining her pleasure. "Why don't you have supper with me?"

"I've already eaten." She stepped further into the room although he sensed she was miles away and the thought stung.

"You can surely have a cup of coffee and wait for me. It's too dark for you to ride to the ranch alone, especially after what happened today. There may be someone else wanting to see Oldham hang."

"Oh, you took care of that." Gladys smiled as she bustled toward the kitchen.

"I'd like to know who the gunman was." Wade sipped his coffee and eyed Amanda who had taken the chair across from him. "That shot was well placed and timely. I just can't be sure Deans won't try again."

"I'll take some coffee, Wade," Amanda said. "It does get a little lonely riding to the ranch, alone." Her blue gaze didn't waver.

Could she have been the sharpshooter? Why not? She hadn't backed down from any situation since she'd come to town, why wouldn't she take on a pack of vigilantes? He wanted to be angry at the thought, but he couldn't. They'd needed what happened too much.

Sadie brought the food and Gladys filled Amanda's cup.

"How was your day at the store?"

"After you left, business slowed a lot. When Stewart returned, he seemed more interested in my knowledge of Oldham than before. Other than that, uneventful."

Her gaze met his as she lifted the cup to her lips which looked soft and sweet and triggered the memory of them beneath his. Dipping into the roast beef and mashed potatoes he wondered if he could ride home with her, and sleep in the barn? He didn't know. He wasn't sure he wanted to.

Fourteen

Wade and Amanda rode toward the ranch in silence. The setting sunlight touched her blond head and made it shimmer with golden hues that resembled a halo. He wanted to run his hands through it, but didn't make an attempt, instead, he wondered again about the unknown gunman. Had it been her?

Although he was thankful someone had driven the men off this afternoon, it agitated him somewhat to think she might be the one. Every time he started thinking of taking care of her, she ended up saving his neck. She acted like her actions were normal, but something about an attractive woman always coming to his rescue didn't seem quite right.

His thoughts traveled to Sarah Jean Sturdyvent. She'd almost clung to him, yet she'd betrayed him. Amanda could take care of herself, be counted on as someone who wouldn't wilt if a problem arose. Of course, she tended to be where she wasn't invited, but almost everything she'd done had proved to be helpful. He admired anyone who would chance placing one shot to deter thirty men. The only person he knew in town with enough guts to do that was Amanda Green Denton.

He looked at her again, trying not to notice the flames in her hair or the flush of her rosy cheeks in the cooling breeze giving her a carefree appearance. Pushing thoughts of later tonight away, he said, "So, you're planning on reopening the bank?"

She slowed Pepper and turned. "Jed says he'll send the money to do it. Gladys has agreed to rent the building."

They neared the ranch property line.

"Why?"

She stopped and stared across Pepper's head directly at him. "I think you know the answer to that, Wade. I'm running short of cash. Besides, reopening the bank might make whoever is in this with Maurice nervous. Maybe they'll lead us to the money."

Exasperation filled him as he watched her sitting there so serious. She almost made him believe she could retrieve the money alone without a concept of how tiny and vulnerable she looked. Did she know what kind of a target she'd make if she put herself in the wrong place at the right time?

Pushing his hat back, he sighed. "I'd like to remind you, we have no proof there's money left."

"I have to think there is." She swung gracefully from Pepper, then walked toward the barn.

"Why?" He dismounted and followed.

"Because, otherwise, I'd be wasting my time. Right now, I can't think about that." Determination filled her voice.

What was she talking about anyway? Didn't she know she was a woman? Women didn't have to worry about their time. He thought of Sarah Jean again. He'd seen her spend hours arranging and rearranging one bouquet of flowers on the front porch. She'd never considered it a waste of time even though he had found it hard to understand how anyone would spend so much time doing so little.

Inside the barn, Amanda unsaddled Pepper as he lit a lantern and placed it near enough to illuminate the horses while they fed and watered them. Taking the saddle off his horse, he placed it on the rack and let the sweet scent of warm hay tingle his nostrils while he tried to keep his eyes off Amanda as she brushed Pepper.

Thoughts of him watching her wash Pepper returned. *Denton, this is getting you nowhere.* He dipped a bucket into the oat bin and poured some in the trough.

"Are you coming in tonight?" Amanda placed the curry brush on a timber. "I thought I'd make a cup of coffee since the night is cool."

Wade looked at her.

She smiled slightly, appearing all soft and feminine standing there in the lantern light.

He shouldn't. Going in that cabin with her was trouble. She'd made it clear, nothing that had happened between them meant a thing to her. He'd be a fool to let it happen again. He hadn't let his heart get involved with her had he? She was just a passing fancy, someone here now and gone tomorrow, wasn't she?

She's your wife, Denton, in every sense of the word. He forced his thoughts back to Sarah Jean. She'd always kept him at arms' length.

Amanda had never done that, not even when she first came to town. "I expect I could use some coffee too. It'll be a long night."

"I'll make enough for both of us."

He stopped working with the horse, and watched her walk out of the barn and across the yard without giving him a backward glance. She acted like she owned the place. He had moved to the barn and replaced her homemade cot with his bed. No wonder she thought she belonged here. Maybe she did.

Amanda lit a lantern, then stirred the coals. Within a few minutes, bright fresh flames leapt from the logs. Would he come in? He acted almost angry. Did he suspect she'd been involved in the dispersal of Dean's men? Why did he care whether she opened the bank or not? He'd made it clear he didn't intend to stay married. She had to survive somehow. The bank would make her a good living.

The door squeaked. She turned away from the fire.

He stood in the doorway just outside the house.

"I won't bite," she said, trying to lighten the tension that had developed between them over the past several days.

"That's a matter of opinion." He stepped across the threshold and closed the door.

"I know, all women bite." Amanda smiled. She couldn't help but taunt him.

"How did you get an idea like that?" He placed his hat on the peg and took a few steps toward her.

"The minute I came into town, people started trying to run me away. The only person who acted like they wanted me to stay is Gladys. She knows what it's like for men to want her gone."

He moved closer. She felt compelled to press this issue further. Just what did he have against women? Wasn't it time she learned? If anyone had a right to know, didn't she? After all, they were married.

"I have nothing against you in particular." His voice grew soft, contemplative. "It's just...." He stepped a few feet closer.

"Just what?"

"It's just that women are nothing but trouble." His dark gaze met hers.

For a moment, she thought she saw sadness in his eyes, but it quickly vanished. "A few times, I think you've been glad I was around."

He pivoted away from her and ran his right hand through his sandy hair. Slowly, he turned back. By the angry stare in his eyes, she thought he'd leave. "I haven't always felt that way."

"What changed your mind?"

He stared at her for several minutes. "Do you have any idea what it was like to lose the war?"

"I helped treat soldiers from the South too. They lost their homes, plantations, their money, but they didn't turn against women."

"I'm not against women, Amanda. I just think they have their place. In some cases, they get out of it."

"Me, you mean." She placed her hands on her hips and met his unmoving gaze. She didn't intend to move until he told her what his real problem with her was.

"Yes, I mean you." His dark eyes riveted her into place and he stepped closer. "I suspect you were the unseen gunman today." He seemed to be looking clear through her as if he could see deep into her soul.

"And if I was?" She lifted her head just a little higher and met his direct stare without flinching.

"If you were, that was a damn dangerous thing to do. You could have fallen off that roof, hit a rock, or misplaced your shot and killed someone." His eyes had grown even darker than normal.

"So, it was dangerous, for whoever did it, right? It did worked, didn't it?"

"Yes, but...."

"I'm not saying I did it, or I didn't. But as long as it worked and stopped the vigilantes, isn't that what's important?"

"Yes, but...."

"The coffee's ready, let's have some." She pivoted toward the fire and lifted the coffee pot off, then poured them a cup. When she turned around again, he sat at the bench behind the table watchfulness in his eyes. She knew he didn't like her evasion.

Why did it matter to him that she might have been on the roof? As soon as the judge arrived, they'd already agreed to separate. He didn't need to think he could tell her what to do in the meantime.

Wade watched Amanda pour their coffee. Who did she think she was fooling? He was almost positive by her avoidance that she'd been the person on the roof, but that didn't concern him as much as how close he'd come to telling her everything about himself. She'd told him about Simon and he had learned more.

Maybe she would understand how Sarah Jean had hurt him, but could he chance the possibility she would think he was a sniveling fool?

Sometimes he thought he was. He had considered the situation with Sarah Jean a lot and he wasn't sure he'd have reacted the way he did, if they hadn't just lost the war, and the family plantation been destroyed. Watching Amanda walk toward the table, he wondered what it was about her that made him forget the resolve he had made and lived by for years?

"When do you plan to open the bank?"

She handed him a cup of coffee, then sat across from him sipping daintily at the hot coffee, avoiding a chip in the cup.

I need to buy some new cups. Maybe I should order some from England. Lately, he'd been thinking about buying some cattle too. The money his mother had deposited in the New Orleans bank had drawn interest for years. She'd put it in his name years before the war, right after her parents died telling him he could use it to make the plantation elegant someday. There was no chance of that. The house and outbuildings had been burned to the ground, the land sold for back taxes.

How his mother had managed to place the money in a bank that didn't fold, he never understood, but she called it luck of fate. He'd never thought of using it until now.

Harvey Griggs had mentioned Longhorn cattle from Texas, said if they could survive in the desert there, they could survive in Arizona Territory.

He took a long sip of coffee. Why, all of a sudden, was he thinking about cups and cattle? He'd been drinking from these ever since he'd moved to the cabin. They had worked fine. His job as sheriff kept him plenty busy too. He had enough to do trying to keep the law and made enough money to cover his expenses and leave him small savings.

Glancing away from the cup to Amanda, he realized, as sure as he sat there she was the reason. Sure enough! No matter how he tried to think she wasn't! He wanted her in his bed every night. He began to harden. *Damn, he'd done it now!*

"I plan to open as soon as Jed sends the money." Her blue eyes sparkled happily into his. "In the meantime, I've got a lot of cleaning to do. Looks like some chipmunks or something have made their home in the empty building." She smiled and took a sip.

"I guess if you're determined to do it, I could help with some of the heavier work." He said the words faster than he intended to, but he sure didn't want some other man in town helping her. There were probably several more than willing.

She smiled pleasure filling her blue eyes.

He really liked the way she looked when she smiled.

"I'd appreciate that, Wade. I've already decided I don't like the teller's box in the middle of the floor where it is. It's a target for robbery. Maybe you could help me move that."

"Just let me know when you're ready." He drained the coffee cup and pushed the bench back. It was time he went to the barn, before he changed his mind. "I guess I'd better turn in."

He stood and walked toward the door. Touching his hat, he started to take it from the peg. He sensed her close. Turning slightly, he saw she'd stepped up behind him.

"You don't have to go out, Wade."

He swung around gazing down at her.

The smile had disappeared from her expressive face. She looked up at him a question in her eyes. "This is your house. We are married."

Reaching out with his right hand, he placed it behind her neck and pulled her toward him. Her lips were soft, sweet, with a hint of coffee she'd just drunk still on them. The kiss was tentative at first, but the desire inside him was too much. He pulled her to him as he drank in the wonder of her. Why sleep in the barn, when it was so much warmer here?

Wade stepped out on the hotel porch just in time to see Amanda walk toward the jail with a food basket on her arm. She again wore the blue and white gingham he'd bought. Her hips swayed slightly as she strolled purposefully toward the building. He smiled to himself.

She's bringing me some lunch. He stepped off the porch to follow her. *I guess I should've waited a few minutes to come eat.*

Smiling to himself, he turned toward the jail. His thoughts drifted back to the last few nights. No doubt about it, he'd never met a more sweet, giving woman than Amanda. She'd worked at the general store in the morning, the bank in the afternoon, then had something good cooked for him to eat when he arrived from the office. The food was only a small part of it. Being married did have some advantages and he was beginning to like them very much.

As he sauntered toward the jail, he felt young, carefree and realized he probably wouldn't tell the judge anything about their legal entanglement if Amanda agreed. He stepped off the boardwalk and picked up his pace. He didn't want to leave her waiting too long.

Smiling to himself, he wondered if he might be falling in love with her. *No, this was nothing like what he'd felt for Sarah Jean.* He hadn't allowed himself to think he really cared for Amanda. Stepping up on the jail stoop, he disregarded the unsettling thoughts. Maybe he could eat a little more lunch, especially if Amanda brought some of the peach cobbler she'd made the night before.

He glanced at his reflection in the window panes then touched the door handle. The door swung open freely. He stopped on the threshold when he saw her standing near the prisoners oblivious to the fact he was there.

"Well, if it ain't Amanda Green," Oldham said. "I wondered when you were going to come see me. It's been a long time, pretty one."

Closing the door quietly, Wade moved further into the room.

The prisoner smiled intimately, through the bars, at Amanda.

Wade's ears warmed. *What the hell is she doing?* Had he been wrong? Did she and Oldham have some sort of relationship?

"I brought you some peach pie." She reached into the basket and pulled out a saucer with a piece of the same pie Wade had eaten the night before.

He couldn't see her face, but sensed she smiled at the prisoner.

Oldham looked tattered, but no longer dirty and he beamed at her. "Always did like peach the best." He reached through the bars and took the saucer.

"I know," she replied.

Anger like Wade hadn't felt in years rushed over him.

Harvey Griggs sat behind the desk looking at him and shrugged. He stood and stepped closer. "I couldn't stop her. She darted in here before I knew she was close."

Amanda didn't seem to hear the deputy or realize Wade was present. Her total attention rested on the man in the cell. "Actually, I have a reason for being here, Maurice," she said, in her sweetest voice.

Wade's stomach churned as rage filled him like none he'd experienced before, even during the war. He turned, reopened the door, and slammed it shut.

Silence filled the room.

He stepped toward the cell.

Amanda glanced at him, innocence written all over her face. "Hello, Wade." She used the same sweet tone she'd used with Maurice. "I thought the prisoners would enjoy some of the pie I made you. You don't mind, do you?" Her blue eyes questioned.

The rage in him had evaporated.

She smiled. "It is our duty feed them."

He stepped across the room, took the basket and set it on the desk ignoring Harvey Griggs startled expression.

"I mind," he said. "I see the prisoners are fed when it's time." He took her by the arm, picked up the basket and gently turned her toward the front door. "Why don't you get back to the general store or banking? I'm sure you have something better to do than visit prisoners this afternoon."

"Your saucer?"

"Forget the saucer." He opened the door, ushered her out, and followed.

She stopped just outside and turned on him.

"What are you doing?" Her voice was stony.

"I might ask the same thing. What the hell do you think you're doing?"

"I'm trying to find out what he did with the bank's money. Since you haven't, I decided to use a women's way." Anger flared in her eyes as she raised her pert little chin in that defiant way she had and didn't move.

"What makes you think you can learn something I can't?" He shoved the basket at her – he should've known – she didn't give up that easily.

"Well, women do have ways." She smiled tentatively, draping the offending basket over her arm. "I just happened to remember Maurice's favorite pie is peach. I thought that I could bribe him into telling me where he'd hid the money. But you...." She sputtered, then turned and started to march away. She took a few steps, then turned back. "You ruined it all."

He could see tears of frustration in her eyes.

"Now, I'll probably never have a chance." Giving her long hair a flip, she turned toward the hotel and stomped away. The basket swayed gracefully in tune with her skirt as she walked away from the jail.

Confusion filled him. What had gotten into him? Why had he reacted that way? Maybe he should have let her talk to the prisoner. She was right, he wasn't learning anything. She didn't slow her pace at the hotel, but stepped off the boardwalk and proceeded toward the bank. What was the matter with him anyway? One word jumped out.

Jealous!

No, he wasn't envious that Amanda might bake a pie for someone else, was he? He watched her disappear into the back of the bank and turned slowly to open the jail door.

Harvey Griggs still stood behind the desk smiling cautiously. "Quite a little woman ya got there, Sheriff."

"In the future, I'd appreciate it if you didn't sleep on the job, Harvey. We've got work to do. If she'd wanted to break those prisoners out, she'd have gotten away with it, before you woke up."

He hung his hat on the peg then walked to his own desk. Sitting, he ignored the humor in Harvey's eyes, then turned to the posters piled on the desk and wished he hadn't spoken to his friend so harshly.

Amanda didn't know when she'd been so angry as she marched down the street. The least he could have done was let her talk to Oldham. Course, he might not have been so determined to see her gone, if she had mentioned what she planned to do ahead of time. *No, no chance of that.* She'd done it the way she had because she knew Wade would be against her getting anymore involved with the prisoners.

Kicking at a pebble she watched it sail into the middle of the street. *Why, he acted almost jealous.* Was he angrier because she'd taken Oldham pie or because she'd tried to question the prisoner?

Too bad he'd seen her. She'd watched him for days and he usually stayed in Gladys' longer. She'd thought she could get into the jail, ask her questions and leave before he left the hotel. Her timing had been wrong. She should have waited when Boyce had come back late from his walk.

Opening the bank door Amanda looked down at the basket. She felt like throwing the pie away, but it had taken nearly a week's pay to purchase the peaches. No, she couldn't waste food like that, but Wade Denton wouldn't get anymore.

Setting the basket on a tiny shelf by the door, she quickly slipped out of the dress and into the shirt and trousers she normally wore. What had Oldham done with the money? Looking around the room, she shook her head. She'd moved every piece of furniture except the teller's box. Nothing. Maybe there wasn't any money. No, she couldn't think of that. Picking up the hammer she had left near the door, she walked to the little divider between the front of the building and the office area.

She'd planned to work on it today so she started to hammer as her mind raced. She had to find a time when Wade wasn't around to question Oldham. Time was running out. The judge would be here any day.

Wade waited for Amanda just inside the front door of the jail like he'd been doing for a week. Darkness came, but she didn't. Was she still angry?

Glancing at his deputy, he realized Harvey acted too interested in what he read. He opened the door and stepped out onto the stoop. No need to let Harvey think she'd stood him up.

He had over-reacted earlier. Would it really have hurt to let her question Oldham? Probably not. She might have even learned something he didn't know after all, she was the one who had pried out Gladys' story about her husband.

He waited a few moments longer then, swung into the saddle and pointed the horse toward the hotel. There were no lights in the bank. He assumed she'd gone to visit Gladys. Stopping in front of the hotel, he dismounted. The tinkle of a piano drifted to him from across the street. A light breeze rustled the dust on the ground making it sift around his feet. He tied the horse to the hitching post, then stepped onto the hotel porch.

The scent of beans cooking wafted to him, but the hotel was quiet. He walked through the lobby into the dining room. In the doorway, he noticed the plates normally left on the table were missing. The stillness was disconcerting. "Anybody here?" He heard a shuffle of feet in the back room.

Sadie stepped in the doorway between the kitchen and dining room. "You lookin' for somebody, Mister Sheriff?"

"Yes, where's Gladys?"

"Pastor Jones, he's havin' a camp meetin'. She went to it."

"I thought maybe Amanda would be here."

"Well, she ain't. I haven't seen her all evenin'. Maybe she's still at the bank."

"No lights. Thanks, Sadie." He walked back through the front door. *Where would she have gone? To the camp meeting with Gladys? Unlikely.* Amanda wasn't religious and she'd told him she didn't especially like Pastor Jones.

Wade mounted. Maybe she'd ridden to the ranch by herself. He'd told her he didn't think it was safe, but since she'd been so obviously angry, maybe....

Amanda watched Wade ride out of town from the darkened bank building. Her heart ached at the sight of his disappearing back. She probably should have told him she was going to start staying in town now she had a place to do it. During the afternoon, she'd realized that her continuing to live at the ranch would only complicate their relationship more. When everything was done, they would go their separate ways.

She lit a lantern, then cut a piece of the peach pie even though she wasn't really hungry. Maybe later, she could slip over to the jail and question Oldham.

Less than an hour later, Amanda was spreading the unbleached muslin on the straw mattress she'd found in the back of the building when she heard a horseman outside. Ignoring the noise, she continued to work with the bed until she heard a peck on the door.

Her heart beat faster as she straightened and looked at the closed door. "Who's there?"

"It's me." Wade's strong baritone penetrated the wooden door.

"What do you want?"

"I want to talk to you, Amanda." His voice sounded more hushed, controlled.

She stepped across the short distance and turned the wooden piece that had been nailed on the inside to keep the door shut and let it swing open. "I don't have anything to say." She stared into his dark angry eyes.

"I think you do. Are you going to let me in, or are we going to talk here, where everyone can hear?"

She heard someone laugh in the street. A distant piano penetrated the night air. The cool September breeze wrapped around her and she remembered how far sound traveled when everything around was silent. She recognized a stubbornness she'd grown to associate with him on his face, and opened the door wider. "Come in." She stepped back. Closing the door gently behind him, she met his gaze.

"Now, will you tell me just what in the hell is going on?"

She heard barely suppressed anger in his voice, but tried to ignore it. Stepping around him, she moved through the tiny bedroom, into the main part of the bank. "I just decided I would be able to do more work on the bank if I stayed here in the evenings." She picked up a rag she'd been using to oil the furniture and stepped to the rolled top oak desk she had been polishing.

His boots scuffed on the floor as he followed her into the room. She peeked up at him. He didn't seem quite as angry. "Well, couldn't you have told me what you were doing?" He stood square in the middle of the doorway looking at her. "I went to the hotel, then rode all the way out to the ranch. I began to think something had happened to you." He had slipped his hat off and held it in with both hands in front of him. His hair curled slightly around his ears and for the first time since she'd met him, she thought Wade Denton looked almost humble.

"Does it matter, Wade? I'm out of your way." She paused for a moment and swiped with the rag at the desk. Why did he come after her anyway? She looked up at him, her gaze not wavering as she fought to keep the lump out of her voice. "That's all I've been since I came to town--in your way. Now I have a place of my own. I should use it."

"Is that the only reason?" He gazed down at her intensity in his eyes she tried to ignore as she continued to dust the desk.

"Yes."

"It doesn't have anything to do with me not letting you question Oldham?"

She stopped dusting and looked up at him. "I was angry for a few minutes, but what it really told me was how little I'm wanted around here."

Their gazes met.

She quickly looked away. Her heart ached, but she didn't want him to see. All afternoon, she had fought the emotions inside. It was time she quit kidding herself. What she felt for the Sheriff was one-sided. The sooner she accepted it and began to live with it, the better off they'd both be. "Since the day I came to town, someone has been telling me to leave. Now, I'm beginning to believe I'd be better off away from here myself. It's advantageous if I stay here at the bank. It will make our legal entanglement easier to get out of.

If I'm still living at the ranch, it will be almost impossible to prove that we mean nothing to each other." She fought hard to keep her voice from cracking.

Without a word, he turned and stalked out.

She heard the click of his spurs on the wood, the squeak of his saddle when he mounted, then the muffled horses hooves on the dusty soil outside. Stepping away from the desk, she let the oily cloth drop to the floor. Yes, it was better to end this now, before it was too late, before there were more than two people involved. She and the sheriff would need to learn to live in the same town, but it would be easier if they weren't under the same roof.

Fifteen

The heat from early October sunlight penetrated Amanda's blue shirt as she applied whitewash to the rough-hewn siding. She loved the feel of the sun as it warmed her skin while she worked. Whoever built the bank had spent little time sanding the boards to make them smooth and she had high hopes of making them look better.

The last several weeks passed slowly for her. She hadn't tried to interrogate Oldham anymore but the situation between her and Wade remained less than congenial. Occasionally, she saw him in town during the day, but for the most part, they kept their distance from each other.

Boyce Stewart agreed to let her work mornings only and the afternoons she renovated the bank. Another telegram had arrived from Jed informing her he had shipped the money by Wells Fargo. She could expect to receive the shipment before winter. Excited about the prospect of opening the bank, her joy was tempered by her separation from Wade. She realized she had begun to think of their relationship as a real marriage. Her heart ached that it wasn't.

She reminded herself on a daily basis that not once had he indicated he felt anything for her. She shouldn't have opened herself up for the kind of rejection she'd once had from Simon. Although Wade's was different, it was rejection, just the same. Maybe even more than Simon's had been because she had never had an intimate relationship with Simon.

Of course, she'd always suspected the problem wasn't with her. During the war, she'd seen men who preferred the company of other men and sensed Simon was like them, but he'd gone to his grave without confirming her suspicions.

When her monthly passed without coming, she convinced herself it was because her life had been so unstable lately. She couldn't think of forcing herself on Wade with a child, but thoughts of him wouldn't leave her as the bank building began to look more like a business.

Being outdoors during the short afternoons was something she really enjoyed. Smiling to herself, she noted that her mother would have been aghast if she knew Amanda had let her skin tan. Boston was a long way away though. Occasionally, she received a letter and she answered each one, carefully avoiding questions about her return to Boston and those involving male prospects.

Applying more paint to the wall, Amanda thought of the last letter. Her mother had urged her to return to Boston trying to entice her by mentioning the formation of the first Young Women's Christian Association in the United States. There were many projects underway to help others and her mother assured her a young woman, like her, would fit in very well.

Amanda doubted that. She had given the matter little thought as she'd stuffed the letter in the bottom of the saddlebag where she kept them all. In the few months she had been in Mineral Wells, she'd become as much as part of this town as anywhere she'd ever lived. No, she didn't plan to return to Boston, today or any other day.

Splashing the whitewash on the building, she fell into quiet reflection. Although Walt Brauns had volunteered to paint for her, she had protested, saying she had to fill her afternoons with something since she'd asked Boyce for the time off. She'd sensed Walt didn't really approve of a woman doing such work, but when she'd asked him how to mix the whitewash, he'd readily shown her.

She swatted at a fly, then brushed a wayward strand of hair back into place.

"It's a shame, a little woman like you doing men's work," Boyce Stewart's gruff voice interrupted her reverie.

Glancing at him, she smiled. She still didn't really like or trust him, although they seemed to have grown used to each other and he didn't tell her she could leave every day anymore.

"I've found, Mr. Stewart," she glanced over her shoulder at him, "that the best way to get a job done, is to do it yourself." Continuing to paint, she wondered why he'd stopped by. Until now, he'd made no pretenses of interest in reopening of the bank.

"It's a waste, if you ask me." He took a puff on his ever-present pipe, filling the clear air with a gray haze of smoke.

"Why?"

"Cause, it'll just peel off. Paint and whitewash don't last in this country. It's too harsh."

"Well, it'll look better for a time," she insisted, continuing to apply whitewash and wishing he'd go away if he didn't have something positive to say.

"Have ya looked at the inside?"

She stopped painting and looked up at him. "Of course, why?"

"I just wondered. When Oldham owned it, he had some of the fanciest furnishings in the territory. I wondered if they were still there."

"Take a look for yourself. Animals have chewed some of the benches pretty badly. I had Charlie Johnson come and work on them. He did a good patch job."

"No." Stewart added tobacco to his pipe. "Was just wonderin'." Abruptly, he turned and walked across the street to his store.

Now just what did that mean? She crouched low to paint the bottom boards.

Thrusting the brush back into the whitewash, she worked with a vigor she hadn't had before. Completing that side, she let the brush drop into the bucket, leaned back on her knees, and inspected her finished project. The building had absorbed a lot of the whitewash, but it looked better and even Stewart would have to admit that.

"Looks good." Wade's voice came to her from a few feet behind her where Boyce Stewart had stood a few minutes earlier.

"Not to hear some say, it doesn't."

"Who?"

"Boyce Stewart. He says I'm wasting my time, it'll just peel off anyway." Turning slightly, she glanced at Wade. He had changed his tan shirt and pants for buckskin and felt Stetson replaced the straw hat he'd worn during the summer. The scent of leather drifted to her from him. He looked rugged and handsome standing there in the bright afternoon sunshine Peacemaker strapped to his side.

Her heart raced even though she willed it to slow as she wondered what she looked like. Embarrassment rose in her at the thought. She'd swiped at her hair a few minutes before, probably leaving whitewash on her nose. Her hands and arms were dotted with the paint. "I can't say I understand what Stewart's visit meant." She stood and pushed another strand of hair away from her face.

"What do you mean?"

Turning toward him, she met his gaze and kept her voice level in spite of her pounding heart. "Since I've been working on the bank, he's rarely asked me anything about it. He's almost ignored the fact I'm getting ready to open." She placed her hands on her hips. "This afternoon, he came over. Tells me I'm wasting time painting the building and asks about the furnishings inside. When I tell him he can have a look, he scurried away like someone was chasing him."

She saw a tolerant glint of humor in Wade's dark eyes as he gazed down at her. "I assume you've looked for the money?"

"Of course. Found nothing but dust, even in the safe, which isn't too safe. I sent a telegraph to the manufacturer in San Francisco this morning. I'll need it repaired before I can trust money in it."

"Maybe Stewart is just curious." Wade started to step away.

Her heart ached. She'd been hoping he'd come to see her, not talk about her employer. "Maybe so, it's just I can't push the idea he's involved with Oldham out of my mind."

"Maybe you're hoping too much, Amanda." He pulled a cigarette paper out and began to roll a smoke.

"Maybe I am at that. Have you heard any more from the judge?"

"Should be here any day. I sent another wire day before yesterday. He's somewhere between here and Prescott. Has other cases on the way." He inhaled and gazed out toward the mountains.

She thought he looked reflective, but decided she was putting her thoughts into his actions again, which wasn't good she reminded herself. This visit was natural. As Sheriff of Mineral Wells, he should be interested in progress in the bank. It would give him additional work.

"You mentioned once that you wanted to move the teller's box. Did you still plan to?" He tossed the cigarette butt on the ground and stomped on it.

"Yes. If you're available, maybe we could do it tomorrow evening, before you go to the ranch. I've got the divider repaired and oiled until it shines. I just want to move it a few feet backward."

"That would be fine, I'll stop by when I leave the office."

"Fine, I'll prepare a stew."

"Whatever." His gaze caught hers and held for a moment. Then, he turned and walked briskly away.

Just exactly what did that mean? He acted almost like he'd do anything she agreed to. Picking up the bucket of remaining whitewash, she went inside.

Wade strode down the street with purpose in his step. But, he couldn't wipe the picture of how fetching Amanda looked with that spot of whitewash on the tip of her nose from his mind. If he hadn't gotten out of there when he did, he'd have tried to wipe it off, and every time he touched her, his body betrayed him.

After the last few weeks, he was beginning to think his need for her would never cease. Obviously, they couldn't expect the judge to annul their marriage at this point, but did she want to stay married? She certainly didn't act like it. Before she had moved into the bank there had been times when he thought she wanted to stay with him, but now, he wasn't so sure.

Life had certainly gotten complicated since she'd come to town. He often found himself thinking of her, how it would be to have a real ranch with her waiting at home at night, a couple of children or maybe even more. The image of a younger version of Amanda flashed before him again. A blond curly headed girl.

A smile slipped out as he strolled down the street, but right beside it stood the nagging suspicion she was in danger, possibly grave danger. It was his job as sheriff to see nothing happened to her, but as her husband, he realized he'd give his life for hers.

You've got it bad, Denton. He stepped on the boardwalk in front of the hotel. *Yeah, guilt over beddin' her that's all it is.* Maybe he'd just question Oldham again.

Walking toward the jail, he pushed thoughts of Amanda away as he pondered questions he'd ask the prisoner. He'd come to the conclusion Oldham waited on something or someone, but who? Wade hadn't been able to decide. He'd run every possible suspect through his mind, time and again. Del Deans, with his early threat to take the law into his own hands then the uprising had since proved to be completely docile.

He'd eliminated George Morgan the telegrapher and Abe the barber/undertaker as suspects. Why, he wasn't exactly sure, but neither man seemed the type to get involved with lawlessness and they hadn't invested in the bank.

Passing the general store, Wade saw Boyce Stewart step away from the door. He was the one man Wade hadn't come to a conclusion about. Of course, Amanda suspected him and if she had any reason other than the women's intuition she always seemed to rely on, he might be more inclined to agree with her. But even she didn't seem so sure as she had when she'd started working for him. The storekeeper had nothing to connect him with Oldham, other than Gladys' suspicion Stewart had something to do with her husband, Bernard's, death.

Neither Stewart or Deans had a criminal record, but the national criminal record wasn't too long. Either man could have committed lessor crimes and not be known in the capitol.

He couldn't let his personal dislike for Stewart automatically make him a suspect. Opening the jail door, he thought about Amanda again, how innocent she looked standing there beside the bank a few minutes ago. Glancing at Dingy sitting on his cot in the cell, the vision of him over her returned. The rage he'd felt that night swept over him again, like it had right before he'd pulled the trigger.

Never before had he shot a man when he could've apprehended him with an order, but he'd felt a panic before he'd shot--fear for Amanda. If Dingy hadn't listened to the command or one of his friends had turned on Wade he'd have killed them, he was sure of that and he'd never felt such a driving emotion in his life. What caused it? He wasn't sure, and he didn't have time to ponder it right now.

Instead, he strolled to the cell and looked at the prisoners. A motley crew, but they were at least clean. "Oldham, come here. I want to talk to you."

No, he hadn't chanced Amanda's safety then, and he wouldn't chance it now. He'd do everything he could to get a confession from the prisoner. Starting tonight, he'd watch over the bank himself.

"Whatya want, Sheriff?" Oldham snarled, but he didn't move to obey Wade's command.

"What did you do with the money you took from the bank?"

The prisoner's gaze met his.

Wade didn't like the glint in Oldham's eyes.

He chuckled down deep and said, "Wouldn't you like to know, Sheriff? Let me out of here, and I'd be willing to cut you and that deputy of yours in on it."

"Dream on. You could make it easier on yourself if you'd tell who your accomplices were and where the money is."

"Who says I had accomplices?" he roared. The chuckle turned into an angry laugh matching the malicious glint in the former banker's dark eyes.

Wade suppressed frustration rising in him. Maybe there really wasn't any money. He stepped closer. "Don't push me, Oldham."

"No, you might wind up with a bullet in ya," Dingy snorted, from the cot where he sat, fully recovered from the gunshot wound. He was anxious to be transferred. The marshal should be coming from Santa Fe any day for him.

Wade turned away from the cell toward Harvey who'd been dozing when he entered. "Heavy night, last night?" His voice sounded harsh, angry, but he didn't temper it. His deputy had a job to do. Wade had been lenient, now he wanted him to know how important watching the prisoners well was.

"A little bit," he admitted, a sheepish grin lifting his drooping handlebar mustache. "That Mexican food for dinner makes me sleepy too. Guess they have a reason to take a siesta."

"You need to start getting your full rest. As long as we've waited for the judge, we may be due another break-out attempt."

"I understand." His blue eyes had grown serious. "I'll put my personal life on hold until we're rid of them." He nodded toward the cell.

"Appreciate that." Wade walked over to his desk and sat. Why was he so apprehensive? Nothing had happened, but it could, he reminded himself.

The next night, Amanda stirred the pot of stew. The delectable aroma filled the little room at the back of the bank where she'd scrubbed the stove until it was spotless. Her stomach fluttered, and her heart hammered as she waited for Wade. Glancing into the main room she saw the polished handrail leaning against the wall. Once they moved the teller's box, later this evening, she'd reattach the rail and be ready for business.

The room smelled clean from all the dusting, mopping and polishing and she was getting anxious to open, but the question was, when would the money arrive?

Traveling across country was dangerous, and even more so with money. *Would it come? Maybe she had done all this work for nothing.* She stepped away from the tiny stove used to warm the building in the winter, took the two plates off the shelf, then placed them on the flat portion of the rolled top desk. Not much of a table, but it would have to do. She walked back to the shelf, took two cups, then heard a knock. Her hands grew clammy as she stepped to the door and opened it.

"Evenin' Amanda." He met her gaze and he smiled slightly.

"Good evening, Wade." She stepped back for him to enter.

He slipped the felt Stetson off and stood in the middle of the tiny room waiting.

For a moment, she felt uncomfortable and sensed he did too. "You can put your hat on the rack by the door, if you want."

"Thanks." He turned and hung the hat.

"Sure smells good." He pivoted toward her.

Their gazes seemed to burn together.

Did he mean the food or the toilet water she wore? Walking into the other room, she placed the cups on the desk. "I hope you don't mind eating off a desk since I don't have a table." She looked at him.

He stood in the middle of the doorway, his broad shoulders filling the space. "I wouldn't mind eating anywhere, Amanda, as long as you're there."

She fought the urge to fling herself into his arms. Instead, she said, "I know you've always liked my cooking."

He took a step toward her. "We really do need to talk."

"About what?"

Their gazes locked and the need in her rose.

"Our marriage. I expect the judge soon."

She stepped around him and to the stove where she took the stewpot, and walked back into the other room. She'd dreaded this moment from the day they'd been married. Together they'd have to decide what they wanted the judge to do. "Have a seat, and we'll talk about it, after dinner." She sat the pan on a hotpad then took a chair beside the desk.

Wade pushed back from the desk and wiped his lips with the linen napkin Amanda had given him. She'd kept cheery conversation going throughout the meal and sidestepped his statement about wanting to spend time with her very well. In the last few weeks, with plenty of opportunity to think about her, his feelings and their marriage, he'd decided the idea sounded better than it once had.

He'd even considered asking her to return to the ranch with him although he hadn't gone so far as to believe he loved her. He admitted he missed her and for more than the food she cooked and the way she warmed his bed.

She challenged him in a way Sarah Jean Sturdyvent had never come close. He found that stimulating. When he let himself, he could imagine Amanda working alongside him to make his property profitable. Glancing at her, he fought the urge to step around the desk and pour his heart out to her.

But the memory of her making pie for Oldham stopped him. She had to know the prisoner personally to remember that was his favorite dessert. Instead, he said, "Where do you want that teller's box moved? I need to work this supper off."

"Actually, I just wanted to move it back a couple of feet, to make more room for customers. I can't imagine why it was put so close to the front door." She stood and walked to the box which was a small three foot by three foot cage with a top on it about four feet tall placed approximately three feet from the front.

"Maybe Oldham didn't want to encourage customers."

She smiled endearingly. "Well, I want to invite as many as I can."

"What about the rest of your life, Amanda? Are you going to let banking take up all your time now?" Their gazes welded together and his heart pounded loud enough she should be able to hear it. Did he dare open himself up for her rebuff?

"I hope to have a private life too someday." Her voice had grown soft, hopeful.

Could there be something between them? He began to hope. Maybe his chances were better than someone else's, after all he was her husband. Stepping in front of the teller's box, he pushed at it. It didn't budge. "Maybe it's nailed down."

"I thought of that, but didn't find any nail heads."

A heady whiff of toilet water filled his nostrils. He fought the urge to wrap his arms around her, pull her close, and forget everything except her. Instead, he pushed on the stubborn piece of furniture again. It didn't move, but he felt it tip. "I think I've broken it loose."

"Let me help." She stepped up beside him and turned her backside to the box. Together they pushed once.

It didn't move.

"Harder!" Her eyes glowed with excitement.

Wade pushed with all his might. The box moved, but he wasn't expecting it, then it tipped and he along with the box started falling. They crashed on the floor and he collapsed on top.

"Oh!" Amanda cried, then he felt her on his back. She laughed as they wrestled around on the floor trying to untangle.

He looked into her eyes, sparkling with humor, not more than six inches away and didn't want to move, now or ever. "Are you hurt?"

The soft smile confirmed she wasn't injured.

He touched her waist with his right hand. Her soft, feminine heat burned through the thin dress fabric inviting his attention. Slipping both arms around her, he pulled her close, covering her lips, tasting of the finest nectar, with his. He couldn't let her go.

Amanda slipped her hands around his neck, urging him pull her closer. He heard her heart pound close to his ear as the smell of her filled him with a heady sense of belonging. His tension evaporated as she returned the kisses with passionate ones of her own. Pulling away for a moment, he looked down at her. "This isn't a proper place for a girl from Boston. I'm giving you one chance, if you want to move."

She pulled his head to hers and kissed him boldly.

He groaned deep and let his hands roam up and down her back, working with the many buttons. His kisses covered her eyelids, her cheeks, chin, and rained down her throat. The dress loosened. Pulling carefully on the fabric so he wouldn't tear it, he finally exposed one creamy shoulder and kissed that spot. "We've got to do something about this. I can't go on this way," he moaned.

She moved away from him and slipped the dress off then rejoined him. "We are doing something about it, Wade." She kissed him again, opening her mouth to his intruding tongue.

With skillful hands, he removed the drawers, tossing them into the pile with her dress.

For a moment, he turned away from her, slipped out of his boots, the vest and his doeskin trousers. Laying them carefully, smoothly beside her, he looked into her eyes, then his gaze trailed down to her freed breast. He bent and placed a gentle kiss on the throbbing nipple then he nipped playfully, sending shivers of pleasure through her.

"Oh," she groaned low.

He lifted her gently off the bare floor and moved her to his clothes. "Amanda, you're the most beautiful woman I've ever seen."

His mouth came back to her, seeking first the orb in the middle of her being, then moving to the V of hair at the entrance of her womanhood. The calluses of his hands made her inner thighs tingle as his fingers moved along them, causing her wanting flesh to seek their comfort.

She looked at him in the lantern light. His sandy hair was mussed now as he bent over her. When he lifted his head and gazed at her, his dark eyes were even darker with passion. She arched toward him. "Please Wade."

But, he wasn't ready. Instead of moving on her, he stretched out next to her, letting his hand rest at her most sensitive place. "Amanda, you have to know, this is more than a fake marriage. I can't let you go." His voice was hushed and close to her ear. "I've tried, but I can't."

"I don't want you to." She looked into his eyes then his lips covered hers again. His fingers caressed her into frenzy like she'd never known before. As the spasms peaked then subsided he moved over her. With purposeful movements, he spread her legs. With deliberate strokes, he thrust into her. Together they rode to a height she had never dreamed existed.

The lantern was dim when Amanda awoke. They lay close together on the cot at the back of the bank. He had his arm draped protectively over her, his dark blond hair curled boyishly against his cheek, and he snored quietly. Bending toward him, she kissed his cheek, then closed her eyes again. Yes, she loved him. Whether he felt the same for her or not she would move back to the ranch. He wouldn't have to ask again.

She sighed deeply as her thoughts returned to the night before, their loving, their dinner, and the teller's box. They'd moved it and hadn't set it up again. Carefully, she crawled from the cot and walked into the other room. It was a mess. The teller's box lay to one side, her clothes were piled on the other and Wade's rumpled buckskins lay in the middle.

"What's the matter?" He called.

"I just woke up and remembered we hadn't finished moving the box."

"Come on back to bed, we can do that in the morning."

"I'm not worried about that, but I remembered something." She walked further into the room, picked up Wade's doeskin shirt and wrapped it around her. Crossing to the place where the teller's box had been she bent to the floor and began to examine it.

"What is it, Amanda?" He stood in the doorway. His hair was disheveled and he'd wrapped the quilt they'd covered with around his waist.

"I think I felt something move as I fell on top of you."

"You've got to be joking." He stepped further inside. "Everything happened so fast, I don't know how you could have felt anything except...." He let the words drop off as he smiled sheepishly.

"Oh, yes, I felt that, but I felt something on the floor too," she insisted sliding her hands across the floor. Then she felt it, a small slit, the size of the teller's box. "Here it is."

"What?"

"I don't know, but I think it moves." She pulled at the flooring, but it wouldn't budge.

"Let me see." He bent and examined the place on the floor. "I think you might have something, Amanda. Get my knife. It's in my pants pocket."

She found the knife and handed it to him.

Several seconds later, he lifted the wood neatly from the floor. "What about that?" he gasped. "I don't know how you felt it, Amanda, but this hole was obviously put here for a purpose. Bring the lantern closer."

Excitement filled her as she grabbed the light and took it to him.

He held it in the opening, then looked up at her, shaking his head. "Nothing, just an empty hole."

"I don't believe it. It can't be, Wade. The money has got to be here."

"Amanda, I tell you there's nothing here. Look for yourself." He handed her the lantern and stood.

She bent forward and looked inside, but she couldn't see anything either. "Well, we found a secret hole, I can't understand why someone would cut a hole and not put anything in it."

"Unless?" Wade knelt beside her and bent further into the opening. "I don't want to run onto a rattler, or a nest of scorpions."

Sixteen

Wade took the lantern from Amanda and lowered it slowly into the hole being careful not to touch the sides for fear of torching the dry wood. This wasn't a good idea and he wasn't comfortable with it, anything could be under there snakes, scorpions, spiders. He shivered. He sure didn't want Amanda doing this alone and he sensed she would if he didn't help. On three sides, the light disappeared into the darkness, but on the fourth, it reflected back from something.

"Do you see anything?" Amanda's excitement filled voice demanded.

Pulling the lantern out, he sat it several feet away. Looking at her, he smiled, although he'd have rather kissed her she looked so fetching there in his shirt, her cheeks rosy with energy, her eyes ablaze with anticipation. "As a matter-of-fact, I think I did see something. I'll be right back." Standing, he picked up his crumpled trousers and walked to the tiny bedroom where he removed the quilt and slipped into them.

Returning to the main room, he saw her standing, staring into the hole. She looked tiny, vulnerable and oh, so sensual in his shirt. His body reacted, but now was not the time to let romantic thoughts overrule his head. "I needed to be presentable. I have no idea what's under there." He knelt again, moved the lantern to the opposite side of the opening, then laid flat extending his arms under the floor until he touched the object.

"What is it?" Amanda stood over him, her long shapely legs plainly in view.

He had trouble concentrating on the task instead of the woman and when he touched the object, it crumbled beneath his fingers. "A wooden box." He sat up and moved the lantern down into the hole again.

The space between the floor and the ground was not big enough for him, but he saw the broken box and behind it something shiny. "There's something else there too." Pulling his hand away, he sat up. "I can't reach it. We'll have to cut another opening." He looked at the floor several feet away.

"I'll bet I can reach it." Amanda stepped closer.

"You're too little. If I can't reach it, you sure can't."

"Someone needs to be small to crawl inside."

"No, Amanda, you can't do that." Fear gripped him.

"What if there's a rattlesnake or scorpion under there?"

"You didn't see any, did you?" Determination flashed in her blue eyes.

"No, but...."

"It'll take hours to cut a hole, maybe for no reason. I can get down there in a couple of minutes, then we'll know."

"No!"

"Yes!" Her blue gaze sparked into his.

He might as well approve, she'd do it anyway. "You can't do it in that." He pointed to the shirt.

"It'll only take a minute to change." She raced in the room without giving him a chance to answer.

"If there was any other way...." He continued to study the situation, but decided she was probably right.

She peeked around the wall. "There isn't."

Lying on the floor he tried to reach the object again, but his fingers were inches from touching what appeared to be a metal box.

"I'm ready." She stood over him, wearing her faded blue shirt, baggy trousers, and heavy boots. Her eyes sparkled with excitement.

He moved away from the hole.

She stepped closer.

"You slide in and I'll hand you the lantern. If you see or hear a thing, I don't care what it is, get out - now."

"I will. It'll be all right, Wade." She smiled reassuringly, those blue eyes that always got to him, whether they should or not, tugging at his heart-strings no, no matter what good sense told him to do.

As she descended into the hole, he tried not to let himself think about how dangerous what they were doing could be. A whole nest of rattlers might be behind the metal, getting the lantern too close to dry wood could start a fire. The thought of Amanda beneath a burning building frightened him as a confrontation with a rattler did.   The expression on her face told him she was committed, there would be no stopping her.

Silently, Amanda slid from the floor into the inky darkness, ignoring the fear that rippled through her. The area was cold, damp and she had trouble breathing, but she attributed her feelings to unreasonable apprehension. She'd never been frightened in tight places before.

Calm down, she told herself. *This won't take long.* Pushing the fear she'd seen in Wade's eyes for her away she slid her feet away from the metal object and moved to the right. "Lower the lantern."

For seconds, she lay in total darkness, then the lantern slid through the opening. She thought she heard something, so she stopped and listened.

Nothing.

Swiveling her head as much as she could she saw the rough side of the flooring boards, cobwebs, dust, and the broken box.

"Can you reach it?"   Wade hovered over the hole, inches overhead.

"I've got to move." Carefully wiggling so she wouldn't hit the lantern, she slid her hands above her head and pushed the crumbling box aside. "I see it." Moments later, she touched the metal sending shivers through her. "It's a metal box. I don't know how you saw it."

"Don't worry about that, just get it and get out of there."

Scooting further, she placed a hand on each side and tried to pull, but she didn't have enough strength to make it move. "I'm need to turn over."

"Maybe it's nothing. Why don't you come back up here and let me cut a hole in the floor. It's almost daylight."

She ignored his protest, carefully rolling herself over. The flooring scrubbed her shirt on top and the sand sifted beneath, but she wiggled until she lay flat on her stomach. Placing a hand on each side, she tugged. It wouldn't move. Again, she sensed something nearby, but she pushed the thought away and continued to tug. Running her right hand along the front, she removed sand where it had settled into the ground. She tugged harder and it moved slightly. "I've got it!"

"Leave it. I don't feel good about this."

"Move the lantern, I'm coming out!"

The light above disappeared. She wiggled toward the opening, but did not relinquish her hold on the box. It was heavy, but she tugged, three, six, twelve inches, then it wouldn't move.

"Come on, Amanda." Wade's anxious voice was directly above her. His hand was at her waist.

"I've almost got it. Why are you so frightened? I've got everything under control?" She pulled the box a few inches further.

"It's probably close enough I can reach it now, leave it be!"

Fatigue gripped her and suddenly she couldn't move the box further. She paused knowing she was close enough to sit she worked her way around until she lay flat on her back, then sat up. "It's something." She smiled wanting to wipe the concern away.

"I don't care. I just want you out of there." Bending over he lifted her from the hole and stood her on the floor.

Standing in front of him, she brushed the dirt and sand away, somewhat shaken by his rough treatment. "You should've waited to be sure it was close enough to reach."

Anger boiled in his dark eyes. "I shouldn't have let you go under there."

"But it's all right. Nothing happened."

"It could have been different. It's not worth it, Amanda, no matter how much money might be there."

He sounded almost like he cared. She hadn't dared let herself think of the possibility. Although the thought lingered, she couldn't dwell on it as she turned back to the hole. He'd made it clear he had no more intentions of keeping this farce of a marriage going than she. Although there had been times, like last night, and this morning when they seemed to share the same feelings for each other. The idea that he might still want to end their marriage saddened her, but she didn't have time to think about it. Looking at the hole, she saw the box was much closer. "Let's get it out."

The first hints of gray dawn filtered in the window, but not enough to illuminate the room and the opening.

"You handle the lantern, I'll do the work this time." Wade's voice was firm when he picked up the lantern and handed it to her.

He reached for the box and pulled it out. "I think I heard something." He glanced at her.

"What?"

"I don't know. Hold the lantern in the hole."

As she lowered it, a snake slithered across the illuminated area.

"We're lucky the weather's cool."   Wade stood beside her watching the serpent disappear.

"Is it a rattler?"

"Yes, a sidewinder."

She shivered as the reality of what might have happened soaked in. "At least, we've got the box."

Wade dropped the piece of flooring back across the hole. "For whatever its worth."

Amanda's thoughts raced. What had she read about rattlers? Did they climb?

"I'll take care of your visitor sometime later today," He straightened. "Snake Man lives up in the mountains.   I'll send someone for him."

Glad to know she was safe, she glanced at the floor again, then to Wade. "Good, now let's see what we've got."

He picked their find up and carried it to the table. "Opening it may not be that easy."

A large padlock slipped through a hasp on the side secured it.

"You didn't happen to find any keys as you cleaned, did you?" Wade looked down at her, earlier hints of fear and anger now gone.

"I'm afraid not."

"Then I'll probably have to cut this off."   He examined it carefully.

"But Wade, we might have need of the box again.   Wouldn't cutting it cause damage?"

He stepped back and stared down at her.   "Just what do you propose?"

"Maybe we could pick the lock."

He checked it closer. "Rusted."

"All the better. Rust weakens metal."

"Have you ever tried to pick a lock, Amanda?"

"No, but...."

"It's not easy. We tried it once."

"When?"

He frowned then looked at the lock again. "In a Yankee prison. Didn't have anything to do but think of getting out anyway."   His voice had grown harsh.

"Then you could probably do this one, too."

"It'd be easier to cut it or maybe use a big rock. That lock's pretty rusty."

"If there's money in there, that means Maurice Oldham put it under the floor. No one just coincidentally put it where it was."

"That's true," Wade looked at her and smiled.

Her heart thumped wildly, whether from her reaction to him or to the thought that maybe they'd found the money, she didn't know, it she couldn't slow it, no matter how much she wanted to.

"If you'd let me have my shirt, I'll see what I can do."

She darted into the bedroom and retrieved the buckskin shirt up from the cot.

When she returned to the other room, he sat at the desk, putting on his boots and watching her. "We've got to talk about this, Amanda." His voice was husky and she sensed his sincerity.

Her hand trembled as she held him the shirt for him to take. "Right now, we've got to find out whether there's any money in that box or not." Her voice was firm.

He stepped toward the door. He took his hat and put it on. "We will, but I expect you out to the ranch tonight so we can get this settled."

She nodded, but anticipation filled her making her feel giddy. He'd never sounded so serious before.

Wade walked out of the bank shaking his head. What was it about Amanda that got under his skin so? He'd been ready to tell her he loved her, wanted to put the whole idea of a divorce out of her thoughts, but she didn't seem the least bit interested in talking about them. All she could think about was money.

He picked up a good-sized boulder, one solid and smooth yet small enough to grip easily and tossed it in the air then caught it.

Should do.

Turning toward the building, his thoughts focused on her again. He sure didn't intend to make himself vulnerable to another woman. If she didn't want a marriage, that's the way she'd have it. Strolling inside, he stopped. She'd combed her hair and the fine gold strands fell loosely about her shoulders, nearly touching her waist. He remembered watching her bathe when he'd been hurt. He'd wondered if it was soft. Now he knew it was, just like the rest of her.

Fighting the urge to step across the room, and love her again, he walked past her. She glanced at his hand. *No, he couldn't compete with this obsession of hers--money.* "Let's see if there's anything in this box worth worryin' over." Stepping back to the desk, he looked at the padlock a little closer, then lifted the rock and brought it down

hard where the top joined the body. The lock didn't budge. He
swung again, once, twice--nothing. Stepping a half-pace back, he
raised the rock higher and crashed it against the lock with all his
force.

The lock sprung open.

"You did it!" She squealed with delight and danced around the
room.

He slipped the lock from the hasp and opened the lid. The
hinges creaked and dust, accumulated over the years, sifted to the
desk. He saw a ledger first, then a journal. Laying the two books
aside, he looked at Amanda who seemed to be holding her breath.

She reached inside and pulled out a cloth bag. "This is it," she
sighed. "I can tell by the weight." She clutched it to her chest and
exhilaration filled her face. "We did it, Wade."

"Yes, we did."

Carefully, she lifted eight cloth bags of coins out and laid them
on the desk. "I'm sure Simon gave Maurice state bank notes, this
feels like coins." Amanda pulled at the strings on one of the bags.

He looked inside. "Slugs! That's good, since most bank notes are
now worthless."

"Slugs?"

He picked an octagonal piece of gold up and turned it over. "An
eagle on one side, rays on the other. Gold coins used primarily in
California. Looks to me like Mr. Oldham turned your bank notes
into something valuable, even after the war. They're worth about
fifty dollars each."

"But Jed was going to make our bank notes good."

"It's gold, he won't have to."

"This is it." Her blue eyes sparkled as she looked up at him.
"Do you think this is all of it?"

"I don't know. Let's count it."

"We need to wait." His voice sounded stern, even to his ears, but
suddenly the situation had changed drastically. Amanda had the
money she sought so fervently, but having possession of it
presented another problem. Someone knew it was here and she
had said the safe needed repair.

"Why?"

"It's almost time for you to go to work. I'm late already. You've
been punctual. You don't want Boyce to think there's anything
different going on, do you?"

"No, but...." She stared up at him, clearly unwilling to leave the treasure.

"And there's the matter of the unwanted guest under the floor."

Amanda shuddered. "What do we do with the money?"

"Nobody knows the safe isn't safe, except maybe Oldham. He's in jail. We can put the money there and count it tonight." He could tell by the scowl on her face Amanda didn't like the idea but Wade couldn't see an alternative.

"All right," she said reluctantly, "but what do we do with the box?"

"Put it under your cot, we may need it later." Without another word he picked up the box and carried it into the other room, slid it beneath the cot and carefully, draped the quilt to hide it. Stepping back to the other room, he saw Amanda working feverishly with the closed safe. "I thought you said it wasn't all that safe."

"It isn't. I'm just having trouble opening it." She continued to work with the lock.

"I'll return this evening." He stepped closer knowing he had to get his point across. "You realize I should take the money into the office as evidence."

She stopped working with the lock and stared at him. "But it's my money. Mine and the people of Springfield."

"It also belongs to the people of Mineral Wells," he reminded her. "Unless you agree to leave it here, I'll have to take it with me."

Amanda turned the lock once more. The door dropped open. She scowled, but lifted the money, one bundle at a time, into the safe. "I'll leave it here, Sheriff." She glared up at him. "You just be sure you do too."

The implication in her words infuriated Wade, but they didn't have time to argue. He was more than forty-five minutes late to work already and glancing through the window he saw Boyce Stewart performing his daily ritual of arranging buckets.

When Amanda stepped on the general store porch Boyce Stewart nearly knocked her down dragging several more buckets outside. She stopped in the middle of the doorway and he glared down at her.

"I won't need your services today, Mrs. Denton." He lifted his head haughtily, and placed the buckets on the edge of the boardwalk then started back inside.

"But why?" She couldn't keep the dismay from her voice.

He turned slightly and stopped, but didn't look directly at her. "Because you're fired."

"Fired!"

"Yes, fired. You're late to work and I don't tolerate tardiness."

"But I've never been late before." Did it really matter? She had money now, could open the bank and that did mean something. Bit she prided herself in keeping the job in spite of their differences.

He placed his hands on his hips and stared over the crook of his pipe. "You may come inside long enough to collect your belongings. I'll bring your wages to the bank, later today. Its time you acted like the sheriff's wife and let him support you."

Taken aback, Amanda couldn't respond. She thought about not going inside, but her pride wouldn't allow that. She'd left her shotgun, a hat, pair of trousers and shirt she sometimes wore when she did work that would ruin a dress.

Stewart walked briskly around the counter and watched her retrieve her belongings.

The room felt cold, much cooler than she'd noticed before and something thumped under the floor. "What's that?"

"I've had skunks under the store since it got cooler." He lit his pipe and puffed. Smoke rose to the ceiling.

"Oh, I never noticed."

"Well, I've seen them." He scowled.

"I'd really like you to reconsider, Mr. Stewart."

"Punctuality, Mrs. Denton." He puffed. The smoke curled around his mustache and floated to the ceiling. "I require punctuality. I told you that to start." He let the hand holding the pipe drop to his side as he continued to stare at her. "Besides, didn't the sheriff spent the night with you? That's where you belong."

She took her belongings and walked to the front door. "What I do, Mr. Stewart, is no concern of yours. The sheriff and I are married." Stopping just inside the door, she heard the thumping again and glanced at the floor. "I'll be expecting you before the day's over with my money."

He nodded.

She opened the door. "You really should do something about those skunks, Boyce, before they spray your merchandise and ruin it."

Stepping out into the porch, the early morning sunshine hit her and she wondered what she'd do today? It'd been a long time since she'd had a day with nothing to do, the day she and Wade had gone to the mission near Tucson. That trip had led them to Oldham. She stepped off the boardwalk and walked across the street to the bank and opened the door. Laying her belongings on the cot, she turned to leave. *Why did Stewart fire me? How much money is in the safe?*

Fighting the urge to open the door and count the money, she forced herself outside.   Boyce Stewart stood in the window watching her, but she looked away like she didn't see him. *What was happening? Why had he fired her?*

The minute Wade stepped on the boardwalk in front of the jail, he knew something was the matter. The door stood ajar several inches. Cautiously, he glanced over his shoulder. Town was quite, the street empty. The scent of biscuits and gravy wafted from Glady's, making his stomach growl, but he ignored the need and pushed the open door further. The room was quiet, too quiet and Harvey Griggs wasn't sitting in his chair. "Harvey?" He waited.

Silence.

"Harvey?" He squinted as dread and guilt swept over him. While he'd been with Amanda, something had happened to his friend.

He pulled his gun and eased his way into the room. The cells looked empty, but from this position the prisoners could be sleeping on their cots and not be seen. Carefully walking around the front desk he looked into the first cell.

Empty.

Dingy, gone!

He stepped to the next cell. Harvey was tied to the bunk Oldham had occupied.

The banker and Jose were gone too.

Apprehension filled him, but he didn't see any blood. "Harvey?" Then he saw a slight rocking motion and heard a low groan. Relief filled him. His legs and hands had been tied together. A bandana covered his mouth, a blindfold over his eyes.

"I'll release you as soon as I get the keys." He glanced at the wall. The ring of keys normally hanging on a nail was missing. He pulled out his desk drawers. *Empty.* Then he went to Harvey's desk. *No keys.*

Thoroughly checking the room he satisfied himself were nowhere in the building. He went to the cell. "Are you all right?"

Harvey moved appearing to nod.

"Do you know where the keys are?"

Harvey shook again, but Wade couldn't understand what the action meant.

"I'll release you as soon as I can. I'm have to get my horse and pull out the window."

He dashed away, but closed the door, hoping nobody stopped before he returned. Walking briskly toward the hotel, the severity of the situation became evident. Three criminals and at least one person who had helped them escape were free and Oldham knew about the money under the bank floor. Furthermore, he didn't want anyone to know about the escape until he had a chance to talk to Harvey, but more importantly, that Amanda was in grave danger.

"Morning, Sheriff," Delbert Deans stepped up on the boardwalk by the hotel. "Checking on the prisoners?"

"Yes." Had Deans released the captives?

"Heard anything from the judge?"

"He's due any day."

Del reached for the hotel door, but it burst open.

An elderly gentleman wearing a three pieced black suit and matching felt hat stepped out. Glancing over his shoulder, his gaze fell on Gladys who had followed. "If I'd known I'd get such fine eats, I'd have come to Mineral Wells sooner, Miss Gladys." He smiled making his silver goatee bounce as he grasped the lapel of his coat.

"We've all been waitin' a while for you, Judge Tucker, glad you finally arrived. Its time we cleaned our jail out too, been givin' them scallywags free room and board long enough." She looked like a schoolgirl, flashing him a starry-eyed smile, a flush of crimson coloring her cheeks.

Wade barely heard the exchange beyond the man's name. Then she was introducing him and Del. The older man grabbed Wade's hand and pumped it like he was priming for water. All Wade wanted to do was free himself, get his horse and break Harvey lose, but he couldn't run out on the judge after waiting all this time.

Gladys chattered away, "What a great day. Calls for a good breakfast for you two and another cup of coffee for the judge."

"I do need to talk to the sheriff before I go look at the prisoners, and your coffee...." Judge Tucker beamed at her again.

With a lace handkerchief, she dabbed at perspiration forming on her upper lip.

The judge opened the hotel door for her.

"I have an errand I need to take care of, I'll be back in a few minutes." Wade tipped his hat, then darted toward the bank. Behind him, he could hear them talking, then the door closed. Hopefully, they'd all gone inside and that would give him a few minutes.

Crossed between the hotel and the bank, he glanced toward the general store and saw Stewart standing in the window gazing out. *Where's Amanda?* He couldn't tell her of the escape in front of Stewart, but he'd have felt better if he could see her. Hurrying past the store he focused on what he had to do first—free Harvey.

Seventeen

Amanda stepped out of the hotel and turned toward the jail. What had happened to Wade? She distinctly heard him tell Judge Tucker he had an errand and he'd be back.

The judge was still talking with Gladys who seemed quite taken by him, but Amanda had grown so apprehensive she couldn't stay inside any longer. The one thing she'd learned about Wade Denton was he was a man of his word. If he said he'd return right away, he would. What had happened? She glanced at the bank. Nothing looked disturbed so she turned toward the jail.

Suddenly, the street seemed to come alive. In the distance, clouds of dust billowed around the wheels of a stage making the tomato-red paint look dull. Two men holding shotguns rode on top, clutching their hats and teetering precariously as if they'd fall off. Behind the stage rode three men on horseback. They rolled past the saloon and jail, then jerked to a halt in front of the telegraph office. The horses snorted and one of the riders barked orders to the other men. A crowd had begun to form around them as the dust settled, and the door opened. The gold lettered words 'Wells Fargo' caught Amanda's eye.

Excitement filled her. Could it be the money?

Gladys, Del Deans and Judge Tucker strolled out of the hotel and Abe Martin stepped out of the telegraph office. Across the street, Boyce Stewart stood on the general store porch watching.

Tossing an angry scowl his way, Amanda turned toward the stage. If nothing else, maybe she'd have a letter from her mother. Even that would be welcome today.

"I guess I'd better see what's keeping the sheriff," Judge Tucker said from behind her. "I can't stay here forever. I need to be back to Prescott soon."

"Well, don't forget supper's at six, judge," Gladys reminded him.

Amanda stepped away as their voices faded into the noise.

A tall dark-haired man crawled from the stage, his eyes taking in the whole town in one swift move. The black mustache and matching shoulder-length hair made him look ominous then her gaze fell on the badge. *The marshal from Santa Fe for Dingy?*

"We have a confidential shipment for the First Bank of Mineral Wells," the driver said.

"I'm looking for the sheriff," the marshal interrupted.

"So am I." Judge Tucker stepped around Amanda to the man. "He seems to have disappeared."

Glancing past the stage she saw Wade and Harvey Griggs going inside the jail. Harvey's hat was missing and she sensed something wrong.

"There's the sheriff and his deputy now." Abe Martin pointed down the street.

"I wonder why he didn't come back to the hotel?" Judge Tucker walked to the marshal. They shook hands and started toward the jail.

"We don't have much time," the driver boomed. "I have a letter that tells me we're to leave this strongbox with a woman by the name of Amanda Green. Does anyone know her?"

Thrilling at the sound of her name, she stepped forward. "I'm Amanda Green."

The driver looked down at her. "You can't be Mrs. Green, she's supposed to be a widow-woman."

"My first husband died at Shiloh, sir." She stepped closer. "My brother Jed shipped what you have."

"But, I expected...."

"Does it matter what you expected?" Amanda met his gaze and didn't waver. "I'm Amanda Green. I plan to open the bank. Now, if you'll follow me." She turned and marched toward the bank.

What would she do? The safe was no more secure now than it had been earlier. Strolling down the street with the stage following her, she noticed a man on a donkey ride into town. Another new person in town and he seemed to be having trouble controlling the animal.

Everything appeared to be happening at once.

"Just exactly what happened?" Wade asked Harvey who had sat down at his desk, regret clearly filling his face.

"I guess Rosemarie has been keeping me awake a bit too much lately." The deputy tried to smile, but his face flushed as he slipped on his right boot. "I'm sorry, Wade. I must have dropped off to sleep for a few minutes. The next thing I knew I woke up in that cell tied like you found me. I could hardly breathe. My head hurts like hell."

"So you didn't see or hear anything?"

"Nothing." He pulled his other boot on then stood and reached for his hat.

"Where are you going?"

"After them."

"But you don't have any idea who it was or which way they went."

"Tracks?".

"I looked all around the building before I freed you. There weren't any." Wade strolled over to his desk and sat. "Whoever did this planned it well. When they took the keys they'd made it nearly impossible to free you." He looked at the cell. Pulling the window out had ruined the wall and it would need repair before holding anymore prisoners.

The sound of boots on the boardwalk outside drew his attention. The door burst open and Judge Tucker entered followed by a tall dark-haired stranger.

Agitation crossed the judge's face as he stepped into the room.

Wade stood slowly.

"What happened to you, Sheriff?" The judge demanded, crossing the room.

Wade hadn't forgotten him, he'd hoped to have information on the prisoners before seeing the man again. He pulled out a cigarette paper and rolled a smoke. It had been a long time since he'd felt this kind of pressure. The judge stared at him, waiting for an answer. Wade lit the cigarette, breathed smoke into his lungs, and said, "We've waited all this time for you, Judge. Now we have a problem."

"What kind of problem?" He looked at the empty cells, raised an eyebrow at the open wall.

"Who's he?" Wade nodded toward the second man.

"John Nance, Marshal of Santa Fe, New Mexico Territory." The man stepped forward and they shook. "You have a prisoner, Wilbur Blackburn, better known as Dingy incarcerated. I've come to take him back to stand trial for murder."

Wade couldn't believe his ears or his fortune. They'd waited more than two months for the judge and almost that long for the marshal. Why did they have to arrive on the same day, right after the prisoners escaped?

"Well, gentlemen," Wade turned away from them and moved back to his desk. "As you can see, we have an empty jail. Last night, someone decided to visit my deputy. I found him locked in this morning." He pointed to the destroyed wall. "Apparently, they took the keys. I had to pull the window out to free him."

The judge walked over to the cell and examined it closer then turned to Wade. "What do you plan to do about this?"

"First, I plan to keep the prisoners disappearance as quiet as I can. Then I intend to stake the bank out."

"Why?" Judge Tucker scowled at him. " The bank isn't even open."

"I have reason to believe one of the prisoners knows there's something of value there even though its not open. I think he'll come back for it." Wade walked to the gun rack, took a shotgun, checked to be sure it was loaded then picked up a box of shells and started for the door.

Marshal Nance had stepped further into the room. "That might be a good place to start. If there wasn't something valuable there earlier, I'd bet there is now."

"What do you mean?" Wade stopped.

"From the number of armed men guarding the stage I came in on, I'd suspect they carried a shipment of money. I understand it started in St. Louis."

"Amanda's money from Jed to open the bank." He glanced at the marshal, a big burly man who looked competent. "What happened to it?"

"The little woman. The one who'd been in the hotel led the men to the old bank building." Judge Tucker had stepped away from the cells.

Apprehension filled Wade. Amanda with all the money and Oldham on the loose. He reached for his hat. "I've got to check this out. We have a real problem." He didn't voice the question utmost in his mind. *What was Amanda doing in the hotel in the middle of the morning?* Could Stewart have given her a break? He doubted it. Stewart wasn't that generous.

"What would you like us to do, Sheriff?" The Judge asked.

Wade slipped on his hat. "Maybe you and the marshall could wait here a few minutes, then we'll decide what to do together."

"I'm with you." The marshal sat in the straight chair at the end of Harvey's desk. "I could use a little rest. Ridin' that stage through the night isn't exactly the most comfortable sleep I ever got. I suspected it was money or something valuable on that stage. It's not often five armed men travel with a stage through the night even with a full moon." He yawned and leaned back in the chair.

"I'm willing to help, Sheriff Denton, all I can." He folded his huge arms across his chest. "I've never wanted to go home empty handed. I understand that Blackburn, Dingy latches on to whomever he happens to come in contact with. I expect he'll stay with the other prisoners until something forces them apart.

"I'll appreciate any help I can get." Wade opened the door and stepped out. In the distance the stage had just pulled away from the bank stirring the dust as it turned and started toward him. Jed must have paid a bonus to get the Wells Fargo to come this far from their normal path.

Amanda moved the gold away from the door as she counted it. More than enough to open, but she wasn't sure where to put it. If only she'd sent for the safe repairman earlier. After she'd counted the money, she slid it under the cot although the area was beginning to get crowded. She considered pulling out the metal box Wade had put there earlier but someone knocked.

"Who's there?"

"It's me, Amanda. Open up."

She recognized Wade's voice and let the quilt drop down over the money. Walking to the door she opened it slightly. "What do you want?"

"What are you doing here in the middle of the day?"

Why did he care that she wasn't working? She opened the door and moved back for him to enter.

Stepping inside, he looked up and down the street behind him, then closed and bolted the door, but the action was lost on Amanda as anger at the unfairness of Stewart's dismissal washed over her. She couldn't do anything about it, but it still infuriated her. "Boyce Stewart fired me for being late this morning." She stepped away from him to the opening for the main room. "I guess it doesn't matter. I can start the bank tomorrow if I want."

"I don't think that's a good idea." He started to follow her, then paused and turned around. Taking the shovel she kept behind the door from its nail he walked into the main room strolled over toward the window and looked out.

What's he doing with the shovel? "And why not? I've waited too long for you to tell me what to do now."

He didn't answer, but turned away from the window and looked at her. "We've got to put that box back." A frown crossed his angular features.

"But--the snake?"

"That's a problem. If it moves, I'll chance shooting it." He laid the shovel near the hole in the flooring then strode back into the other room and returned with the box. Without a word, he sat it a few inches from the loose board then knelt.

"I don't understand what's happening, Wade. You told me you'd get Snake Man to take care of the snake." She stepped closer.

He glanced up at her, lit the lantern then began to work with the piece of flooring, obviously intending to remove it. "Things have changed, Amanda. You just have to trust me on this one." He removed the wood. "Can you find something to do away from here this afternoon?"

"I have nothing to do except get the bank ready." She stepped closer as he lowered the lantern into the hole. "Unless you tell me what's going on, I have no alternative but to stay. You told me we'd go to the ranch tonight, but I didn't have money here then."

He didn't seem to be listening as he examined the ground. Apparently satisfied the snake wasn't near, he moved the box closer, opened it and tossed the boulder he had broken the lock apart with inside. Digging into the sand, he added several shovels full. He paused and looked at her. "The marshal thought there might be money on the stage."

"From Jed. The cash and bullion to open the bank arrived on the stage."

He stopped digging. "How much?"

"About twenty-thousand in bills and coins."

"Where is it?"

"Under the cot, beside the box. I'm surprised you didn't see it. It's heavy."

Wade closed the lid on the box and picked it up like he weighed it. "Just right." Setting it back on the floor, he slipped the broken lock through the hasp and forced it closed. Turning the container the way it had originally been Wade slipped it back into the hole. Using the shovel, he pushed it closer to where Amanda found it, then brushed at the ground to wipe out the evidence they'd taken it out recently.

Frustration built in her. "What're you doing?"

He replaced the piece of wood over the hole then carefully moved the teller's box back into its original place. When everything looked as it had the evening before, he turned toward her. "I don't have time to go after Snake Man today." He strolled past her and hung the shovel on the nail behind the door.

"What's happening?" She stepped between him and the door.

Stopping he looked down at her.

She could tell by his set expression he didn't want to talk about it, but she was determined to know before he left.

"The less you know, the better off you'll be. I want you to go to the hotel and stay there until I tell you it's safe to come back here."

"I will not!" She placed her hands on her hips and stood her ground. Who did he think he was, trying to order her around? Her whole future was in this building. She'd had come too far and waited too long to find the money to go to the hotel and leave it now.

"Amanda," he pleaded. "You've got to trust me. The money will be safe. I'll see to that."

The determined, far away expression told her he wouldn't give in easily, but she had to know, she had a right to know. "Wade Denton, I won't let you out of here unless you tell me what's happening."

His eyes grew stormy, but she didn't budge. He stared at her for a moment, then turned around rubbing the back of his neck with his right hand. For a moment, she thought he would leave by the front door, but slowly he turned around. "The prisoners escaped last night. Someone hit Harvey over the head then locked him in a cell. They even took the keys." He stared down at her and she heard caring in his voice. "You aren't safe here. Oldham knows about the money being here. That's why I put the box back. I'm hoping he'll think we haven't found it."

Fear gripped her, but she didn't let it show. How could Wade think she could walk out on a problem like this? "Nobody is going to come for the money in broad daylight. I'll be fine here until dark. You can spend the night. No one will think anything of it. If I went to Gladys' we'd be advertising that I'm away. Everyone in town knows there's money here now." Amanda watched what she'd said soak in.

He turned away from her, then pivoted back. "The rest of the money's under the cot?"

"Yes. I had a telegraph the other day. The safe repairman was in Tucson. He's due any day."

"I don't like it, not one little bit, but you have a point." He stepped toward her and placed his right hand on the back of her neck, cradling her gently next to him. His voice husky, he said, "I don't want anything to happen to you, Amanda. You're too important to me."

She looked up at him without moving away from his warmth and comfort. "Nothing's going to happen to me, Wade," she said, with more confidence than she felt. "I'll wear the pistol and keep the shotgun handy."

He cupped his hand under her chin and pulled her face toward him. "Do that and keep the door locked until I knock. Don't open it for anyone except me. Understand?"

"Yes."

His lips came down on hers with a fervent kiss that left her trembling. Abruptly, he turned and stepped outside. She carefully locked the door behind him.

Wade strolled toward the office, trying to appear casual although every nerve in him was on edge. He examined the street for anything unusual, but everything was quiet, too quiet. Gladys' chickens pecked at something in the middle of the street, a light wisp of smoke rose from the hotel chimney. What would Gladys and Del do when they learned that the prisoners had escaped? They had hired him to capture Oldham, and now he'd let them down.

He'd have felt better if he could have convinced Amanda to spend the afternoon at Gladys', but she was right, her being there might draw suspicions. He didn't want to do anything to draw attention to her.

"Sheriff," Abe Martin called, as he stepped in front of the telegraph office.

"Yes, Abe." Wade stopped and looked at the man.

"I thought you might want to know that in addition to Miss Amanda receiving money today, you got some too. I guess you could be the first depositor in her new bank."

"What do you mean?"

"I mean that money you sent to Louisiana for several weeks ago. It came on that stage too. Sure has been a busy morning." The man smiled a toothless grin, then turned to go back inside. In the tiny room the sound of a telegraph coming in drew his attention.

"Sure has, at that," Wade said. The money was from his mother's bank in New Orleans. He planned to use to start his herd.

"I could keep it here, if ya want," Abe said, sitting in the chair behind the counter and turning to the pecking machine. "At least until Miss Amanda gets the bank open."

"I think I'll have you do that." Wade didn't really want to take time for this, but he didn't want to cause suspicion even more. "Maybe I should count it though, just to be sure it's all there."

"Sure has been a busy morning, Sheriff." Abe pulled a small pouch from the tiny safe and placed it on the counter.

"Yes, it has." Wade opened it and hastily counted the money. Just about what he'd expected. Enough to pay for the cattle coming from Texas and enough left over to enlarge the cabin. The week before he'd received permission to use ten thousand acres of semi-arid land and Harvey had told him about a man who knew how to bring the water from the San Francisco River onto the land. Pushing the money back into the pouch, he handed it to Abe. Could he convince Amanda to stay with him? He hoped so, when all this business with Oldham was over. He loved her and there was nothing he could do about it. "Take care of it for me, Abe. I'll be back soon to retrieve it. Right now I've work to do."

"Sure thing, Sheriff. Just wanted you to know it was here. I'll put it safe." He took the pouch.

"Thank." Wade walked away, but he'd taken only a couple of steps, when he saw Del Deans coming down the street. By the angry expression on his face, Wade knew the secret had escaped.

"Where are they?"

"If I knew, I'd have them back in jail." Wade stepped around him to walk to the jail.

"I expect you to find them, and soon." Deans matched his step. "If you'd done what I wanted, we'd have had this taken care of a long time ago."

"Judge Tucker is here. That's the only proper way to have taken care of this, Deans, no matter what you think." They stepped in front of the jail. Wade turned toward the saloonkeeper and stared down at him. "Just exactly how did you learn that the prisoners had escaped?"

He pulled his lapel back and extracted a cigar then placed it between his lips. "Everyone knows."

"I don't think so." Wade scrutinized him, could he be the one. "Harvey, Judge Tucker, Marshall Nance, myself and Amanda. Those are the only people I've told about the escape. How do I know you didn't help?"

The man's blue eyes sparked. For a moment he looked at Wade cautiously. "What have I to gain by helping them escape? I had money in the bank. Oldham took off with a lot of my money. That's why I wanted to hire you, just like Gladys."

"Then, how did you know about the escape?"

"I just happened to be riding out of town a few minutes ago. I saw that hole in the wall. No, Sheriff, I wasn't involved with it, but I've been expecting it." He lit the cigar. Smoke circled his head and he waved it away then gazed off down the street.

"I'd appreciate it if you'd keep the information to yourself. We're searching for the men and someone in town had to help."

"Anything you want, Sheriff. Are you going to form a posse?"

He appeared to be sincere, but Wade didn't know whether to believe it or not. "Not yet. Don't know which way to hunt for them."

"If I was tryin' to get out of town, I'd head for them hills." Deans pointed to the mountains north of Mineral Wells.

Wade had thought of that himself. The land south of town was flat with small bushes, often not tall enough to hide a man, not to mention four. It wasn't uncommon to be able to see someone following you for days. That's how Wade had spotted Amanda, what now seemed an eternity ago.

Mineral Wells lay in a valley between two mountains. It was unlikely anyone would try to climb the cliffs on either side, but north of town were juniper, scrub pines, and further up, ponderosas. If someone wanted to escape, they'd probably go north.

"Why aren't you sending a posse out?" Deans seemed determined to know every move.

"I have reason to believe, the prisoners will be come back to town." Wade opened the door and stepped inside the jail.

"Why?"

"That's a professional confidence. You aren't a lawman, Mr. Deans. If you'll excuse me, I need to consult with my deputy, the marshal, and the judge." He closed the door in the saloonkeeper's face.

But, Deans wasn't to be deterred long, he pushed on the door and opened it right behind Wade. "Well, I want to talk to them too." He stepped into the room, scrutinized the two visitors and asked, "Which one of you is the judge?"

"I am." Judge Tucker sat up straight in Wade's chair.

Deans crossed to him. "Something needs to be done, judge, right now! I've been patient with the sheriff, but it's time we found the prisoners. You're here they're gone. We need to get them tried, this situation taken care of once and for all."

"And who are you, Sir?" Judge Tucker looked over his spectacles at the irate man.

"I'm Delbert Deans, owner of the establishment across the street. As long as those prisoners are on the loose, I won't have the business I usually do. Besides that, I had a lot of money invested in that bank. I want the person who took it prosecuted to the fullest extent of the law."

"We'll take care of it Mr. Deans." Judge Tucker stood and sauntered across the room to Wade.

"What to you plan to do, Sheriff Denton?"

"It's almost noon, Judge. I plan to stake out the bank."

"But why?" A puzzled expression crossed his face.

"I have reason to believe Oldham will not leave town without visiting there."

"Isn't that preposterous, Judge?" Deans had stepped between the two men. "While they're hiding up in the mountains or skirting across the desert, Denton is staking out the empty bank, just in case Oldham returns. *For what?* He took our money and this sheriff doesn't have any intentions of getting it back for us."

Wade looked at the Judge, but by the question on his face, knew he was listening to Deans.

"He's just concerned about the bank because his wife lives there now. He's not wanting anything to happen to her."

Wade felt his face flush. *Damn, that man! Leave it to him, to put me in a pinch.*

"Is that right, Sheriff?" The Judge's gaze met Wade's levelly.

"Yes, Amanda is trying to open a new bank. Money came this morning to finance it. If we go out of town looking for the criminals, that will leave her without protection."

"I don't think Oldham is going to try to rob the bank in the middle of the day. He'd know we're looking for him." Dean's beady gaze met Wade's again.

"Do you have someone who could watch the bank? We might split up and ride out a little ways. Since there's no evidence here, we might pick up some sign outside of town. If we don't, we'll know for sure that they're still here." Marshal Nance had joined the conversation.

Wade knew when he'd been outnumbered. "I could get Walt Brauns to watch the bank. I don't expect these men are unarmed."

"I'll stay at the hotel, and watch the back of the bank," the Judge volunteered. "Nance and your deputy can ride one way, you and Mr. Deans the other. As soon as you decide whether or not they've ridden away, you can return. The days are short, but you should be able to decide by dark and be back here in time to surround the bank for the night."

Overpowered, Wade relented.   Judge Tucker held more authority in the territory than he, but he still didn't like the idea of leaving town, even for a moment, but Deans had made it almost impossible not to.

"I'll have some lunch and talk to Brauns. We'll leave at one. If you're riding with me, Deans, you'd better put on some riding clothes and have a good mount." Wade strode out and to the hotel. The street was quiet, too quiet for his liking.

Eighteen

Amanda hammered the last nail into the railing forming a small separation between the front of the bank and the teller's box. Since Wade had put the box back where it had originally been, she decided she might as well put the railing in place. The work also gave her something to do in her confinement.

He had brought her a bowl of beans for lunch and told her he and Harvey were each taking a small posse in opposite directions out of town to see if they could find any hoof prints the escaped prisoners might have made. He'd told her he would be back by dark and again cautioned her not to open the door to anyone but him.

She set the hammer down and examined her work. The railing was still too close to the front, but until they got this thing settled, it would have to do. Someone knocked at the front.

Walking through the tiny door in the railing, Amanda stepped to the window. Normally, people had been coming to the back. Looking outside, she saw Boyce Stewart standing there. He wore his black bowler and suit-coat. "What do you want?"

"I have your pay. I told you I'd bring it later today." He glanced north down the street, then south.

Did Wade's warning include Stewart too? She didn't think so - he owed her money. Stepping forward, she pushed the bolt lock back and opened the door.

Stewart stared at her then again glanced each way down the street. "May I come in, Mrs. Denton. I really don't like flashing money around, as you should know."

"I don't think so, Mr. Stewart."

"Then, I'll just have to hold it for another time." He turned and started to walk away.

Amanda gazed out onto the street. Two of Del Dean's girls sat on the saloon porch. Otherwise, the street was empty. "Oh, come on in, Mr. Stewart. I guess it's time we got this taken care of." She opened the door wider, then he stepped inside. Closing it behind him, she didn't relock it. He wouldn't be inside long enough to bother. She stepped to the teller's box.

He held an envelope toward her. "Count it, I want to be sure we're in agreement that it's all here."

"Mr. Stewart, you never shorted me on my wages before. Why should I suspect you now?" She opened the envelope, took the money out, and began to count.

The front door burst open.

"Stand back," Maurice Oldham ordered. He pushed the shotgun he carried into her ribs. Two more men rushed in behind him and the door closed again.

"That worked perfectly, Oldham, just like I told you it would." Placing his hands on his lapels Stewart stepped back to make room in the narrow space for the three men. No doubt he was the man who had broken them out of jail.

"What's happening?" Amanda asked, although obviously, her words were a waste. Fear rippled through her and the magnitude of what she'd done by not following Wade's instructions hit her – she was in grave danger.

"I guess you could call it the skunks under my floor," Stewart laughed.

The men looked ferocious. Dingy snarled showing his ugly jagged teeth, the little Mexican relocked the door, and Oldham scrutinized the room as if to familiarize himself.

"As I remember it," Oldham stepped a little closer to Amanda and stared down at her. "I heard you talking to the sheriff one night after you had captured us. You told him you thought the money might still be in town." He chuckled, his beady eyes sparked into hers. "Well, you were right. I've finally come to get what's mine."

"But the safe...?"

"Yeah," he laughed. "That safe isn't worth the metal in it. I'd never put anything there. Push that teller's box over, boys, there's a gold mine under that floor."

"Why'd you hide it there?" Amanda asked.

Maurice glanced at Stewart, then back at her. "A bit bulky for a quick escape. I figured a time would come when I'd return. It has."

His lips lifted in a snaggle-toothed grin and he turned away from her.

Oldham and Stewart stepped back as Jose and Dingy worked with the teller's box, first taking the hammer and knocking away Amanda's fresh construction. After it was removed, they began to push on the box. They grunted and pushed, but it didn't budge. After three tries, the two men stopped and looked at Oldham. "We can't do this by ourselves. Help us, Boss."

"Can't," Oldham said. "I've got to keep my gun on her. She's crafty, you know that."

"I'll help them." Stewart stepped away from the window where he glanced out occasionally. Together the three men pushed the platform. After several shoves, it fell over, much as it had when Amanda and Wade had moved it.

"Now what?" Jose asked.

"Now," Oldham moved away from Amanda and the window. "We take this piece of wood out and remove the money box." He handed the shotgun to Dingy. "Keep this on her. If she makes a move of any kind, let her have it."

"Be delighted to," the near rapist sneered.

Oldham worked with the loose piece of wood and finally removed it. "Now, for the fun part." He wedged himself into the hole. Since being arrested, he'd gained some weight and was thicker than Amanda, but not nearly as big as Wade.

"Can you see anything?" Stewart bent anxiously over the opening.

"I know where I put it, Stewart. Don't think I'm an idiot." Oldham glared at the storekeeper and slid to the ground.

Hostility between the two men permeated the building.

"I didn't mean a thing," Stewart said. "I just thought a light might be helpful."

"Just keep watchin' the street and leave retrievin' the money to me, Stewart." Oldham slid down further, much as Amanda had done, then he disappeared.

For a few minutes, everything was quiet, then Oldham reappeared. He stood and smiled. "It's here. Almost like I left it. The wooden box has fallen apart, but that's why I didn't put money in it. Step away boys, I'm comin' up."

Jose and Dingy moved back from the hole.

"Ouch!" Oldham screamed, looking toward his right leg.

"What's the matter?" Jose stepped closer, ready to help.

"Somethin' bit me." Oldham climbed out and pulled at his trouser leg.

A chill ran through Amanda.

"What was it?" Dingy moved closer and peered into the darkness, then he quickly turned away and grabbed the wood that had covered the opening. "The biggest damn rattler I ever did see." Fear filled his ugly eyes as he slammed the board across the hole.

"How bad is it?" Stewart stepped away from the window.

"It's on my leg." Oldham pulled up his trousers.

Amanda saw two tiny bloody holes about two inches apart.

"A big one." Dingy examined the wound, but kept his distance from the injured man.

"Sweet Mary, Mother of Jesus." Jose crossed himself and moved away. His skin had turned an unnatural ashen and sweat popped out on his forehead.

"Well, I want that money." Stewart stepped to the hole and started to reopen it.

"Is there a doctor here?" Oldham moaned. "What about Abe Martin? I'll bet he knows what to do. I've heard of people livin' but I've got to be bled." Perspiration had formed on his upper lip, and panic filled his blue eyes.

Stewart removed the piece of flooring. "You should've thought of that before you got so smart, Oldham. I offered to shine something into the darkness. Someone watch the street and keep your eye on her. We don't want anyone interrupting us. I may have to shoot that snake."

Dingy pushed the gun into Amanda's ribs again.

Stewart knelt on the floor and lowered the lantern he'd lit, taking his time to examine it thoroughly. "Don't see a thing," he reported. Quickly, he bent and tried to pick up the box, then let it fall back. "One of you's got to help me. It's too heavy."

"Not me." Jose stepped away further.

"You watch the street and keep her covered. I'm not afraid of a snake." Dingy handed Jose the gun then moved to the opposite side of Stewart. Together, the two men pulled the box into the room.

"Sure is heavy." Glee filled Stewart's normally unemotional dark features.

"Let's open it now." Dingy still held onto the treasure.

"Can't!" Stewart continued to hold his side. "We need to get out of here before someone finds Brauns in the stable."

"What about me?" Oldham had tied a neckerchief around his leg, just below the knee. "Half or more of the money is mine."

"We'll divide it with ya." Stewart motioned for Dingy to set the box down. "Go get the horses, Jose, and be sure you keep them between us and the stable. I don't want that judge sittin' on the hotel porch seein' us."

"Yes sir." Jose darted out the front door.

"What're ya goin' to do with her?" Dingy had again taken possession of the shotgun.

"She's comin' with us." Stewart grabbed her arm and jerked Amanda toward the door.

Wade turned his horse back toward Mineral Wells. He and Deans had ridden more than five miles north of town and covered the area between the mountains thoroughly. They hadn't found any fresh tracks, at least anything indicating the three prisoners and their accomplice could make them. He'd had enough. "I'm going to town whether you want to or not." He spurred his horse.

"I guess we might as well. I can't understand why we didn't find anything though." Deans turned his horse and rode up beside Wade.

"Because, they didn't come here, Deans. Can't you get that through your head? They're still in town. I'll believe it until it's been proved differently." Wade slapped the reins against the horse's shoulders and rode away. He hadn't been comfortable for one minute since he'd ridden out of town, and he wouldn't until he saw Amanda again.

The sun had begun to dip. The little valley would be dark soon. He rode past the stream where Amanda had nearly been raped without slowing. At the edge of town, he did slow enough to let his horse start to cool. As soon as he got to the stable, he intended to take the animal to Walt Brauns, get him a good rubdown and regular meal, just in case he was needed later.

He stopped and surveyed Mineral Wells from the distance. It looked the same as earlier except shadows lay long across the hotel. A wisp of smoke floated gracefully from the chimney and the chilled autumn air ruffled his Stetson. Gladys would be cooking supper, people would be settling in for the evening. He walked the horse to cool him and to not be noticed as the sound of laughter floated from the saloon. Everything seemed the same. Maybe he'd been worrying about nothing.

He rode up in front of the livery stable and dismounted. Glancing at the bank, he noted Amanda hadn't lit the lantern. The glass window paned front was dark. He'd talk to her as soon as he saw Brauns. Maybe she'd trust him enough to watch over the money while she went for supper.

Deans rode past him. "See you later, Sheriff. When are you going to check with your deputy and the marshal?"

"As soon as I take care of my horse." Wade gave the man an angry scowl. "I don't tell you how to operate your saloon. It's time you quit trying to tell me how to run my jail."

Deans paused, and stared down at him. "I will, as soon as my money has been returned."

Wade turned away from the angry man and strolled into the stable. "Walt!"

Silence.

He tied the horse to one of the stall doors then started to leave. Walt had said he'd keep an eye on the bank. Where was he? Maybe he'd gone to his house behind the stable. Wade started to walk out the back door then he heard a grunt in the corner near the front.

"Walt?"

This time, Wade heard a thud. Pulling his gun, he walked toward the sound coming from the furthest corner of the barn. Walt had wiggled his way from beneath a straw pile.

"Walt?" Wade slid his gun into the holster and brushed straw away from the stable owner.

Tied much like Harvey had been earlier in the day, Brauns, looked dusty and dirty as if he'd been there awhile. He rolled over and stared up at Wade as he freed his hands and removed the bandana.

"Am I ever glad to see you." Walt gasped. "I was beginning to think no one would ever come. I didn't know how long an afternoon can be." He sat up.

Wade offered his hand. "What happened?"

"I'm not exactly sure. I was cleanin' in the front door, just to look busy while I watched the bank. All of a sudden, I woke up, all tied just like you found me." He rubbed the back of his neck. "Sure got a bump on my head."

"Who did it?"

"Don't know. Didn't see or hear a thing."

"I'd better check on Amanda. Do you know when it happened?" Wade turned to walk away.

"Must've been early. I've been awake for awhile."

Wade stepped in the doorway and looked across the street at the bank. Gray darkness lay heavy across the valley, but no light shone in the window. Apprehension filled him. "Feed this horse, Walt, and saddle my other one. I may need him."

"Sure thing, Sheriff." Walt rubbed the back of his head. "And, I'm sorry about not watchin' the bank for you. I didn't think there would be any harm in workin' here for a few minutes. I guess I was wrong."

"Whoever is doing this has it well planned." Wade strode out the door and across the street. Strolling around the building, he knocked on the back door.

No answer.

He knocked again.

Still no answer.

He pushed. The door was locked from the inside. He pushed harder.

"What's the matter, Sheriff?" Judge Tucker had crossed the street.

"Somebody hit Walt Brauns over the head and tied him up. I was just checking to see that Amanda is all right. She's not answering."

"Did you try the front door?"

"No, I always come in the back."

Together, they walked around. Wade pushed on the door that fell open easily. Looking inside, he saw the teller box lying in the floor and turned back to the judge. "Did you see anything this afternoon?"

"A few miners rode into town from the south. They stopped at the saloon. The preacher came back. Otherwise nothing." He rubbed his neck an apologetic expression on his face. "I'm sorry, Sheriff. I did the best I could. Maybe I should have patrolled the area."

"Are you sure you didn't see anything else?"

He thought for a moment. "Well, I did see that storekeeper 'bout mid-afternoon, he took all his shovels, buckets and things inside, then put the closed sign out. I didn't think it unusual figured a man who owns his business can close anytime he wants. He went to the stable, and I never saw him again."

* * *

Amanda was exhausted. It had been a long, slow trip since they had ridden out the back of the livery stable and started to climb in the rough shale rocks. The sun had set hours ago and she was cold.

"Can't we stop?" Oldham moaned from beside her.

"We've got to get as far away from Mineral Wells as we can before morning." Stewart stopped and viewed his partner critically.

"I'm very sick, Stewart," Oldham gasped. "I need a doctor bad."

"Well, ain't that too bad." The storekeeper's laugh interrupted the tranquil night air eerily, then quickly subsided as the musical hum of ponderosa pines returned, making Amanda feel confident she would survive this trek in spite of their constant threats.

The cool pine scent which normally made her feel refreshed and alive tonight only made her colder, but she tried not to think of it, concentrating instead on chances to escape if one came. Progress had been slow but in the illumination of a full moon she saw that instead of the mountains being behind them, they now rode atop the hills. Stewart had led the tiny party of escapees and his one captive to a canyon leading to a hard to see natural trail in the cliffs behind the livery and his store.

"Why don't we just split the money now?" Oldham teetered in his saddle. Without medical attention, he couldn't possibly last long.

Amanda felt some sadness for this, but tried to be philosophical about it. If he hadn't been trying to steal money that didn't belong to him, he wouldn't be in this kind of situation.

"I can take my money and go back to Mineral Wells. I'm ready to face whatever punishment they give me. I just want to live." Oldham slumped forward and fell silent.

"No!" Stewart seemed oblivious to the other man's need.

Amanda had known him to be a cold man, but she'd never thought of him as cruel until now.

"I'd like my money too," Jose offered, his voice sounding tentative and frightened.

"Me too," Dingy joined in. "After all, I've got a marshal lookin' for me." The men had formed a circle around Stewart on their horses.

"'Pears to me the only one who has nothing to lose in this is you, Stewart." Dingy pulled his gun and leveled it on the storekeeper. "No one knows you helped us escape. Oldham probably ain't goin' to make it. A bullet apiece could take care of the rest of us, wouldn't it?"

Boyce squirmed in his saddle.

Although she couldn't see his face clearly, he appeared to be rethinking his position in the situation and she hoped he decide to stop for awhile. Maybe they'd at least free her feet. They'd been tied to the stirrups as her wrists had been to the saddle-horn.

"Now, I have no intentions of anything like that." He toyed with his pipe. Amanda had seen the gesture before and knew he was nervous. "If you'll just put that thing down, I'll prove it. I'll open this box and see what's in it. We'll split here and now. I don't see any reason for keepin' company with the likes of you anyway. As you say, I'm a respected businessman."

Dingy lowered the gun and Stewart swung off his horse. Jose dismounted, then grabbed Pepper's reins and tied her to a nearby tree.

"Help me down, someone," Oldham groaned.

"Leave him be," Stewart ordered. "He ain't goin' to last long enough to split with us anyway." He untied the box that he'd secured to an extra horse. "What is this?"

"What?" the three men chorused.

"The lock's open." He stripped the remaining ropes and lifted it to the ground.

Dingy lit the lantern and held it so they could get a better view of the contents. "Open it," he insisted, "let's see what we've got."

Stewart pulled the lock from hasp then let the lid drop open. "Move that light closer."

Dingy stepped forward and held the lantern above the box.

"What's this?" Stewart roared, as he bent over and dipped his hand into the sandy contents. "Sand!" The grains drizzled through his fingers. He dug deeper and came out with the stone Wade had used to crack the padlock. Throwing it back inside, he slowly rose, and turned to Oldham who still sat on his horse. Reaching up, Stewart grabbed the sick man's shirt and pulled him down.

He fell to the ground with a thud.

Stewart bent over him, shaking him. "You did it, didn't you? Where's the money?"

"I don't know," Oldham groaned, took a deep breath, and stretched out lengthwise.

"We've got to help him," Stewart cried. "He's the only one who knows where the money is. Bleed him, Dingy."

"I've told you all I know," Oldham groaned, rolling into a fetal position. "Don't touch me. I saw what you did to Bernard. I don't want that done to me."

"Bernard?" Dingy looked at Stewart.

"The hotel owner, over a gambling debt." Oldham writhed on the ground. "Poured liquor down him until he couldn't walk, then whacked him in the back of the head where no one could see it. I'd rather die from snakebite."

"Bleed him!" Stewart ordered. "Saving his life is the only way we'll find where he hid the money."

"We'll have to let him heal some, even if I do bleed him." Dingy knelt beside the sick man, took a huge knife and cut the trouser leg from hem to knee.

"Don't have time. Have to keep him alive long enough to find the money."

Oldham screamed.

Amanda cringed. "I was a nurse during the war, maybe I can help him."

"Why didn't you say so sooner?" Stewart demanded.

"You didn't ask, and we're hardly friends." Her hands felt numb, her legs weak, and training from long ago told her there was little she could do, but she had to try if they'd let her.

"Untie her, Jose."

The Mexican walked over and quickly removed the restraints around her feet first, then her hands.

Rubbing her hands and shaking her legs, Amanda slipped to the ground, relieved to be out of the saddle for awhile. She walked to where Maurice lay. Even in the moonlight she saw the leg was swollen beyond normal size and the poison had plenty of time to fill his body.

"What can you do?" Stewart stepped over her.

"Not much, maybe amputate, but I've never done that before. I'm not a doctor, I'm a nurse."

"Is he going to live?" Stewart stood over her, staring anxiously at the sick man.

"I really don't know. I didn't say I could cure him. I just hoped I could make him more comfortable." She felt of Maurice's forehead. It was hot with a temperature.

Stewart pushed her away. Standing over Oldham, he glared down him. "Tell me where it is!"

"I don't know," Oldham moaned. "Do you think I'd have chanced getting snake bit if I'd known the money wasn't there?"

Stewart thought about that statement for a moment, then he turned toward Amanda. "Maybe he's telling the truth." He grabbed her hair, pulled her roughly and made her stand. "The lock was open. Maybe you found the money and have it."

Amanda didn't flinch. Fear gripped her, but she had no intentions of admitting to anything especially to Stewart.

"That's it, isn't it, woman?" He snarled close to her face. His hot breath singed her cheek, repulsion filled her and her head hurt from him pulling her hair, but she didn't whimper. He'd have to do more than that to get her to talk.

"Talk to me, woman!" he demanded again.

She didn't budge.

"That shows it's true." Dingy stepped up.

In the brush, Amanda heard a rustle.

"What's that?" Stewart turned away from her long enough to look behind himself.

The sound of hooves riding away echoed against rocks.

"Come back here, Jose!" Stewart ordered.

"Didn't get in this to attack women." The Mexican's voice got fainter as he rode away.

"What're we goin' to do, Mr. Storekeeper?" Dingy asked.

"We're goin' back to town. I'm sure she's got the money hidden somewhere."

"But the marshal is there...and the sheriff."

"All the better. The sheriff ain't a goin' to let anything happen to her. She's his wife."

"But they was forced to marry."

"At the time, they were, but anyone can see by the way he looks at her, he's in love with her. I'd say we've got ourselves insurance as long as we got her."

"Insurance?"

"Oh, forget it, Dingy. Just get her on that horse. I want to get back to town about dawn. Catch that sheriff unaware. He'll do anything to protect her."

Amanda couldn't believe her ears. Was what he said about Wade true? Did he love her? Would he do anything to protect her? He'd said they'd talk. Was that what he meant?

Dingy hustled her over to Pepper and boosted her up. "I might get my chance with you yet," he laughed near her right ear.

A shiver ran through her.

"What we goin' to do 'bout him?" Dingy pointed to Oldham who lay silently on the cold ground.

"Take his horse and leave him. Probably won't last 'til morning."

Oldham groaned.

Stewart kicked him in the ribs then mounted his own horse.

"Now ride, Dingy!" he ordered. "We don't have much time and it's a steep trip down.

The night had been long for Wade. By the time he discovered Amanda missing it'd been too late to try to track the kidnappers. Wandering off in the darkness, even with the aid of lanterns, could have covered valuable tracks that might be the only clue he got. While he'd waited, he had shot the sidewinder he'd found curled up in the teller's box, assured himself the money was still safe and tried to get some sleep. He and Marshal Nance had taken turns watching the bank and although Wade couldn't sleep he'd forced himself to rest realizing he needed all of his strength and brain power to track the fugitives.

Although it was still more than an hour till daylight, he had already eaten and saddled his horse. As soon as the first sign of daybreak came, he'd be off. He had moved all the money to the hotel and Gladys had prepared breakfast as well as extra food for the trail. Walt Brauns told him of another way out of the valley, a tiny canyon behind the stable and general store. Wade tried to find Stewart and discovered him missing, so he was fairly convinced Amanda had been right, the storekeeper was involved with the missing money all along.

To be sure the town was covered, Wade stationed Harvey Griggs at the south edge, Marshal Nance at the north and Judge Tucker at the hotel to look out for the money. He'd tried to put aside his feelings for Amanda and think of her only as a kidnap victim, but he hadn't succeeded. Memories of her kept flashing back, how she'd looked in his buckskin shirt, her blond hair with sunlight shining on it, her smile.

He loved her and he'd waited way too long to tell her. She was his wife in all ways and it was time he let her know. Whether she loved him or not, he didn't know. At this point, it didn't matter. It was too late for any resolves he'd ever had about getting involved with a woman to mean anything.

She wasn't anything like Sarah Jean Sturdyvent, and his feelings for her were completely different too. Sarah Jean had hurt his pride. If something happened to Amanda, his heart would be broken irreparably.

He mounted and rode to the edge of the stable, then directly behind the general store turned toward the mountains. Stopping long enough to light a lantern, he bent low to look for tracks. Seeing none, he moved toward the canyon anyway, not letting himself think that he might already be too late. In this loose shale, tracks of any kind would be hard to see. He'd just have to trust that since Stewart knew of this way from town, this was the way they'd gone. Carefully, he urged his horse up the narrow canyon.

"I'm hungry," Dingy grumbled again.

They'd been riding all night and Amanda was hungry too, tired and chilled to her very core, but she hadn't given up. In fact, she'd regained courage as with every step, they drew nearer to Mineral Wells and help.

"We're almost to the top of the canyon," Stewart said. "I've hardtack and jerky in my saddlebags. We'll stop and eat there, let our horses' rest some. That climb down is rough."

"You could've come in from the north. It would've been easier." Dingy had said this before too.

"The sheriff will be covering that direction and the south too. It's doubtful he knows this way into town. He's only been there a few months and the canyon isn't easy to see."

"I don't care, just as long as I get some food. Are you sure there's still money, Stewart?"

"Oldham said there was. I expect Mrs. Denton knows where it is. She's just not willin' to tell."

They had reached a ledge.

"This is it," Stewart said.

"What?" Dingy stopped his horse near the edge.

"Where we rest. We've probably got an hour or so before daylight. As soon as the sun starts to come up, we'll start down since darkness stays in the valley longer than it does here."

Dingy pulled Amanda roughly from Pepper.

The horse whinnied.

Amanda wanted to comfort the animal, but Dingy jerked on her arm and forced her to walk to a small clump of bushes.

"Check for snakes," Stewart ordered. "At the moment, she's worth something to us. One person snake bit is enough."

Dingy kicked the bushes then tied her to a tree. After he'd secured her, he walked to his own horse and tethered it loosely in the tall grass. She wished they'd do the same for Pepper, but neither man did.

"Here," Stewart walked over and dropped a piece of hardtack and one of jerky in her lap.

"How do you expect me to eat that?" She nodded toward her hands, tied behind her back.

"Feed her, Dingy." Stewart laughed. "She should love that."

Nineteen

Amanda fought to stay awake. She'd eaten the hardtack and jerky Dingy had poked into her mouth. It was tasteless and dry and he hadn't bothered to give her anything to drink, but it had soothed her growling stomach enough that her body wanted to rest, even though she didn't.

Dingy snored, leaned against a nearby tree. Only Stewart seemed to have an access of energy. He had been working with his saddle and the gear on the packhorse for the last ten minutes. He turned and glanced at the other man. "Wake up!"

Jumping awake, Dingy sat and rubbed his eyes. "You don't have to yell at me, Stewart." He stood and walked to the storekeeper. "If you don't treat me good, I might run out on you like that little Mexican did."

Stewart stopped working with the buckle and turned to him. "Don't try to fool me. I know you've got a reason for goin' back just the same as I do, and that's money. Course you're chancin' the marshal catchin' ya, but you figure if you can't get the money Oldham said is there, I've got some stashed."

Rising to his feet, Dingy walked to the storekeeper and watched him. "I figure the two of us against three, maybe four of them. We've got a good chance if we can pick them off one at a time, but it takes money to get anywhere."

Stewart walked away from the horses.

"I could leave right now." Dingy had followed Boyce as he stepped closer to Amanda.

"But you won't." Stewart turned back to him. "If anything happened to me, that money would be yours, and you know it."

Dingy didn't nod or acknowledge his statement.

"Now, I think it's time to go. Untie her." Stewart pointed toward Amanda. "Tie a bandanna around her mouth, too. We don't want to chance lettin' her give us away."

Untying the filthy scarf he wore around his neck, Dingy walked to Amanda. He wrapped it across her mouth and secured it behind her neck, then he loosened her from the tree.

"Help her on the horse, Dingy," Stewart ordered. "We're burnin' daylight."

The trail was narrow and rough and nearly impossible to pick out hoof-prints but Wade led his horse up it anyway. This had to be the canyon Walt Brauns had told him about. At the mouth of it, Wade detected faint prints, but he hadn't been able to determine whether they were from horses a deer or some other animal. Even though this trail was steep and he couldn't make any time it was more hidden than any other and therefore the most likely escape route.

He held the lantern close to the ground as the horse worked its way upward. Overhead, the sky started to lighten, but even with the lantern, the nearly dark canyon made riding treacherous. Any other time, he'd have waited for full daylight before climbing a trail like this, but waiting might mean Amanda's life. He wasn't willing to chance that.

"How far is it down?" Dingy asked.

"Only a couple of miles, but this loose shale makes it take awhile."

"I think we should've come in from the north."

"You know what I said, now keep ridin'." Stewart led the small caravan down the mountainside.

Amanda feared that Pepper would lose her footing and they'd be thrown over the side of the mountain. Coming up the trail had been treacherous, going down was even more so especially when she wasn't allowed to hold the horse's reins. She leaned back as far as she could and held her feet as far forward as being tied to the stirrups would allow.

Stewart stopped abruptly. Pepper slid on the rocks, trying to keep from running into the storekeeper's horse. Amanda gripped the back of the saddle to keep upright and tried to relax for a moment.

"What's the matter, Stewart? Why'd ya stop?" Dingy, his horse, the packhorse and Oldham's mount were close behind her.

"I thought I heard something."

Daylight slowly illuminated the sky, a bright rose color seeping over the mountaintop announcing a new day, soon it was replaced by a radiant iridescent yellow then cloudless azure. Any other day, she would have enjoyed the shear brilliance of new awakening, but Amanda was too tired and too frightened to give it more than an uninterested glance. To their right several boulders protruded from the mountainside, but not enough to hide three riders and five horses.

"Maybe it's the sheriff." Dingy had slowly worked his way up beside Amanda.

"If we can move to those rocks," Stewart pointed to a small plateau about twenty yards in front of them. "We should be able to see anyone coming up the trail."

"Sounds like you've done this before, Mr. Storekeep." Dingy chuckled under his breath.

"It's no concern of yours what I've done." Stewart scowled and urged his horse forward.

It took several minutes to go the few feet to the ledge as Stewart stopped three times to listen. Amanda didn't hear a thing, but by the way he shook his head she could tell he wasn't happy about their situation. "Tie those horses and take her off this one." He slid from his saddle and tied his horse to a scrub pine. "Someone's definitely coming and I don't want them to see her."

Dingy tied his horse and the two he led to an outcropping, then walked up to Amanda, roughly pulling her to the ground. Pushing her ahead of him, he tied her behind a rock fastening her hands to her feet. She couldn't see anyone and they wouldn't see her. At this point, she hadn't seen or heard a thing, but obviously Stewart thought there was a threat of some kind.

"Climb up over there." Stewart pointed to a rock above the trail.

Dingy followed his instructions. "If it's anyone other than the sheriff, shoot 'em. If it's him, I want him alive. We might need him later."

A shiver ran through Amanda at his words. She had to try to help Wade, if she could. She began to work trying to loosen the ropes holding her wrists and feet together.

* * *

Wade blew the lantern out and set it alongside the trail. Daylight illuminated the path enough he could now see where he was going. The shale shifted beneath his huge bay horse. He couldn't actually see hoofprints in the shale, but the periodic interruptions could be places where horses' feet had moved the rocks.

Examining the trail ahead, he urged his horse onward. On the left, he saw a plateau. Maybe they'd rest there for a few minutes. Possibly he could get a look at what was ahead.

The bay whickered.

Wade patted his neck. The animal obviously wasn't used to this kind of climb and didn't like such unsure footing. He glanced at the horse's ears that were laid back indicating he didn't like their situation. Forcing the bay to keep walking, Wade scrutinized the area. Perfect place for an ambush. Stopping, he listened. All was quiet. Slowly they moved on.

Wade hoped this ride was fruitful. He hated to think he might be on the wrong trail. He wouldn't let himself think of Amanda, what could happen to her. The horse climbed slowly on, snorting occasionally. When they reached the edge of a plateau, Wade turned toward it and continued to examine the ground.

Fresh hoof prints.

He heard a noise behind him, then his horse reared. Wade held tight to the reins, threw his weight forward over the bay's withers to help the animal to retain his balance, but to no avail. The horse bucked and Wade fell off. Then the animal came down on Wade's right leg.

Excruciating pain ripped through his limb as the animal writhed in the loose shale trying to regain his balance. Wade tried to move away, but the frightened horse had him pressed into the mountain. His head hit something and he lost consciousness.

Helplessly, Amanda watched, in horror as Wade's horse ground him into the rocks. Pain ripped through her renewing the memory of him being shot weeks before. Then Stewart stepped over the stunned sheriff and brought the butt of his six-shooter soundly down against the back of Wade's head. He crumpled and fell silently against the rocks.

"Grab the horse!" Stewart ordered.

Dingy jumped from the rock where Stewart had stationed him to the huge bay. He had thrown the rock that caused Wade's horse to spook.

"Did you kill him?" Dingy asked, grabbing the reins. "Whoo!" He jerked the reins and forced the horse's head around. The animal tried to rear again and fought to bite Dingy's hand, but couldn't reach him.

"Naw, just knocked him out. Thought I'd put him outa his misery for awhile." Stewart slid his six shooter back into the holster. "I imagine that leg smarts. He'll be more cooperative when he wakes up."

"What're we goin' to do with him?" Dingy had joined him, standing over Wade, still holding his horse's reins.

"Well, since he so conveniently rode up to us, I think we could all use some rest. We'll take the remainder of this trail just before dark. Sheriff's probably got a broken leg. That can only help us. Tie him don't want to chance him gettin' away. We want him awake when we ride into town."

Amanda fought to remove the filthy rag from her mouth, but couldn't. Wade groaned as Dingy moved him away from the rocks and tied him a few feet away from her. His right leg flopped at a crazy angle. At least, he was alive. She leaned against the rocks and closed her eyes. Fatigue took over. She drifted off to sleep.

The trail was even steeper than it seemed going up. They had tied him to the saddle with his hands behind him, although he couldn't understand why. He wasn't a threat to anyone in his current condition. Even his shoulder hadn't hurt as much as his leg did, and when he tried to make it do what he wanted, it wouldn't.

Stewart tied a bandana around Wade's mouth like the one on Amanda. There was no chance of either of them escaping. He couldn't walk, had barely been able to throw his injured leg across his horse's back. Excruciating pain ripped through his head where someone had hit him, but his real concern was for Amanda.

He tried not to watch her. Every step Pepper took sent a shiver of fear through him. How she'd been able to stay on the horse, he hadn't been able to figure out. A new admiration for her filled him. He wondered if he would ever have an opportunity to tell her. At the moment, talking to her seemed to be the only important thought he had. He would do everything he could to see she was not harmed.

The sun had slipped behind the cliffs on the opposite side of the little valley when Mineral Wells came into view. What little Wade could see of the street was empty. They were approximately a hundred yards up and behind the general store, still in the tiny hidden canyon.

Stewart stopped riding and turned toward them. He leveled his shotgun on Wade, but spoke to Amanda. "All right, Mrs. Denton. I've been patient. Now where's the money that was under the bank floor?" He kept the gun on Wade but rode back to her. Bending over long enough to slip a sharp knife from his boot, he leaned toward her, slit the bandana and growled, "You'll tell me, or I'll shoot your husband."

Amanda turned and looked at Wade.

The hammer on the gun clicked. Obviously, Stewart meant business.

If the storekeeper shot him, would Amanda be safe? Wade doubted it. Vigorously, he shook his head, no.

Her gaze locked with his. His heart went out to her. In her eyes, he saw the love and yearning that had tugged at his own heart for weeks. He continued to shake his head no hoping to convince her not to tell their captor where the money was.

"Now, Mrs. Denton." Stewart raised the gun and pointed it at Wade's heart.

"It's in the bank safe."

"Oldham said the vault wasn't secure, wouldn't hold a combination"

"It won't, but it was the only place we had to put it. We knew Oldham wouldn't look there."

Stewart lowered the shotgun and slid it into the holster on the side of his saddle. "Tie them horses, Dingy."

Dingy tied the packhorse and Oldham's to a mesquite sprout jutting from the rocks.

"I want you to ride ahead and see that blacksmith is taken care of." Stewart handed Dingy the knife he'd used to cut the bandana from Amanda's face. "Know how to use this."

"Oh, yes." Dingy's eyes glowed with excitement.

"Stay behind the general store or the stable. They're probably lookin' for the sheriff by now, but they can't cover everything." Stewart pulled his six-shooter and aimed it at Amanda. "Just in case you get any notions about trying to ride away, Sheriff. It'll only take one bullet to fix her and I can hold the whole town off from here."

Wade nodded. Stewart was right. The cliff walls were so straight up anyone looking for him would have to come to the top of the mountain by the north or south to catch him. It was unlikely they'd find this particular canyon even then.

"Now, you two, get off your horses," Stewart ordered.

"We can't, our hands are tied, and Wade can't walk." Amanda sounded about as frightened as Wade had ever heard her and he wanted to assure her they'd make it, but couldn't even if he'd been free. He didn't think he'd ever felt so vulnerable before in his life.

"I'll show you how." Stewart slid from his saddle then walked to Amanda. Roughly, he pushed her to the rocky soil. "See, I told ya." He laughed.

Wade didn't wait for the same treatment. As easily as he could move his broken leg, he worked it across the saddle-horn and slid off the other side. When his weight hit the injured leg, pain sliced through him, but he pushed it aside. He didn't have time to think of that now. He had to save Amanda.

"The sheriff learns quickly." Stewart chuckled.

Wade wanted to knock the smirk off the man's face, but at the moment, he couldn't.

Amanda stood at the side watching and Wade was relieved to see she was relatively unharmed by her fall.

Stewart stuck the pistol in her ribs and said, "Now, walk. And don't get any ideas about yelling. I can kill both of you before anyone gets here."

Amanda walked from the little canyon into the dark valley still hoping she could do something to help herself and Wade. Dingy disappeared into the stable as a whiff of fried chicken drifted to her nostrils. They were close to help, but not quite close enough. Her stomach growled and she shivered. The evening air had begun to cool, but she knew the shudder had come from fear, not cold air.

"Follow Dingy," Stewart ordered, "and don't get any ideas about running. I've got my gun on your husband."

"I won't," Amanda replied, "but you don't need to think you're always going to be boss, Boyce. Your time's running out."

"Oh, that's what you think. As long as I've got you and the sheriff, I've nothing to worry about. That judge and marshal don't want a woman's blood on their hands."

Amanda crossed the distance between the canyon and the stable as slowly as she could to help Wade. He hadn't made a sound, but his pain must be intense. He leaned heavily on a wooden stick he'd picked up and dragged his injured leg behind him. She hoped Walt

Brauns could fight Dingy off, but she feared for the stable owner's life.

They had almost reached the door when Dingy reappeared. "Ain't here, Stewart. The blacksmith is missing and so are all the horses. Looks like the whole town is empty."

"What makes you say that?" Stewart pushed Amanda and Wade inside.

"I looked out front. Not a soul on the street."

"Well let's hope it remains that way while we visit the bank." Stewart hustled them through the stable.

Each step Wade took was an effort as he moved toward the bank.

"Help him!" Stewart motioned toward Wade.

Amanda wanted to help hold him up, but when she started to step toward Wade, Stewart pushed the gun into her ribs and said, "Not you – him."

Dingy stepped back. "Why would I want to do that? I don't owe him anythin'."

"Cause I said so." Stewart turned the gun toward his accomplice.

"I didn't mean anything by that." Dingy stepped up to Wade and slipped an arm around his middle. Wade leaned into him and seemed to walk a little taller although he still grimaced.

"It'd be better if we untied his hands, Stewart," Dingy grumbled. "I wasn't made to be a crutch."

"Quit your complainin'. We don't have long." Stewart pointed toward the stable front with his gun. Dingy passed them, pulling the sheriff against him.

"Now you." Stewart motioned with the six shooter to Amanda, then the door. "And don't do anything heroic. I'd hate to have to shoot a perty thing like you."

Amanda wondered how she'd ever thought she'd been wrong about him. He was everything she'd thought and more. She visualized Oldham lying up on the mountain, probably dead by now.

At the open stable door, Dingy stopped. Stewart stepped beside him, still holding the gun on Amanda. "Look outside."

Dingy pushed Wade away and took a couple of steps forward. He stopped and peered out. "Nothin'."

"Good, now get him across the street."

"Why don't we just leave them here? We know where the money is. A hurt man and a woman, they's a slowin' us down."

"I told you to quit tryin' to tell me what to do." Anger had risen in Stewart's face. "Who's running this operation."

"Yeah, I know. But I don't owe ya my life, Stewart." Dingy stepped up to the storekeeper seeming to have forgotten both Wade and Amanda for a moment. Anger and concern wrinkled his hairy brow. "I saw what you did to Oldam. How do I know you won't do to the same to me? After all, you just threatened me. I ain't one to take a threat lightly."

For a moment, Amanda thought the men were going to fight in the doorway of the stable.

"You ought to know me better than that by now, Dingy." Stewart stepped away. "The reason I pointed the gun at ya was to let ya know I meant business. I wouldn't harm ya. There's more than enough money for both of us. You've done a lot for me."

"Well, you jes' be sure you keep that in mind. Like I said before, I know how to use this pig sticker." Dingy held the knife Stewart had given him earlier in front of his grizzled face.

A shiver ran through Amanda. Was this ever going to end? Was the money she'd spent so much time looking for worth this? She didn't think so. She'd never intended for Wade to be hurt or Oldham to be killed. Mrs. Satterly, Opal Worthington, Mr. Baxter and none of the other depositors from Springfield would want that either. Her father certainly wouldn't want her to get this far even to fulfill Simon's obligation.

Stewart pushed the gun into Amanda's ribs again. "Now start walkin' toward the bank and don't stop until you get inside. We left the door open."

Amanda followed his command and stepped out into the street. As Dingy had said, it was empty. In the distance, someone played a piano. A bird chirped from the palo verde tree just outside the bank, that tired, late evening songbirds use just before settling for the night, otherwise the town was quiet.

"Push on the door," Stewart commanded, shoving Amanda forward.

She stepped up on the wooden porch and pushed. It didn't open. "It feels like it's locked."

"We left it open."

"That's far enough," a graveled voice, Amanda didn't recognize spoke from behind them.

Stewart pulled the hammer on his gun back and shoved the tip of it more firmly into Amanda's ribs. She tried to take a deep breath, but couldn't. "I don't know who you are, but if you want this pretty woman and the sheriff to live, you'll put that gun down," Stewart said, his voice sounded firm and determined. "My partner's got a pig sticker in the sheriff's ribs. He knows how to use it."

Amanda held her breath.

"Throw the guns on the ground," Stewart commanded.

The sound of metal hitting the wooden porch filled what had been silence a few moments before.

"Count the men and see if the guns are all there, then pick them up, Dingy." Stewart pushed the gun further into her ribs.

She couldn't see Dingy, but she heard the scuffle of his boots on the porch.

"Now, if you'll excuse us, gentlemen," Stewart said, "we'll just retrieve what belongs to us, then you can have your town."

He pushed on the door again. It didn't open. With the six-shooter, he broke a pane from the front window. "Reach inside and open the lock, Mrs. Denton. I'm gettin' anxious to be away from here."

Amanda did as she was told. Taking care not to cut herself, she stuck her hand through the broken window. It was a long reach to the wooden knob that held the door closed, but she stretched and finally it moved. The door swung open slowly.

"Inside!" Stewart pushed her in front of him, then stepped to the side, holding his gun on the other men as Wade and Dingy entered the building. He slammed the door behind them, then turned the lock.

Dingy laid the guns he'd collected in the floor, keeping one for himself.

Amanda heard voices outside, but no one else came in.

Stewart stepped behind her again.

Faint light filtered into the room.

"Light the lantern, Dingy," Stewart commanded.

Dingy walked to the rolled top desk and lit the lantern. The light flickered then filled the room.

"Now, Mrs. Denton, I've waited a long time. Open that safe. I want to see the money."

Amanda walked across the room. "I can't very well open it with my hands tied."

"Untie her, Dingy."

Dingy stepped up and cut the rope around her wrists.

She rubbed her hands together trying to restore circulation.

"Enough of that. Open the safe." Stewart pushed her to the huge metal safe.

"Most any combination works." She stepped forward.

"Then open it!"

She twirled the lock, moving it slowly to the numbers she'd always used. Stepping back after she'd stopped at each number, she pulled on the door. It didn't open. Turning slightly toward Stewart, she said, "It doesn't always work the first time."

He glared at her. "Open it, and quit playing games."

She glanced at Wade. He seemed to be telling her something with his eyes, but she couldn't understand what it was. She began to work the combination again. Again it didn't open.

"Let me try it." Stewart pushed her away and stepped up.

"What is the combination?"

"Twenty, three, fifteen, around three times counter clockwise then forty."

Stewart did exactly as she said, pulled on the door, and again the safe didn't open. "What is this?" He pointed the gun at her again. "I want in this safe, and I want in it now!"

Amanda looked at Wade again. His eyes seemed to be pleading with her to do something. She glanced from him to Stewart. "I think the sheriff needs to speak."

Outside, she heard voices, more than before. A crowd seemed to be forming.

"Take that rag off his mouth, Dingy." He seemed to be getting frustrated, beads of sweat had formed on his forehead and the hand holding the gun twitched nervously.

Dingy slipped the knife under the bandana tied around Wade's mouth and slit it away.

"I've been tryin' to tell you, Stewart, that the safe repairman came yesterday. It's been fixed."

"Who knows the combination?"

"Me."

"I don't believe you." Stewart aimed his pistol at Wade.

The men's gazes seemed to hang in the air.

"Well I guess you're going to have to believe someone. I'm the only one besides the safe repairman who knows the combination. I imagine he left for San Francisco after he finished. He was having a lot of trouble riding that burro and he said he hoped to get to Tucson in time to catch the next stage west."

"Take his ropes off, Dingy."

"But...?" The grizzly man stammered.

"I've had about all of that I'll take." Stewart lifted the gun toward him again. Slowly he pulled the trigger.

The man who had assaulted Amanda fell to the floor and didn't move.

The sound of voices outside got louder. "Who shot who?"

Amanda looked at Stewart, but neither of them answered.

"Now, unless you want her to be next, you'll open that safe." Stewart bent over Dingy and picked up the knife that had fallen from his lifeless hand. Straightening, he cut the ropes that held Wade's hands.

Dragging his injured leg, Wade stepped forward. Amanda glanced at Stewart, then back at the still form on the floor. Stewart continued to hold the gun, and the knife. He seemed to be watching her and Wade, but could he really be?

Wade worked with the combination.

Amanda watched Stewart.

He glared back at her.

The room was quite.

All she heard was the clicking of the combination as Wade worked with the lock. Outside, the crowd grew quite too. Stewart seemed to be getting more nervous with each passing moment.

Wade pulled on the lock. Slowly the safe opened.

"Step back a second. I want to see what's in there." Stewart moved forward just a step, turning his back to Amanda. At that moment, Wade turned on him with full force, hitting the man in the face. Amanda jumped on the storekeeper's back, and began to strike him. Both doors of the bank burst open.

The marshal, Judge Tucker, Del Deans, Walt Brauns and others Amanda didn't recognize rushed in. The gun fell from Stewart's hand. Amanda saw blood spurt from Wade's arm. The storekeeper had cut him, but Wade pounded a fist into Stewart's stomach anyway. He fell to the floor.

Twenty

Stewart groaned.

Wade straightened, gasped for breath, then toppled, coming to rest in the backroom doorway.

Amanda ran to him and quickly examined the cut on his arm.

It still bled profusely. She applied pressure and the bleeding slowed somewhat. The cut was obviously deep and she remembered seeing Union doctors sew wounds up with silk thread and a needle. To her knowledge, there were no such supplies in Mineral Wells. "Someone get Abe Martin!"

In the back of the room, she heard retreating footsteps.

"Oh, wouldn't it be too bad if the sheriff didn't make it." Someone had pulled Stewart to his feet. He gazed down at them. "I guess he'd just be another man I can add to my list." He laughed.

Walt Brauns laid a horse blanket he'd brought from the stable over Dingy's face.

"Yes, I think we have a great deal more than bank robbery to charge you with." Judge Tucker stepped toward the storekeeper. "Murder, I'd say and attempted murder of a peace officer, accomplice to theft, who knows what more."

"Well, I didn't kill Oldham," Stewart roared. "I might have if I'd ever been able to find the money. Couldn't imagine that anyone would hide it right where it was supposed to be." He laughed chilling irony filled the sound that was neither joyous nor sad, but resolved.

Marshal Nance started to lead him toward the front door. Stewart's gaze fell on Gladys. "Well, I guess you finally got what you wanted. Oldham was the only one who knew. I did feel a bit of fondness for that husband of yours. I couldn't really help what happened to him."

"What happened?" Gladys asked.

He stopped and stared down at her. "I guess I should tell ya. I'm dead meat anyway."

The room became silent.

Glancing around accusingly at the people standing in the little bank, he chortled again. "I took all of you and nobody noticed. Charged three times what my goods were worth. What the market would bear, right?" He laughed hilariously. "Had quite a nestegg. For weeks, me and Oldham and Bernard had been playin' poker game in the backroom of Deans' saloon. I kept gettin' in deeper and deeper. Did all right though, until Bernard started pushin'. He'd still be alive, if he hadn't kept naggin'. One night, he said he'd waited long enough. I had lost all the money and more, plus the store. Couldn't give it up though. I'd worked hard for all that."

"But Bernard let you work off what you owed for the store, why didn't you make a deal with him again?" Glady's words seemed to vibrate in the silent room.

"And go through all that act again?" Stewart laughed a sickening mirthless sound that sent a chill down Amanda's spine. "It was all an act. Did you really think I cared for you or Bernard?" He snarled. "I guess I fooled ya, just like I did Bernard that night, before I killed him. I'd had enough of bein' beholdin' to your old man. Enough of lookin' up to him like I appreciated what he did for me. I earned everythin' he gave me. I didn't intend on actin' like that son he never had again."

Amanda noticed a tear had formed in Gladys' blue eyes.

Stewart must have seen it too. He looked away. "Lock me up, Deputy." He stepped forward.

Harvey Griggs moved toward the door and took him by the arm as several more men congregated around them. There was no need for rope he didn't stand a chance of running away.

Abe Martin stepped in the doorway. "Somebody need stitched up?"

"Yes, the sheriff." Amanda released her hold on Wade's arm slightly. Blood welled up, but not as fast this time.

"Looks like I got a customer too." Abe stepped through the crowd, looking down at the body then to Wade.

"Which is worse, Sheriff, your arm or your leg?"

"He needs his arm stitched then his leg set," Amanda said.

"That's it." A week later Wade added the last bundle of bills to the stack on the rolled top desk. "Looks like what's left is yours and the depositors back in Springfield. How much did you say you owed them?" His gaze fell on Amanda.

For the first time since they'd captured Stewart, she felt terribly uncomfortable. "I don't believe I ever told you." Amanda felt herself warm with embarrassment.

The last time he'd asked that same question, she'd flatly told him she didn't trust him enough to tell him. Their circumstances had certainly changed since then. Although she still wasn't sure about their relationship, he had proved himself too many times for her to do anything but trust him now.

She told him the amount.

He opened the ledger they'd found in the money box and looked at the final entry. "Looks like Oldham almost broke even. I guess you can just add that to the money Jed sent you. Now, I think it's time we opened the door and let these people who have waited so long have their money."

"But, my friend's money should be set aside first." Amanda stared down at him.

"Why? It's the same money."

"We should count theirs out first to be positive there is enough." Amanda laid the little ledger she'd carried in the bottom of her saddlebag all the way from Illinois on the desk. "They've been owed longer."

Wade looked at her an expression of disbelief on his face. "But these people are here, now. They want their money."

Amanda heard the faint hum of voices outside the front door. "There should definitely be enough money for both, but mine should get theirs first." She didn't move. She saw the frustration on Wade's face but she didn't budge.

"You don't trust me, do you?" he asked levelly. He laid the pen he'd been using down and stood. "We've traveled all over this territory, you've saved my life and I yours, but you don't trust me with the thing most dear to you--money." He spat the words at her.

"That's not it, Wade. I just feel my friends...."

"The hell with your friends, Amanda. You're really talking about yourself."

Outside they heard the rumble of an approaching coach.

"That'll be the stage," Amanda said.

"The stage?"

"Yes, I wired the Wells Fargo the money would be ready. We'd better get it counted out."

Wade sat down and together, they counted out the money to be shipped to Springfield, leaving the portion that had been withdrawn from Simon's personal account in a separate stack.

Amanda tried to push thoughts she had offended Wade away, but the nagging realization kept returning. When they finished counting the money, she packed it in the strongbox the money from Jed arrived in, went to the door and signaled for the drive to come inside. Two of the three men with the driver hoisted the box onto the stage. Amanda paid for the shipment.

She stood in the doorway and watched the stage disappear out of town then she turned back toward Wade. "I guess we can let the townsfolk in now."

"I guess we can," he muttered.

Strolling to the front door, Amanda opened it. This was the first time the bank had been accessible. Exhilaration filled her although she'd have preferred Wade to be more enthusiastic.

Del Deans stood first in line, then Gladys with Judge Tucker directly behind her.

"It's about time you opened," Deans growled.

"If you will form a single line, everyone whose name is in Oldham's ledger will receive their total deposit back," Amanda announced, stepping past the teller's box that had been moved back several feet and secured with the gate she'd once polished and installed herself.

"Wonderful!" The cry filled the air.

When the voices had again grown silent, she continued, "I'm sorry to say, there's not enough money to pay interest but I'm sure you didn't think you'd get this much back."

"We sure didn't, Amanda," Gladys interrupted, "and I think we should all be grateful that you and the sheriff were willing to sacrifice your lives for our property."

"Yes!" The roar went through the crowd, followed by a happy cheer.

"We're just glad that we could do it." Wade had hobbled to the doorway on the saguaro spine crutches Abe Martin had made him when he set the broken leg.

Amanda felt his warm hand on her shoulder. Her heart rate increased and she leaned back against him slightly relishing in the feel of him.

"I've got to tell you though," Wade continued. "If it hadn't been for Amanda's perseverance, we'd have never found the money. I gave up on it. She didn't."

A cheer rang out again.

Amanda looked up at him.

He smiled and winked.

Her heart made a crazy little flip, but she couldn't quite smile back at him. A nagging memory of their earlier disagreement halted her response. Did he really think she loved money more than she did him?

"Now, let's get these folks their money," he whispered.

"Yes," she replied. "We've got a talk that's long overdue."

The last of the money had been distributed. Wade pushed back from the desk, then pulled up on the crude crutches.

"Well, your money's distributed," he said. "My official duty as sheriff is over. I think it's time I went to the ranch and got some rest."

"I'll come with you." Amanda locked the front door then walked to the safe where she began to stash the remaining money. "Like you said quite some time ago, we have a lot to talk about."

He paused for a moment and watched her. Today, she wore a red and white gingham dress Sadie had made. She had never looked prettier to him, but he knew he'd never be the man she needed. He was grateful to be alive and thankful they'd found the money for the townsfolk. He'd never love another woman, he was sure of that, but he had no illusions that Amanda Green Denton sought anything more from him than he'd already done.

"I don't think that's a good idea," he said, although he had to force the words out.

"But you said...." Amanda's words dropped off a crestfallen expression crossed her fair features.

"I know what I said." He started toward the door. "That was when I thought I meant more to you than money."

The door on the safe closed, then Amanda said, "You do."

Turning slightly, he stared at her. "Prove it. From the first day I met you that's all you ever talked about. Now you've got the bank and the money to run it, you don't need me." Leaning heavily on the crutches, he hobbled toward the back door.

"Don't go." Her voice quivered.

He couldn't turn around, instead he opened the door and stepped out onto the alley. Slowly, he walked around the building toward the stable. Fatigue slipped over him, but he continued to walk away. When he neared the front of the bank, he heard an unusual sound coming from the east. Looking up, he saw a herd of cattle entering town. *The Texas Longhorns I ordered. So much for that plan.* He shuffled across the street.

Walt Brauns stood in the stable doorway. "Looks like someone's gettin' some cows."

Wade nodded.

"Could you saddle my horse and give me a boost up? I need to go to the ranch and rest."

"Sure. Should I saddle Pepper too?"

"No, Amanda will be staying at the bank."

Amanda looked around her. The words Wade said still seemed to echo through the building.

You've got the bank and the money to run it.

She sat in the chair beside the rolled top desk. Of course she had the money, but what would having it be like without him? He'd never told her he loved her and yes, she had wanted to see the money owed to the people in Springfield going there before they handed that owed out to Mineral Wells residents, but that didn't mean she loved money more than she did him. Would he go to Judge Tucker and start divorce proceedings? Her heart broke at the thought.

She stood and walked to the back door. She had to wire Jed and tell him the money was coming along with a list of who should receive it. She also had to answer his all-important question.

Twilight illuminated the little valley as she walked toward the telegraph office, stepped through the doorway and looked around.

Oscar Miller sat behind the counter listening to the tick, tick of the telegraph machine, but he glanced up as Amanda entered the room. "Evenin' Mrs. Denton." He moved away from the Teletype machine.

"I didn't mean to interrupt, Mr. Miller."

"Oh I was just listenin' to what came over the wire, no message for us. I like to hear the sound of people talking to one another a long way apart." He smiled.

She returned his smile. "Then, I need to send a wire to my brother Jed in St. Louis."

"What would you like to say?"

"Shipped money and ledgers today STOP Please distribute STOP Answer to question two - yes STOP"

"Is that all, Mrs. Denton?" Oscar read the message again.

"Yes, how much do I owe you?"

"Two bits."

Amanda lay the quarter on the counter and started to turn away.

"Did the sheriff want me to continue to hold his money, Mrs. Denton?"

Amanda stopped walking and turned back toward the telegraph operator. "What money?"

"Oh, I guess I shouldn't have asked. Came in on the same stage as yours, but from New Orleans. I assumed it was to fix up the ranch so you all could start a family. I understand those funny lookin' cows that came into town earlier today were the ones the sheriff ordered."

"What funny looking cows, Oscar?"

"Texas Longhorns. Sure created a stir around Preacher Jones and his family earlier. The sheriff though, he took care of it. They followed him out of town."

"Oh, I was busy with the bank. Many of the people we returned money to deposited it again after we closed I had book work to do."

"A great day. Mineral Wells is growing and that's wonderful. More customers for the telegraph office." The operator smiled again.

"Yes," Amanda said, turning toward the door. "Have a good evening." She stepped out and looked down the street. It was empty except for a couple of horses tied in front of the saloon. Her stomach growled. She was hungry but hesitated to go to the hotel. Lately, Gladys and Judge Tucker looked so happy together. With her own current unhappiness, how could she be around them?

Turning toward the hotel anyway, she pushed the thought away. She had to eat. Gladys might not have time to talk, but she didn't have to stay long.

Wade secured the wire around the top post of the gate.

"Fine looking critters if you don't mind rangy cows," Manuel Mendoza the valquero who had led the cattle drive said.

"Yes, fine heifers and those two bulls aren't bad either. I hope you don't mind Mr. Mendoza if we wait 'til morning to settle up.

I'm a bit stove up and my money's in town." Wade stumbled slightly as he turned toward the cabin.

His head hurt, his arm throbbed and his leg ached, but nothing felt as bad as his heart. Admittedly, he felt better physically than he had a week ago, but he wasn't well enough to hold down his full-time job yet. Harvey had kept watch on the town. Earlier in the morning, Marshal Nance had ridden out with Stewart, taking him to his new home, the Yuma Territorial Prison.

The thought of living without Amanda the rest of his life was what had made Wade's heart ache so, and he knew it. Probably had something to do with the intensity of his other aches and pains too, he'd decided. He hadn't been able to get her out of his mind all the way home. He told himself he really should have expected something like this. Sarah Jean fell in love with a Union general. Amanda, well, she loved her money.

The valquero gazed at him, a question in his eye. "Are you all right?"

"Yeah, just tired. Rough day." He turned toward his house, staggering slightly.

"I could give you a hand."

"I'm fine." Wade forced himself to walk straight putting his full weight on the crutches.

"No problem about the money," the valquero said. "My friends and I could use a couple days rest. They want to try out the saloon in town and we could all use a good meal. Is there anywhere to eat?"

"The hotel serves until seven-thirty or eight-o'clock each night. Gladys feeds everyone. I'd offer you something myself but my wife's not here and I'm not much of a cook when I'm feeling good." Wade paused to rest a moment.

"That's all right. I know the men would rather have a drink than eat anyway." The Mexican smiled. "Looks like you need some rest. We'll see you in the morning."

"In town?" Wade asked.

"Si." The man swung into his saddle. The other men joined him and they rode away.

Wade hobbled toward the cabin. When he touched the door handle, dizziness swept over him. He stumbled, then pushed on the closed door. Stepping inside, the cool interior of the room chilled him. He staggered across the room and sank down on the bed. A little sleep and he'd feel better.

* * *

"Not eating much tonight," Gladys observed, adding fresh coffee to Amanda's cup.

"I'm just not hungry." Amanda pushed the barely touched plate of food away.

"Couldn't have anything to do with the sheriff ridin' out of town without you awhile ago, could it?" Gladys raised an eyebrow and stared down at Amanda knowingly.

Amanda took a sip of her coffee. "How did you know?"

Gladys laughed. "Wasn't hard. He looked about as miserable as you do sittin' here all alone."

"We had an argument."

"There isn't a married couple that ever was who haven't had a disagreement at one time or other. It'll heal."

"I don't think so." She pushed away from the table and stood.

"Now, what could be that serious?" Gladys sat the coffee-pot down and stared at Amanda.

"Wade said I'm in love with money and I am, at least for what it can do for me and others. All I wanted to be sure of was that those depositors back in Springfield got theirs first. Everybody got his or her money but Wade couldn't accept that. He wanted people here in Mineral Wells to be first."

"Oh, is that all," Gladys picked up the coffee pot and started toward the kitchen door. "Sounds like he just wanted to be first to me. Wanted to know he meant enough to you to heal his wounded pride. These last few days have been a physical strain on him. I suspect there's some woman back in his life who still haunts him too."

"Why?"

"When he came here, didn't have a thing to do with women. Stayed as far away as he could, that is until you came. You changed things, and him." Gladys smiled knowingly. "I suspect he's afraid now."

"Afraid?" Amanda couldn't imagine Wade apprehensive about anything.

"Yeah, you two been so busy chasing criminals you haven't had a chance to be husband and wife yet."

"But we aren't...weren't like you mean, Gladys. You know you all forced us to marry."

Gladys' eyes twinkled as she smiled.

"Oh there you are, darlin'." Judge Tucker stepped in the doorway.

"George." Gladys smiled at him.

Amanda saw adoration in her eyes.

"I'll be right with you."

"Sure." He stepped away.

Gladys turned back to Amanda. "I know what you mean, but if we hadn't forced the wedding it would have happened anyway. We just got it out of the way quicker than you two would have."

"Oh, I don't think so, we have a plan, as soon as the judge comes."

"But the judge has been here for more than a week," Gladys smiled at her. "Has anything happened?"

"No."

"Enough said. Now I've got to meet George." Gladys stepped through the double doors into the kitchen while Amanda stood and watched the doors swing closed.

Twenty One

This was crazy, Wade surmised, swinging his aching leg over
the saddle.   The full moon had slipped above the mountains
lending a glow to the cattle in the pen and the log building around
him. He'd tried to put Amanda out of his mind, go to sleep, ever
since he'd come home. The bed felt empty and he couldn't close his
eyes, much less sleep, no matter how tired he felt.

Trying to convince him he didn't love her had been a useless
endeavor.   Finally, he'd decided money didn't matter, nothing
mattered but her. He was hopelessly in love and if she would
continue to be his wife, he wanted her. Even if she did insist on
running the bank her way, nothing mattered except her.

He spurred the horse and pointed the animal toward town. It
was late, almost midnight, he thought, but some things couldn't
wait, and this was one of them.

The night air settled around him. Not too far away, an owl
hooted. Wade pulled out a cigarette paper and rolled a smoke, lit it
and spurred the horse again. As he drew the smoke into his lungs,
the horse lunged forward. The jerking motion made his leg hurt,
but he didn't care, at this point he deserved any pain he got.

He'd covered about half the distance to town when he saw
another rider coming toward him.   He cautiously slowed and
readjusted the six-shooter where he could reach it easier although
he thought the rider was probably someone who had too much to
drink at Deans' saloon. Jose was still on the loose, but Wade had
decided the little Mexican had probably fled back across the border.

Wade moved closer and realized the rider wasn't a man. The
moonlight formed a halo affect on her blond head as she darted
from the trail into the brush. He couldn't see her. "Amanda!"
Night air hung silently around him. For a moment, he thought he'd
been wrong. Then he heard a horse move toward him.

"Yes, it's me, Wade."

"What are you doing out here in the middle of the night?"

"I was coming to the ranch."

"But I told you."

"I know what you told me, but...." Her voice trailed off.

"I was coming to the bank to see you." His voice had grown husky. He wanted to jump from the horse, pull her from hers, and crush her to him, but his aching leg stopped him.

"Then why don't we ride back to the ranch together?" she asked

"Sounds good to me." He turned the horse, and they rode slowly, silently away.

Amanda slid the saddle off Pepper's back and placed it on the side of the stable stall. Beside her, Wade worked doing the same for his horse. His crutches clumped on the dirt floor. The scent of warm horses, sweet oats, and fresh straw filled the barn.

What if he didn't want her? That's what he'd said earlier, wasn't it? A memory of Simon threatened to invade her thoughts along with her mother's harsh criticism, but she pushed them away. She was a grown woman. A married woman and she wanted her man.

After Amanda had talked to Gladys, she'd tried to sleep. She had tossed and turned on the tiny bunk until she finally decided what she had to do--come make Wade talk whether he wanted to or not. She turned away from Pepper and nearly stepped into Wade who had moved closer.

"Amanda," he said, his head just inches from her. He leaned precariously forward on the crutches, but what she saw in his eyes made her heart leap.

"Yes, Wade?"

He touched the side of her cheek, then bent toward her. His lips covered hers. She felt a yearning deep within. Moving closer to him, she wrapped her arms around his neck and pulled him close.

The sound of a crutch hitting the gate then the dirt floor seemed to vibrate through the stable. He stumbled slightly, but Amanda held on to him. "Amanda, we've got to talk. Oh, how we've got to talk." His lips covered hers again.

When they pulled apart this time, she said, "I think we should get you into the house."

"Not yet." He took a deep breath. "I've got to tell you. I love you, Amanda. I think I've loved you since the day you stood on the step in front of my office and told me you were looking for Oldham.

I don't care about the money. I don't care about anything except I want you to be my wife in all ways."

Amanda's heart soared as joy filled her. "I love you too, Wade."

"I'm sorry about what I said about the money. I don't think money's that important to you. I don't know where my head was. That day Stewart brought us back to the bank, when he held his gun on me, you told him where the money was. That alone proved I meant more to you than the money, even when you didn't know if you had enough to pay the depositors."

Amanda moved away from him slightly.   "Trust, that's a problem we've had all along."

"Yes."

"I didn't trust you because of the way Simon and his friends used me and the fact I could never be what my mother wanted. Dad instilled the thought in men that sometimes we have to do what's right to fulfill someone else's injustice. I went a little overboard and could've gotten innocent people killed. He wouldn't have wanted that, nor would those depositors back in Springfield. Mother expected me to be a dainty little lady. I wasn't made that way. As long as I can remember, she was disappointed in me. Dad went the other way, not cuddling, but teaching and loving. Simon was his friend and in a way, I feel he betrayed Dad with his actions." She stopped speaking for a moment and looked at him. "You haven't trusted me, but I don't know why."

Wade sighed, long and laboriously, then turned and picked up the crutches. "Come into the house, I'll tell you why."

Together they walked crossed the distance, oblivious to everything around except themselves. Once inside, he leaned the crutches against the wall, then looked at her. "Come here." He opened his arms, and she moved into them. He lifted her chin so he could look into her eyes. "I've been so wrong, Amanda. Can you forgive me?"

"I love you, Wade. Yes, I can forgive you."

Using her to balance, they walked toward the bed together. She realized he was tired, very tired, but a determined glint in his eyes told her, he had no intention of resting until he'd told her why he hadn't trusted her.

"First, I got the idea I could never do anything right." He sighed, took a deep breath and continued. "My little brother, Jamie. He was eight and I ten. I was supposed to watch over him. He fell into the pool of water by the creek. We weren't supposed to be near it, but

Jamie wanted to. He was insistent for his age. I tried to pull him out, but I couldn't. I didn't know how to swim. He drowned before mother got there."

He stopped speaking for a moment. Amanda watched as the pain of the memory covered him. She wanted to help, but realized, this wasn't the time, he needed to tell her the complete story. "Mother never blamed me. She told me I was too little to help and said she was grateful she hadn't lost both her sons that day. I kind of put the feeling of failure aside, then I went off to The War. Fred Bessler and I had been friends for years. In a way, he replaced Jamie. He was wounded, but eventually, they had to amputate his leg, didn't matter, he died anyway. I was feeling pretty low when The War ended, but I still had my fiancee Sarah Jean Sturdyvent."

Amanda sat down beside him on the bed. He told the story of how Sarah Jean had promised to marry him two days before he'd gone off to war. He'd waited for her letters, made excuses when he didn't receive them, then the final day when he'd gone to her home and found her pregnant with another man, a Northern general's child.

"That wouldn't have been so bad if I hadn't lost everything else. I can't actually say I blame her for not wanting to marry a loser." His face seemed to clear and he sat a little taller

"I knew some of it, or suspected it." Amanda said quietly.

"How?"

"You had nightmares while you were sick with the bullet in your shoulder. I wasn't sure what had caused it, but I've seen it happen to other soldiers, both from the north and from the south. Where they were from didn't make the pain any less intense."

"No, I guess it wouldn't." He picked up her hands that she'd kept folded in her lap and kissed them. "I've been a fool, I should have told you before. After the war, I guess I hinged everything I had left on Sarah Jean." He gazed into Amanda's eyes. "Now, I don't think I even loved her. At least nothing like I do you. But everything disappeared at once. The Confederates lost then we got to go home to nothing. The plantation had been burned down. Mother sold the land just before the greedy carpetbaggers got there and moved to New Orleans with her sister. My last hope lay in Sarah Jean."

Amanda stood and took a couple of steps across the room. "I know what you mean. My father wanted me to marry Simon. They'd been friends in their youth. Dad thought he was doing what was best for me. My mother and I never did agree on anything. What Dad didn't know was that Simon wanted me for a decoration. I wanted children, a home, family. Everything changed after I married Simon. We didn't have a marriage."

The room was silent for a few moments. Amanda heard the movement behind her then she felt Wade's hands on her shoulders. Slowly he turned her toward him and she looked up at him.

"I want children too, Amanda. My cattle came today, breeding stock to start a ranch. Raising cattle to supply the soldiers should bring in enough money to support a family. Sheriffin' is a little dangerous for a man with responsibilities. I never thought of having a wife who owned a bank, but that doesn't matter to me anymore, as long as you can take some time out for me and our children."

Amanda smiled at him. "I'm glad to hear that, but it's not really necessary. My brother Jed, when he sent the money asked me if he could come take over the bank. Seems he doesn't think Arizona Territory is so bad a place to live anymore, now that I've survived as long as I have. He says Springfield is getting a little crowded for him. When I wired him the money was on the way to Springfield, I told him yes, he could take the bank over. I figure he'll get here about the time I need to quit anyway."

"Quit?"

Amanda smiled, and the excitement she'd been keeping for weeks filled her. She'd worried about this, now she realized she'd been wasting her energy. "Yes, quit. Unless I've calculated wrong, that should be about when our son or daughter arrives."

"What?" A smile like Amanda had never seen before on Wade's face creased it. He started to lift her, but an expression of pain when he leaned on his bad leg crossed his face, instead, he pulled her to him and wrapped his arms around her. Together, they moved toward the bed. He sat down, then pulled her onto his lap.

"I love you, Amanda Green Denton, and I'll do the best I can to take good care of you and our children."

Photograph by Angelina Ridenour Monckton

Elizabeth Butler lives in Illinois, but her heart is in the west. She, her husband and daughter lived in Arizona for ten years and she takes frequent vacations to Montana and Wyoming. She loves to ride horses although she'd never ridden them much until a couple of years ago and doesn't yet own one. In addition to her husband of nearly 35 years and her daughter she has a granddaughter who lives in Missouri where she plans to retire one day. She is an Administrative Secretary at the University of Illinois. Elizabeth looks forward to hearing from her fans. You may contact her by writing her at B & E Publishing Company, P. O. Box 391, Arcola, IL 61910